Bolan hit the deck immediately

He felt grass against his cheek, the bullets snapping overhead. A second's hesitation, and the gunner would have nailed him, cutting him in two.

Bolan was grappling with his carbine, wrenching it toward target acquisition, when another automatic weapon opened up behind him, firing short, repeated bursts.

He waited for the searing impact that would end his life...but nothing happened. In a flash, he realized this gunfire was directed toward the wall and his enemies. He saw the hardmen jerking, twitching, tumbling with the impact.

Someone had intervened to save his life.

Now all he had to figure out was who and why?

MACK BOLAN ®
The Executioner

DON PENDLETON'S
EXECUTIONER®
THE
SHADOW TARGET

A GOLD EAGLE BOOK FROM
WORLDWIDE.

TORONTO • NEW YORK • LONDON
AMSTERDAM • PARIS • SYDNEY • HAMBURG
STOCKHOLM • ATHENS • TOKYO • MILAN
MADRID • WARSAW • BUDAPEST • AUCKLAND

First edition September 1999
ISBN 0-373-64249-0

Special thanks and acknowledgment to
Mike Newton for his contribution to this work.

SHADOW TARGET

To hazard much to get much has more of avarice than wisdom.

—William Blake
Some Fruits of Solitude

If your desires be endless, your cares and fears will be so too.

—Thomas Fuller
Gnomologia

The enemy is risking everything for all the marbles, this time. And it's time they learned the taste of fear again.
—Mack Bolan

For Officer Robert D. Sanderson, Birmingham Police Department, assassinated by terrorists on January 29, 1998. God keep.

PROLOGUE

The hit team had been driving for an hour, due west from St. Louis, more or less, on Highway 70…or, was it Highway 40? Hedeon Chapaev had been spotting signs that bore both numbers ever since they left the city. Now and then, the signs showed up together, on the same pole, as if deliberately intended to confuse.

Americans.

Chapaev reckoned he'd never truly understand what made them "tick," as the expression went, but he wasn't concerned about enlightenment where the *Amerikanskis* were concerned.

He knew enough about his enemies to kill them, as it was.

What more did any soldier really need?

He wasn't a soldier anymore, the nagging voice in Chapaev's brain reminded him, but he ignored it. He'd always be a soldier where it mattered, in his heart and mind, regardless of the views expressed by those who cast themselves as his superiors. What did it matter if they stripped him of his rank, his uniform, his hard-won decorations? What did soldiers care if parties toppled and a stupid wall in Germany came down? While Hedeon Chapaev lived, they couldn't rob him of his training or the will to fight.

The only difference was that now, when he went off to war, he was rewarded for his efforts in accordance with the ultimate result. Success meant wealth—in fact, beyond Chapaev's wildest dreams—and allowed him to keep the lifestyle he had lately come to cherish.

Failure, on the other hand, would be repaid with death. Chapaev knew that, understood it and accepted it.

The more things changed, the more they stayed the same.

Their vehicle, a Chevrolet Suburban, had been purchased from a used-car lot in Louisville, Kentucky, where the salesman was delighted to accept a three-inch stack of hundred-dollar bills. The license plates were recently stolen, from a strip mall in St. Louis, to avoid provoking undue notice from police or passersby.

From all appearances, the five men in the black Chevrolet truck were nothing special. Fresh off work on some assembly line, perhaps, or on their way to watch a sports event, perhaps to check out one of the local bars where women shed their clothing and caressed themselves for money, while a crowd of drunken strangers watched and cheered them on.

A casual observer drawing any such conclusion would've been at least half right, in Hedeon Chapaev's case. Tonight was business, though the crew was on its way to work, not heading home. At the same time, it was a game of sorts to Chapaev—hunting men.

The gray gym bag between his feet contained a Heckler & Koch submachine gun, the MP-5 SD3 model with a telescoping metal stock and built-in sound suppressor, already loaded, plus a dozen extra magazines with thirty rounds apiece. The pistol slung beneath his left arm in a Galco horizontal shoulder holster was a BDA 9, the double-action version of the classic Browning Hi-Power. Two extra magazines, each holding fourteen rounds, balanced the shoulder rig, beneath his right armpit. The ski mask rolled up in his pocket was a cheap one, scratchy wool, but it would have to do.

Tools of the trade.

"We're almost there," the driver, Uri, told him, speaking English.

Chapaev didn't ask if he was certain. It was Uri's job to know when they had reached the target. He had never let Chapaev down before, and there was no good reason to suppose tonight would be a first.

"How long?"

"Perhaps five minutes to the intersection," the driver said. "From there, perhaps another five, ten minutes. It depends on speed."

"Obey the signs," Chapaev said. "Create no difficulties."

What was five more minutes, when they had all night?

An airlift to the target would've saved them time, but there was more expense, more paperwork, involved in picking out a helicopter. Besides, a helicopter might alert their prey and make the job more difficult.

Surprise was critical if they were going to succeed. And failure, Chapaev told himself, wasn't an option. If he wanted to be paid—if he intended to survive—he could not fail.

They left the interstate a few miles west of Warrenton, turned south toward the Missouri River, running through farmland where houses stood a quarter mile or more apart. The harvest season had already come and gone, the fields all barren now, except where weeds had sprouted in the place of cultivated crops. It had been nearly ten o'clock before they left St. Louis, well past 11:00 p.m. now, and most of the Missouri farmers were in bed. That didn't mean their targets would be sleeping, but the darkness gave Chapaev and his hunters an advantage.

"Here," Uri said, poking out his chin to indicate a narrow access road to their left. "If we weren't misled, this is the way."

"Drive past for half a mile or so," Chapaev ordered him, "then kill the lights and double back. We need a place to leave the vehicle."

"I'll find one," Uri replied. "Don't worry."

But the hit team's leader wasn't worried. He was looking forward to the next half hour with a sense of grim excitement.

"YOU WANT A SANDWICH, Baker?" Special Agent William Jones was up and moving toward the kitchen as he spoke, at ease in slacks and shirtsleeves, moving as if he had somehow managed to forget about the automatic pistol on his hip.

The man called Rory Baker grimaced at the sound of his

own name—no matter that he had selected it himself. It didn't suit him, and it tasted sour in his mouth, but he managed to reply with an approximation of civility.

"Not hungry."

"Suit yourself."

"I'll take one, while you're up," said Special Agent Phil Tomlin, sitting in the Barcalounger recliner with his shoes off, watching football on the television.

"That'll be the day," said Jones.

Baker wondered what it was that made these agents "special." Every federal officer he had encountered in the past twelve months was Special Agent So-and-so, regardless of the agency he served. It didn't seem to matter whether they were FBI or ATF, from DEA, the Secret Service or Internal Revenue. Each one of them was "special"—although some, apparently, were more special than others.

Two such had stopped by unexpectedly to visit him this evening. Aside from Special Agents Jones and Tomlin, Fletcher and McCarty, he was now confronted by Special Supervisory Agents Jaworsky and O'Neill.

"Nervous?" Jaworsky asked him, putting on a crooked smile.

"Why should I be?" Baker answered.

"Just wondering. We see that, sometimes, when a case gets wrapped. It's like a letdown, see? I mean, it's natural, but still…"

"I'm fine."

"Okay," Jaworsky said. "No problem, then."

"Your face all right?" O'Neill inquired. Then added, hastily, as if afraid that he might have offended him, "I mean, you look good, stitches out and all. A whole new you."

That was the plan, of course. New name, new face, new life. Betrayal had its price, and Rory Baker had held up his end of the bargain. He had been paid, in part—the plastic surgery was fair enough, although it still gave him a start to see a stranger staring at him from the mirror—and he was preparing to collect the rest of his debt.

Tonight.

"We've got the relocation all arranged," Jaworsky told him, opening an imitation leather briefcase that sat on the cheap coffee table between them. He withdrew a fat manila envelope and spilled its contents onto the table. "Driver's license, passport, birth certificate and credit cards—you've got an A+ rating, by the way—Social Security card, employment résumé, that goes back twenty years…the whole nine yards."

"You're very thorough," Rory Baker said.

"Hey," Jaworsky said with a shrug, "it's what we do."

"You took Perrugia down," O'Neill put in. "Without your testimony—"

"You were very helpful," Jaworsky said, interrupting his enthusiastic comrade, "and the deal's all set. We take you out tomorrow morning, bright and early. San Francisco's what you asked for, and we got it for you."

Baker smiled and felt the tug around his eyes, on both sides. It would take time, the plastic surgeon had advised him, for the nerves and muscles to respond in normal fashion.

"Very good," he said.

"So, you'll leave at 6:00 a.m.," Jaworsky said. "You've got a flight out of Jefferson City at nine o'clock sharp. Touch down in Frisco at half-past ten, Pacific Standard."

"That's with the time-zone change, you understand," O'Neill put in. Jaworsky half turned in his seat to stare at him, while Baker kept his new face deadpan.

"It would seem that everything has been arranged," he said.

"You're covered," Jaworsky replied, his own plastic smile flicking on and off.

"There's nothing left to say, then, I suppose…except goodbye."

The door burst open with a crash, a black-clad figure entering behind an automatic weapon, two more gunners crowding in behind him. At the same time, from the kitchen to his left, Baker heard another crash—the back door, latch and dead bolt splintering—followed by sound-suppressed gunfire and another crash, as Special Agent Jones went down.

His partner, Tomlin, was already lurching from the recliner when a spray of bullets slammed him backward, crimson spouting from his ventilated chest.

Jaworsky and O'Neill had swiveled toward the gunmen in the doorway, reaching for their own holstered weapons, but they never had a chance to draw and fire. Short bursts of automatic fire, delivered with precision, knocked them sprawling from their chairs. One of the rounds—a head shot to Jaworsky—spattered Baker with blood, the warm drops clinging to his cheek.

The leader of the hit team crossed the room to stand before him, peeling back his ski mask to reveal an almost-handsome face. His smile was crooked and devoid of warmth.

"There were two more," Baker said, "outside."

"Both dead," the hired assassin said. "And so, it would appear, are you."

THE FIRST NEWS BULLETIN told Dr. Louis Marx that it was getting on toward panic time. He didn't have to wait around for details, though the information that he picked up from the first, sketchy broadcast was bad enough. Six dead and one missing in Missouri, with the vanished victim more significant than all the others put together.

His patient.

Dr. Marx didn't know the man's name, wouldn't have cared to learn it. He knew the face, though, before and after, right down to the bone and muscle underneath the skin.

And why not? After all, he had designed the new face himself, constructed it from scratch. Not that it did his patient much good in the end.

Marx wondered, briefly, why the man had been abducted, when the shooters could have simply killed him on the spot and left him with the rest. Unbidden images of fiendish torture came to mind, and he regretted even pondering the question.

It was someone else's problem, now. The best that he could do was to wish his former patient a swift and relatively painless death. As for himself...

The sudden panic was irrational, he realized. The government could hardly blame him for the failure of its agents to protect their man. They didn't call it the Witness *Protection* Program for nothing, after all. Marx had done his job, fulfilled his part of the bargain, like always. The leak hadn't originated in his office; that much, he would swear to on a stack of holy books.

Still, there were bound to be some repercussions from the massacre. Shit always flowed downhill, especially in a bureaucracy, and he was near the bottom of the slope. Well-paid for his participation in the program, granted, but the sharks upstairs would be looking for scapegoats, anxious to lay the blame. Suppose one of them got it in his head that Dr. Marx had somehow been at fault?

So, what?

The plastic surgeon knew that he was innocent. More to the point, he had a first-class law firm on retainer, just in case. The possibility of an indictment was remote; the chance of a conviction so far-out that he considered it impossible. There was a possibility that he'd lose the franchise, granted, out of spite, and that would shave a cool six figures off his yearly gross—tax free, through an arrangement with the government—but he would still get by.

So, what was the problem?

Marx prescribed himself a sedative and washed it down with Perrier sparkling water. His Rolex watch told him he was running late, and that would never do. This morning's mission was to lift the breasts—and the morale—of a dowager whose real-estate holdings included four opulent blocks on the Loop. Marx couldn't make the woman young again, but he could do the next best thing. Arresting gravity—if only here and there, a few months at a time—was something of a specialty.

He left his home in Highland Park and caught the interstate, due south. Marx was already halfway to Chicago, passing Morton Grove and Skokie, when he picked up on the fact that he was being followed. It was nothing but an itch at first, then something made him check the rearview mirror, noting that the blue Miata on his tail was running just a tad too close, its driver stubbornly ignoring opportunities to pass on either side. Suspicion turned to fear when Marx glimpsed something that appeared to be the muzzle of a weapon peeking up across the Miata's dashboard, there and then gone.

One thing that Marx had picked up as an intern years ago was that in certain situations there was no time to consider or deliberate a course of action. It was like that in the emergency room, where the patients came in burned and broken, torn and bleeding. If you didn't act, you lost.

And so, without another thought, Marx slammed the accelerator to the floor, kicked his Mercedes S-420 into high gear and blasted out of there before the two men in the blue Miata knew exactly what was happening.

They caught on fast, he had to give them that, and they were after him before he picked up fifty yards, but Marx felt better just for seizing the initiative. He started weaving in and out among the other southbound vehicles, ignoring bleats from angry horns around him, racing down the freeway like one of those hopheads who were always showing up on *Cops*.

Screw it.

He concentrated on the road in front of him, the cars that swerved to stay out of his path as he sped past. An occasional glance at the rearview mirror was enough to show him the Miata hanging in there, instantly eradicating any doubts Marx might have had that he was being chased down the highway with hostile intent. The gas tank on the S-420 was three-quarters full, and they would have to gun him off the road before stopping to chat.

Of course, that seemed to be the general idea.

Coming up on Marx's left, the exit ramp for Lincolnwood looked like his best chance for survival. Marx had played the life-and-death game more than once, during his internship and residency, before he sought refuge from mortal decision in the specialty of plastic surgery, but even then, it hadn't been his life at stake. If he was working on a gunshot victim or a hit-

and-run and something went awry—let's say the scalpel slipped—Marx still went home alive. He still got paid.

This time...

Marx saw an opening and swung the S-420's steering wheel hard left, veering between a Honda Prelude and a looming Peterbilt truck. The Miata tried to follow, but the semi cut it off, tires smoking, air brakes screeching as the driver fought to keep his rig from jackknifing.

Marx nearly lost it on the exit ramp, but saved it inches short of impact with the guardrail before shooting through onto the next street. A hard right, then a left and left again, convinced him that he had evaded his pursuers—whomever they were.

It was impossible to miss the link between that morning's news flash on TV and the pursuers on his tail. At thirty-nine, Marx was old enough to have lost his faith in blind coincidence. And that, in turn, meant that he couldn't check in with his office.

Not if he intended to survive.

He pulled into a small suburban strip mall, parked the Mercedes in front of a convenience store and reached into the glove compartment for his pills. His legs were shaking, and he didn't trust himself to walk inside the store to buy a can of soda, so he gulped the pill down dry.

Before the drugs kicked in, he had already made a mental note of things to do: stop at the bank, pick up some clothes, perhaps a suitcase. Pay cash for the lot, and skip the paper trail. As for tomorrow and the day after that...

He twisted the ignition key, backed out of there and drove off into the unknown.

THE SUITE OF OFFICES on Lake Shore Drive was high-rent property, top of the line. Three shooters went in wearing business suits, with light raincoats to hide the automatic weapons slung beneath their arms. They rode the elevator up in silence, sharing it with two young secretaries who were whispering and giggling about their weekend dates. The shooters stared at nothing, waiting while the women disembarked, and rode another three floors to the target site.

The elevator stopped on nine. "No witnesses," the middle gunner said, speaking in English with a heavy Eastern European accent. As he spoke, the shooter fished a stocking mask out of his pocket, slipped it on, the flankers doing likewise. They were faceless as they left the elevator car and barged into the waiting room of Dr. Louis Marx.

No plastic surgeon could undo what happened next. Three submachine guns raked the waiting room with short, precision bursts, slamming two patients from their seats, stitching a line of bloody holes across the startled secretary's ample chest. The guns were sound suppressed, emitting sounds like sailcloth ripping, the explosive impacts of their bullets stifling screams.

The shooters didn't linger in the waiting room to double-check their kills. There was no need. The leader moved directly to the only door in sight and shouldered through it, squeezing off another short burst at the nurse who stood before him, gaping, with a slim manila folder in her hand. She went down like a sack of laundry, spilling blood and papers on the pastel vinyl floor.

The four examination rooms were empty, but the shooters checked them anyway, then moved on to the doctor's private office.

Empty.

The physician's files required a room all to themselves, equal in size to Marx's office, double that of the examination rooms. There was no time or inclination for a thorough search. The leader of the hit team reached beneath his raincoat and palmed an incendiary canister.

He nodded toward the doorway, waited for his two compatriots to leave, then pulled the pin and flicked it toward the filing cabinets. Backing out through the doorway, he pitched the grenade underhand, watching it bounce off the farthest cabinet before he turned and hurried after his men.

The blinding flash, when it came, was hot enough to melt the filing cabinets and incinerate their contents. There was no need to search or sort the files. In ten or fifteen seconds, they would all be gone.

Now, all they had to do was find the doctor and finish him off before he had a chance to talk.

The rest would take care of itself.

1

Mack Bolan gauged the drop at nine feet, give or take, and launched himself into the darkness, knees bent to absorb the impact of his landing, one arm out for balance, while the other clutched an automatic rifle to his side. He had determined in advance that there were no attack dogs on the premises, no motion sensors, nothing in the way of infrared security devices.

The only risk he ran, from that point on, was being shot dead in his tracks.

The usual.

It was an hour past nightfall, not as late as Bolan would have liked—the sentries would be wide awake and on their toes—but all his targets had assembled, and he couldn't trust the meeting to drag on for hours, even with the weighty matters that were on the table. After all, the groundwork had been done, the major obstacles removed, skids greased. The juggernaut was rolling.

And it would be Bolan's job to stop it cold, by standing in the way and doing everything within his power to throw the campaign off course.

Again, the usual.

Whatever happened in the next half hour, he had come prepared. Bolan was decked out in his nightsuit, hidden pockets filled with everything from lock picks to stilettos and garrotes. His main weapon for the strike was a CAR-15—the short "commando" version of the standard M-16, complete with telescoping stock—on this occasion fitted with a 40 mm M-203 grenade launcher slung beneath the barrel and a 100-round drum magazine. For backup, Bolan wore a semiauto .44 Magnum Desert Eagle on his right hip, and a customized Beretta 93-R underneath his left arm in a shoulder rig. His combat harness bore the weight of spare magazines for the automatic carbine, plus a Ka-bar fighting knife. The bandoleer slung left-to-right across his chest was fat with 40 mm high-explosive and incendiary rounds to feed the M-203 launcher.

Bolan was dressed to kill, with a major-league party to crash.

The party house was a modest sixteen-room ranch-style, set on fifty wooded acres in Burlington County, New Jersey, due west of a town called Presidential Lakes. Bolan found the name a bit pretentious, since his drive-through recon of the hamlet had revealed neither a lake nor anyone resembling a president. He chalked it up to small-town ego strokes and put it out of mind, his concentration focused on the rich men he had come to kill.

There would be six in all, with two of those preeminent among the others: Baklanov and Donatelli. If it looked like it was going down the tubes, if anything at all went wrong, he had to at least attempt to nail those two.

The rest could wait.

He pegged the distance from his entry point to target acquisition as a rough four hundred yards. It would have been an easy run, two minutes tops, if it was daylight, open ground, no obstacles. In this case, though, he had to do his hunting in the dark. The grounds were wooded, and at least three dozen sentries had been detailed to patrol the fifty acres while the sitdown was in progress. Each stalker in the woods was carrying a shotgun or an automatic weapon, plus a compact two-way radio that linked him to the manor house and more guns, waiting in reserve.

It could have been enough to do the job—had they been soldiers in the true sense of the word. There was a world of difference, though, between a contract killer and a battle-hardened fighting man of military background. One was used to having targets fingered for him, stalking them on urban killing grounds and making a quick, clean tag before a waiting driver whisked him off to parts unknown. The other used terrain—any terrain—and climate to his best advantage, or defied the elements if all else failed, trusting in no one but himself.

A hit man took the garbage out; a soldier grew up fighting for his life.

Which didn't mean, of course, that he was never taken by surprise.

In Bolan's case, this night, he was within sight of the house, its lighted windows seeming close enough to touch, before he hit an unexpected snag and saw it start to come apart.

He had already dodged two sentries, blending with the shadows, slipping past them easily, a pair of city boys caught up in playing Daniel Boone. He could have killed them, either with the Ka-bar knife or the sound-suppressed Beretta, but it would have slowed him, and he was more concerned with picking off the leaders of the pack than thinning out the herd.

Still, number three surprised the soldier, stepping out of cover from the shadow of an ancient oak, and very nearly got him killed.

It wasn't that the guy saw Bolan coming. If he had, and took the time to aim the shotgun he had tucked beneath one arm, he could have been an instant millionaire. He could have pocketed the bounty that had followed Bolan from the first engagement of his private war against the Mafia, beyond a premature obituary, to his present life in limbo.

If.

That would have called for more alertness than the guy could muster, though. In retrospect, Bolan assumed—he hoped—the shooter had been answering a simple call of nature. One way or another, the gunner was yanking on his zipper as he stepped around the oak, into an errant shaft of moonlight filtered through high clouds. His eyes locked on to Bolan, while his lips worked silently.

And then, he dropped his piece.

Scare stories in the tabloids notwithstanding, it's rare indeed for any gun of quality to fire without a finger—or some other object—pressing on the trigger. Most have built-in safety mechanisms to prevent an accidental discharge if the gun is dropped, bumped, kicked—whatever—and the vast majority of shooting accidents reported in the media spring from the foolish negligence of some incompetent who didn't know the gun was loaded.

But the sentry's shotgun went off anyway.

It was a mystery to Bolan, but he had no time to spare for playing Sherlock Holmes. The fire-select switch on the CAR-15 was set for 3-round bursts, and Bolan stroked the trigger lightly, placing three out of three in the chest from a range of fifteen feet.

The impact of those 5.56 mm tumblers punched his target backward, briefly airborne with his arms outflung, before he landed supine, slack in death. The corpse's eyes and mouth were open, though he never spoke a word.

Even as the echo of the shotgun blast and rifle shots began to fade, the soldier could hear his enemies converging on the kill site, shouting back and forth in darkness as they came. Precise triangulation was beyond them, being taken by surprise as much as Bolan and his late assailant had been by the sudden confrontation. But it wouldn't take them long to find the stiff, and any time he wasted trying to conceal it would be time shaved off his own life.

Mouthing a silent curse, Bolan moved past the dead man and headed toward the house, where even now he knew that reinforcements would be scrambling to assist the grounds patrol. Three dozen guns against him when he scaled the wall, and now it would be—what? Twice that?

No matter.

Bolan hadn't come this far to simply turn and run away before he even glimpsed his targets over gunsights.

He picked up speed, until the jog became a sprint, and prayed that he hadn't already lost his chance.

THE SOUND OF GUNFIRE had been muffled, distant, but there could be no mistaking it. Still, when Gaetano Donatelli bolted to his feet, spilling the best part of his Scotch whiskey and soda on the white shag carpet, he demanded, "What the fuck was that?"

No one responded to the foolish question. They were all too busy scrambling from their easy chairs and glancing anxiously at hulking bodyguards. Color was swiftly leeched from faces tanned by sun lamps and Caribbean vacations, hard eyes darting here and there about the spacious library. A casual observer, ignorant of who these people were and what they represented, might have thought they were afraid.

Except, perhaps, for one.

The Russian, Rurik Baklanov, kept to his seat a moment longer than the others, rising with an athlete's easy grace instead of lurching to his feet. His gray eyes didn't seek out Semyon Shurochka, standing off to one side by himself, because he knew his first lieutenant would defend him if the need arose. As for the rest, he almost felt an urge to laugh at their display of nerves.

DeRicco, from Miami, was the worst. Prolonged exposure to the southern sun had nearly mummified the sixty-something mafioso, leaving him with the appearance of a walking corpse that might collapse and crumble into dust in a gust of wind. His fearsome reputation didn't fit the withered dwarf who stood before Baklanov now, flanked by two bodybuilder types with shiny pistols in their hands.

Their host, Gambola, showed a bit more nerve, barking commands at his lieutenant to find out what was going on, but there was still a tremor in his voice, a subtle shimmy to his double chins.

Fortini, out of Cleveland, passed a hand across his shiny scalp, as if to smooth down nonexistent hair. He didn't speak, but stood with feet apart and shoulders slightly hunched, a brawler's stance that matched his crooked nose and forehead seamed with ancient scars.

Peredo, from New York, was dressed in a charcoal suit that matched the color of his eyes. He held himself erect without appearing rigid, confident that not one of his iron-gray hairs was out of place. Behind him, close enough to slap his swarthy face, a shifty-eyed Sicilian peasant-type covered Peredo's back, one hand inside his tailored jacket, clutching gunmetal.

"My boys'll sort this out," Gambola told the room at large. "We should be fine, in here."

"Should be?" DeRicco's baritone was all the more incongruous, emerging from a man his size. "What kind of half-assed guarantee is that?"

"Don't sweat it, Jules," Gambola said. "This place is like Fort Knox."

"You say!" DeRicco rasped.

"You're calling me a liar in my own house, now? That's how you make friends in Miami, I suppose?"

The argument was interrupted by more gunfire from the grounds, the echoes sounding closer this time.

"Shit!" DeRicco said to no one in particular, eyes darting rapidly from one face to another. "If this turns out to be some kind of fucking setup, I can promise you—"

"A setup?" Scowling at the mummy from Miami, Cleveland's Don Fortini spoke through clenched teeth that resembled chips of yellowed ivory. "You want to start accusing someone, say it plain."

More shooting from the grounds, and Rurik Baklanov decided that the argument had dragged on long enough. "Perhaps," he said, "it would be wise if we adjourned this meeting and convened another time."

Gaetano Donatelli picked up on the signal, forcing a grimace that passed for a smile. "Makes sense to me," he said. "Give Gino, here, a chance to put things right. We'll get an escort out of here, and I'll get back in touch with you next week, sometime. How's that?"

"As far as I'm concerned," DeRicco answered, "you can save your fucking quarter. The whole damn thing's a jinx."

"No, Jules—"

"He's got a point," Fortini said. "I've never seen a combination start off this bad and go anywhere except straight down the crapper."

"Look, I'll call you," Donatelli said. "Meanwhile, let's—"

He was interrupted by a blast that sent a tremor through the house. No gunshot. To Baklanov, it sounded like an RPG grenade, or something similar.

"Fort Knox, my rosy ass!" DeRicco said with a sneer, already moving toward the exit, with his two iron-pumping soldiers keeping pace.

"What is this, Gino?" Donatelli asked Gambola.

"Jesus H.," their host replied, "I wish I knew!"

"If we get stuck in here…" Peredo said, his warning left unspoken.

"Nobody's stuck," Gambola said. "Just move to the cars while my boys put it right."

"Your boys aren't on their own out there," the mafioso from New York reminded him.

"Okay," Gambola said aggressively, "so we should get it settled that much quicker, then."

Semyon Shurochka stepped close to Baklanov and whispered to him, speaking Russian. "Let's get out of here," he urged. "It's going bad."

And there was no denying that, from all appearances. The first real meeting called to finalize and formalize the new regime was going up in smoke. Despite the bitter taste of disappointment in his mouth, however, Rurik Baklanov wasn't prepared to fold his hand, admit defeat.

Not now, when he had literally sacrificed his life to come this far.

There would be other meetings, new agreements. The regime would be inaugurated, in due time—sooner than later, he believed. And if some of those present chose to stand against the rising tide, they would be swept away, replaced by others with a more collegiate outlook.

But first, they needed to evacuate the premises before Gino Gambola's house came down around their ears. There would be time enough when it was over to identify the dead and name their enemies. If any managed to survive the night, there would be grievous punishment in store.

Rurik Baklanov would see to it personally.

In fact, he thought, it would be a pleasure.

THE FIRST HE ROUND Bolan triggered from his M-203 launcher found its mark a foot or so above a darkened second-story window, detonating with a smoky flash that shattered half the glass on that side of the house. Before the thunder of the blast subsided, Bolan felt a ripple in the air above his head, ducking the spray of bullets from an automatic weapon that was fired from somewhere to his left.

He scuttled to the side, seeking a target, just in time to spot a pair of shooters rapidly advancing from a range of twenty yards. One of them had an Uzi submachine gun braced against his hip, preparing to fire another burst, the other leveling a 12-gauge riot gun.

It was a toss-up as to which man posed the greater danger, so he shot them both, two light strokes on the trigger, left and right, the muzzle of his weapon barely moving as he tracked from one mark to the other. Bolan's first three rounds surprised the shooter with the Uzi, ripping the fabric of his shirt and spinning him. The dead man triggered off a wild burst from his SMG as he fell, bullets from the Uzi joining Bolan's 3-round burst to drill the second gunner, blowing him away. They sprawled together on the grass, unmoving, as the Executioner spun back toward his primary target.

It was getting tough to concentrate, now, as the other sentries homed in on the sound of the explosion and sporadic gunfire, drawn like sharks to a fresh smell of blood in the water. Bolan didn't stick around to count heads or assess their expertise, flicking the carbine's fire-select switch to full-auto as he ran around the north end of the house. Still running, he jammed a thermite round into the 40 mm launcher's open breech and locked it down, squeezing off his shot in the direction of the broad glass sliding doors that opened onto a flagstone patio.

The fat incendiary canister smashed through the glass without exploding, struck a wall inside and detonated into roiling flames that set the walls and carpet blazing. Seconds later, thick white smoke poured through the shattered windows, spilling out across the patio, and Bolan took advantage of it, ducking through the cloud as half a dozen shooters came around the corner of the house behind him, bent on running him to ground.

It was a fifty-fifty gamble, as to whether those he sought would hide inside the house or take their chances on a break for freedom. If he went inside to find them, Bolan ran the risk of being trapped, cut off, while Rurik Baklanov and company slipped out another way and left him in the trap he had created for himself. Conversely, if they stayed inside and Bolan failed to seek them out, the very best he could expect was to play ring-around-a-rosy with their soldiers for a while before he had to cut and run.

He hoped that lighting up the house would flush them out, but in the meantime, while the precious seconds ticked away, he had to stay alive—and that meant staying one jump out in front of those who sought to run and gun him down.

He cleared the drifting smoke, pausing long enough to swivel in his tracks and fire a sweeping burst, waist-high, back toward the sound of angry voices following him. Someone cried out in what could have been surprise or mortal pain, and Bolan left them to it, loading up another high-explosive round as he ran on, continuing around the house.

Three gunners waited for him, lined up like a firing squad. A heartbeat's hesitation saved his life. One of the shooters bellowed an order to his team, when they could just as easily have opened fire on sight and nailed their target cold. Unfortunately for the ambush party, by the time they got their act together, Bolan had already launched himself, headlong, into a dive that left him prone, below their line of fire, his automatic carbine spraying bullets in a rising zigzag pattern, raking them from knee to chest.

Too close, he thought, but that was how it went in combat. Any fight he walked away from was a victory, and there was nothing to be gained by second-guessing even the most marginal success.

He scrambled to his feet, moved on, judging by weight and

feel how many rounds were left before he had to ditch the drum and call upon a backup magazine.

So far, so good.

Behind him, his pursuers would have cleared the smoky patio by now. Bolan paused long enough to turn and bring the carbine to his shoulder, sighting quickly as he fired the HE round toward the corner of the house. It struck a glancing blow against the wall, but that was all it took to detonate the impact fuse, transforming stately brick to shrapnel in an instant. It would slow the hunters, he thought, but they weren't about to give it up and let him go.

Not while they lived.

In front of Bolan, still beyond his line of sight, he heard the sound of engines revving. In a flash, he pictured limos pulling out, his quarry rolling along the drive, through wrought-iron gates and out of reach. The sudden rush of energy he felt was mostly anger, with the barest touch of panic that his gamble might have been in vain.

Determined not to lose them now, when they were this close, Bolan took off sprinting for the driveway, twenty yards ahead.

THE WAY GINO GAMBOLA saw it, he was getting screwed. Holding the shitty end of the stick was where he found himself, and there was nothing in the world that he could do about it now. The goodness of his heart had prompted him to host the meet—well, that and the anticipation of a hefty profit down the road—and now his house was trashed, a bunch of loonies shooting up the place like there was no tomorrow, while his VIP houseguests bailed out and left him with the mess.

See it another way, though, and the Jersey Mob boss had to laugh. What else could he expect? His guests were big, important men. Most of them hadn't pulled a trigger for themselves in years, and if they hadn't gone soft, exactly, they had definitely grown accustomed to the luxury of giving orders, pushing buttons when they wanted something done and trusting that the matter would be properly resolved.

Gambola felt that way himself these days...most of the time, at least. He was a punk from Jersey City who had come up through the ranks the hard way. Made his bones, then made it big, but there were no such things as overnight sensations in the Outfit. Everybody paid his dues along the way—some more than others, granted, if you have the proper Family connections—and Gambola never felt that anything was handed to him on a silver platter.

Still, it came from somewhere, and that which was given could always be taken away.

He sent the VIPs out to their cars with Tony Sylvestri, sidetracked by the game room, where he kept most of his guns. Nothing illegal, there, in case somebody showed up with a warrant and he didn't have them greased to give him warning in advance. His rifles and shotguns were strictly sporting, while he kept a Smith & Wesson automatic on the night table, upstairs, beside his bed.

Precautions.

When he was a kid, no more than nine or ten years old, Gambola read somewhere that Boy Scouts had a motto: Be prepared. He liked that, even though it never seemed to help the Cub Scouts when he stopped them on the way to school and held them up for ice cream money. Still, he couldn't judge a motto by the wimps who took it for their own. The frailty lay in human flesh, not in the sentiment or words.

He chose a Remington 870, the classic 12-gauge pump, and checked to satisfy himself that it was loaded. There were no kids in the house, and Gambola didn't buy that crap about how loaded guns at home were such a danger to the family. In thirty-something years, Gambola had never shot a relative, on purpose or by accident. It had been close a time or two, with Cousin Mikey, but he counted to ten and let the sticky-fingered little bastard off with an ass whipping.

Tonight was something else entirely, though. Whoever had the balls—and lack of brains—to raid Gambola's house, while he was entertaining half a dozen of his most important friends wasn't long for the world. He hoped his troops would leave a couple of the raiders with enough life in their bodies that he could enjoy the act of snuffing them himself.

And from the sound of things outside, Gambola just might get his wish.

Three minutes, easy, since the shooting started, and it showed no sign of slacking off at all. That made him wonder, as he moved toward the nearest exit with his shotgun tucked beneath one arm, what kind of force his soldiers were confronted with out there.

Not cops. Gambola took that much for granted, as there would have been no shooting in the first place. And he didn't figure any of his VIPs staging a hit against the house while they were all inside. That left some unidentified third party, and a lifetime of duplicity, all backstabbing intrigue that had taught Gambola there were damned few people he could trust. Some capo who had heard about the meet by word of mouth but didn't get an invitation, maybe, and was jealous, even fearful, thinking that his territory might be up for grabs, when everything was sorted out. That left a world of suspects, from Los Angeles to Baltimore, Detroit to Dallas and New Orleans, but Gambola didn't have the time to think about that now.

He had to keep his soldiers kicking ass and taking names, which in the present instance called for him to lead them by example.

Well before he reached the kitchen, Gambola smelled the smoke and knew that something, somewhere, was on fire. Terrific. Now his house was burning down, and the Mob boss knew damned well there was a clause in his insurance that excluded payment if the fire resulted from a war or insurrection. He was wondering if he was covered, when the shock waves of another blast ripped through the house and made him stagger left and right.

He got his balance back and moved on, cursing bitterly, his hands white-knuckled on the Remington. It didn't matter who the bastards were. If somebody thought he could move in and treat Gino Gambola this way on his own damned property, the shithead would be dead before he had a chance to think again.

Outside, the air was smoky too, though not as bad as in the house. Gambola trailed the sounds of gunfire, following the action on his chunky legs, but not running yet, because that would have made him look pathetic, maybe even comical. When he caught up with whoever the hell was causing this, Gambola had it in mind to wipe the smile from every face he didn't personally recognize, and teach the cocky bastards what it meant to treat a boss like he was some street-corner hustler that could be slapped around.

Now, all he needed was a living, breathing target, and—

His soldiers nearly bowled Gambola over when they came around the corner. There were three of them, and they were running for their lives. Looking embarrassed, now that their boss stood before them, scowling, the oldest of them—Rocco Salvi, out of Newark—blurted a warning.

"Jesus, Mr. G," he said, "you gotta find someplace to hide. This fucking guy..."

Gambola didn't have to ask who Salvi was babbling on about, because the "fucking guy" chose that moment to step around the corner, leveling some kind of military-looking weapon from the hip. The weapon seemed to have two muzzles, both of them aimed squarely at Gambola's face.

"Aw, shit!"

Salvi was nearly sobbing as he raised his Ingram submachine gun. Gambola's other boys had nowhere left to run, their enemy before them now, all dressed in black, with some kind of soot or war paint on his face. They brought up their weapons, with Gambola shouldering his way between them, sighting down the barrel of his Remington 870 shotgun.

The world exploded, then, and Don Gambola knew exactly how a football felt at kickoff time. There was a white-hot stab of pain inside his head—the eardrums going—and the blast tore his Armani suit right off his back while he was airborne, tumbling like some kind of acrobat, head over heels.

Gambola landed on one shoulder, with his fat head twisted at an awkward angle. When the snap came, it was loud enough for him to hear it even with his busted eardrums, and it came from the inside, up close and personal. The good news was, Gino Gambola couldn't feel a thing—no pain, nothing—from his shoulders down. The bad news was, he couldn't move, and simply had to lie there, watching, as his enemy retreated, jogging toward the driveway, where Gambola's guests were hastily retreating.

Somehow, the capo of New Jersey found the strength to weep, but he couldn't decide if they were tears of rage or shame.

THE CREW WAGONS were well away, one nearly to the wrought-iron gates, when Bolan came around the corner of the house. He counted four already rolling down the driveway, while the fifth—a Lincoln—was just pulling out, smoked windows hiding those inside.

He didn't need to see them, though, to know that Baklanov was in the gray Mercedes-Benz, up front, about to clear the gate. That would be Donatelli in the black stretch behind him. Bolan only cared about the rest to the extent that they were players and facilitators of the Russian's plan. If Baklanov escaped...

The final tank in line, a Cadillac, was picking up momentum when Bolan fired a high-explosive round from thirty yards. The limousine was armored, but its windows—advertised as bulletproof—were never meant to take an HE charge. The blast ripped through the vehicle, flame swallowing its passengers, before the driver lost control and stalled the engine.

A dozen guns were ranged about the front porch of Gambola's manor house, and all of them reacted instantly to the explosion in their midst. Some of the shooters toppled when the shock wave hit, while others dived for any cover they could find. Still others stood their ground, seeking the source of the explosion, two or three of them immediately spotting Bolan, swiveling their guns around to bring him under fire.

The Executioner chopped them down with short bursts from the hip, skirting the porch and firing on the run. Bolan cared no more for these "soldiers" than the obstacle they posed, blocking his access to a pair of dark sedans—a Buick Skylark and a Pontiac Grand Prix—that waited for him, thirty feet beyond the porch.

The air was filled with muzzle-flashes, winking at him as he rushed across the porch, returning fire at point-blank range. A couple of the shooters panicked, running for their lives, and Bolan let them go, indifferent to their fate as long as neither one of them carried ignition keys he needed for the Buick or the Pontiac.

One final soldier stood between him and the cars, hamhanded as he tried to clear the jammed bolt of a Skorpion machine pistol. He never got it done, as Bolan drilled him through the forehead with a single round and dropped him in his tracks.

Ducking around the Grand Prix to the driver's side, Bolan peered through the window, scowling at the empty slot of the ignition switch. Another moment, and he stood beside the Skylark, feeling an adrenaline rush as he found the keys in place. Bolan laid down another burst of fire to scatter any gunmen still intent on stopping him, then slid behind the Buick's wheel and slammed the door. He gave the key a twist, was rewarded with an instant snarl of power from beneath the hood and dropped it into gear.

Now, all he had to do was overtake the Russian's limousine, take out his target and survive to tell the tale.

No sweat. It would be easy.

Just like falling into an open grave.

2

"That was bad," Semyon Shurochka said. Nothing in his voice or attitude betrayed alarm. In fact, despite the stubby AKSU automatic rifle cradled in his lap, he seemed relaxed, as if out to enjoy an ordinary Sunday morning drive.

"A setback," Rurik Baklanov informed his chief lieutenant. "Nothing more."

But was it? There was clearly more than mere coincidence involved in the attack on the Gambola mansion. Mobsters had their enemies, of course—in the United States, as in the Russian motherland—but it defied all logic that Gambola's foes would choose this night, this moment, to inaugurate a shooting war against New Jersey's ranking Mafia Don.

"Somebody knows we are here," Shurochka stated.

How could they? Baklanov considered asking, but he knew the answer to that question in advance. The leak could have resulted from a double-dealing member of the team he had assembled, with Gaetano Donatelli's help, to organize a New Day in America. Or from any one of their subordinates who suffered pangs of jealousy and longed for a higher rank within the outlaw "family." Another possibility—more likely, in the Russian's view—was that some local warlord excluded from the coalition might have picked up on the scheme and sought to sabotage the merger. Either way, it would remain for Baklanov and Donatelli to identify their enemy and deal with him in ruthless fashion, make a grim example of him, so that no one in the future would be foolish enough to stand against the New World Order of the syndicate.

But first, before they started settling their accounts, the first priority was reaching safety, making sure that he and Donatelli were secure. In time, the smug American would cease to matter, but for now...

"We're being followed," Sasha told them, speaking from the driver's seat.

"One of the other limousines," Baklanov said.

The driver frowned and shook his head. "They went the other way, all four of them."

"Some local farmer, then," the Russian mobster said. "This is a public highway, after all."

"Maybe," Sasha replied. "He's coming very fast, though. Burning up the road."

Reluctantly, Baklanov turned in his seat and peered through the tinted window, checking for himself. The headlights were a mile or so behind him, tiny pricks of light, like fireflies. It required an effort to imagine any danger, sitting in this armored limousine with Shurochka and his two best soldiers packing automatic weapons, ready to kill at the drop of a hat. Even so, Baklanov was known for his precautions, leaving nothing to chance.

"Slow down," he ordered the driver.

"But, they'll overtake us," Sasha protested.

"In this tank," Baklanov reminded him, "a farmer in his tractor ought to have no trouble overtaking us. Besides, we don't know who it is back there."

He pictured a policeman coming up behind them, red-and-blue lights flashing, bent on citing Sasha for a violation of the local speed limit. There had already been sufficient killing for one night, the Russian thought, and while he didn't mind exterminating an American lawman, if the circumstances should demand it, it occurred to him that such a killing, here and now, might only make things worse. At least, if they confined the shooting to Gambola's property, the mafioso had a chance to clean things up before police arrived.

"Still gaining," Sasha announced.

"Be ready," Baklanov instructed his associates. "I won't be stopped tonight, but we must not be trigger-happy, either."

"I know how to do it," Shurochka said, stating the obvious. The lieutenant shifted in his seat, swinging the muzzle of his AKSU toward the nearest gun port.

Baklanov wasn't concerned yet, in the sense of being worried—much less frightened for his life—but he could recognize a problem when he saw one. If the vehicle behind them was pursuing, they would have to stop it swiftly, forcefully, and leave no trace of their involvement in the deed. Tonight could be erased, what the Americans sometimes called a "do-over," and Baklanov could start again, with Donatelli's help, to get their coalition off the ground.

"Gaining." The driver's voice was tense, his dark eyes flicking back and forth between the highway and the limo's rearview mirror.

"Ready," Shurochka told his friend and master, leaning toward the gun port, with the muzzle of his weapon inches from the artfully camouflaged slot. He left the AKSU's skeleton stock folded against the left side of the rifle, knowing there would be no opportunity to aim as if he were competing in a target match.

The other bodyguards, Ivan and Vladimir, were similarly armed, one with a Skorpion, the other with a mini-Uzi SMG. They also carried pistols underneath their jackets, as did Sasha, leaving Baklanov the only passenger of the Mercedes-Benz who was unarmed.

With any luck, the Russian mobster thought, he wouldn't be required to soil his hands.

"Coming," Sasha announced, holding the limousine rock steady at the speed limit, a sluggish fifty-five.

"Be ready," Shurochka told his soldiers, reaching out to slide open the gun port as he spoke. "And shoot to kill."

IT WAS A FIFTY-FIFTY gamble which way he should turn once he was through the gate. A pair of puzzled sentries gaped at him, neither one of them sure whether they should wave him on or try to stop him with a hail of bullets. Playing safe, they let him go, and Bolan had two seconds flat in which to make his choice.

If he turned west, the road would take him into Camden, across the Delaware to Philadelphia. Eastward, it wound through Presidential Lakes, the Lebanon State Forest, Whiting and a half-dozen more hamlets before it ran into the sea at Point Pleasant. Urban or rural? Would Baklanov try to get lost in a crowd, or hide out in the dark?

The soldier flipped a mental coin and swung his liberated Skylark to the east, standing on the accelerator. If his choice was faulty, he had blown the game already, but at least he ought to know within a few more moments, one way or the other.

Even if he caught up to a fleeing limousine, there was a chance that it would be the wrong one, one of the Sicilians who had cast his lot with Baklanov. That wouldn't be a total waste, but he could take the mafiosi anytime, at home. It was the Russian who commanded his attention, as brains and driving force behind the sit-down that had drawn Bolan halfway across the country, from another job in Arizona, to disrupt the master plan.

That much had been achieved, at least, if only for the moment. Bolan cherished no illusion that the firefight at Gambola's hideaway would scuttle Baklanov's design. It would be rated as an irritation, nothing more, unless he managed to decapitate the serpent he had come to slay.

A mile or so ahead of him, he spotted ruby taillights in the darkness, winking brighter for an instant as the driver tapped his brakes. Bolan considered switching off his headlights, running up behind them in the dark, but it would be too risky on an unfamiliar rural highway, farms and homes on either side, driveways and access roads unseen, perhaps livestock and deer wandering about. If he couldn't conceal himself, then, Bolan opted for the other course and flicked on the Skylark's high beams, burning a tunnel through the night.

The vehicle in front of him made no attempt to bolt and run.

That could mean that the driver had no link to the fiasco at Gambola's, or he could be playing it cool, waiting to see who was approaching from behind. Whichever, Bolan would find out within another sixty seconds.

Driving with one hand on the Skylark's steering wheel, the other resting on his CAR-15, Bolan began to think the coming confrontation through. If he was gaining on a crew wagon, regardless of the passengers' identity, the limo would be armored and impervious to bullets from his automatic rifle, much less either of the side arms he was carrying. The M-203 launcher could effect a kill, but he'd need both hands—however briefly—to steady the weapon and fire.

So be it.

Barring some dramatic intervention from the target, Bolan reckoned he could keep his ride on track and on the blacktop long enough to make the shot.

He had already closed the gap to half a mile, and he was gaining rapidly on what might prove to be some local resident out driving with his lady love. The taillights didn't look like any kind of pickup truck he was familiar with, but that left countless foreign and domestic cars to choose from, and the distance was too great for Bolan to identify the make and model.

Closing.

If it was a crew wagon ahead of him, the soldiers riding in it would be on alert for any hot pursuit. The borrowed Buick had no armor plating, and he would be vulnerable to a single bullet, much less any blaze of automatic fire designed to sweep him off the road. If all else failed, by simply holding him at bay until they reached a settlement with lawmen cruising on the night shift, Bolan would be forced to disengage and make a run for it, involving risks beyond a simple clash with mercenary guns.

Which simply meant that he would have to finish it before they reached a town.

The Skylark's engine had some heavy-duty power to it, Bolan found, as he accelerated in pursuit of the retreating taillights. Good acceleration, and the power windows were a bonus, letting Bolan lower the glass on the passenger's side without leaning across the empty seat. If he had been relying on the CAR-15 itself, he could have braced its muzzle on the windowsill, but that would place the M-203's trigger well beyond his reach.

No problem.

He could trust the Buick to run straight and steady for the brief time he would need to aim and fire the 40 mm launcher. Call it two, three seconds, maximum. Of course, there could be trouble if the limo fishtailed, slamming into him while he was roaring down the straightaway in no-hands mode.

Forget about it.

He would do what was required of him, and damn the risk. It would be worth it if his target was Baklanov's Mercedes-Benz. And if it wasn't…well, then, Bolan would make do with what he had.

There was no danger that the Russian would attempt to flee the country; he was confident of that, at least. His target had too many deals in progress, too many high-level irons in the fire, to simply bail out and abandon his investments. Besides, he had worn out his welcome at home. Short of fleeing to some Third World backwater, where would he go?

To hell, perhaps…and soon, if Bolan had his way.

He had the crew wagon in sight, now, and there was no doubt whatsoever that it was a limousine. In another moment, Bolan was rewarded with a clear view of the world-famous Mercedes emblem, telling him that Lady Luck—or maybe Mars, the god of war—hadn't deserted him.

His left hand gripped the Buick's steering wheel and held it steady, while his right slid out to find the CAR-15 by feel. Its weight was reassuring, and he hoped that it would be enough to do the job. One shot was all that he could count on, even with the Lady and old Mars together in his corner. After that, it would be anybody's game, and Bolan could as easily wind up the loser, joining those he had already killed tonight.

He blanked that prospect out and concentrated on his driv-

ing, running up as close as possible behind the limousine before
he made his move to pass.

One chance to win.

One chance to live.

He focused on that single shot and vowed to make it count.

"I DON'T LIKE THIS one on my ass," Sasha announced to no
one in particular.

"The car," Shurochka said, then closed his mouth, as if the
two words should have meaning in and of themselves.

"What of it?" Baklanov demanded. "Speak coherently, for
God's sake!"

"It's familiar," Shurochka said, appearing to take no offense. "I think...."

"What do you think?" It was a challenge, just to keep from
shouting at him.

"I saw it at Gambola's house," the gunman said. "Yes, it's
the same one. The Buick that was parked in front."

Baklanov twisted in his seat, squinting in the glare of headlights that were drawing closer by the second. How could Shurochka tell the chase car was a Buick, much less one from the
Gambola motor pool?

The Russian spoke his doubt aloud. "Why would Gambola
send a man to follow us?"

"I don't say that he did," the lieutenant replied. "I recognize the car, that's all."

But if Gambola had dispatched a car to follow them, what
did it mean? There were at least two possible solutions to the
riddle. First, he might have sent an escort to protect them, albeit
a tardy, insufficient one. Or, second, Gambola might have some
part in the ambush that had broken up their meeting. If he was
a traitor, masquerading as a friend...

"You're sure?" Baklanov asked. "About the car?"

"I'm sure enough," Shurochka said.

"How many men are there inside?"

"I can't tell that," Shurochka replied. "That model seats

four comfortably. You can squeeze a fifth one in the back if you don't care that it's cramped.''

Baklanov didn't like it, but kept the thought to himself. A show of strength before his men at all times was the first rule of command. The first display of indecision, doubt or weakness would come back to haunt him, someday, when his flunkies got up nerve enough to challenge his authority.

"Gambola would be foolish to send someone after us," he said at last.

"Or something worse," Shurochka said.

Thus validated, Baklanov had only to decide how he would deal with their pursuers. Knowing that the limousine was fully armored, he could let the Buick—if it was a Buick—trail them through the night until its occupants dredged up the nerve to make a move. Whatever happened after that, even if they were killed, it would be simple self-defense.

Of course, there were a hundred reasons why he didn't wish to deal with the American police, and that meant he should see the problem dealt with promptly, while they still had darkness and the open road to shelter them. A quick, clean finish to the problem, here and now.

"All right," he said, his mind made up. "Get rid of them."

Shurochka grimaced—his approximation of a smile—and flicked open the gun port with his long, pale fingers, deftly sliding the AKSU into firing position. On the other side of the limo, to Baklanov's right, Vladimir had taken his position at the other gun port, cocking his Skorpion with a loud click of the bolt. That left Ivan, without a window of his own, hunched on the jump seat directly across from Baklanov, the mini-Uzi cradled in his lap. It seemed to Baklanov that he was pouting like a child.

"Cheer up, Ivan," Shurochka said. "You'll have your chance another time."

It crossed Baklanov's mind to take issue with that, maybe argue the point that his whole grand design was meant to eliminate blood feuds and running battles, but he was wise enough to keep his mouth shut on that score. Whatever happened down the road—a year, five years from now—it would take blood to grease the way for institution of his new regime. The old guard mafiosi in America wouldn't roll over and surrender all that they had worked for, killed for, without putting up a fight. The fact that he had managed to recruit a handful of important allies early on, for all the good it did him, still wouldn't allow him to escape the coming war.

Nor, frankly, did he wish to win a bloodless victory. What glory was there in divesting spineless men of their possessions, looting those who dared not stand and fight? He had been counting on a struggle when he came to the United States, and every move made in the interim had been designed to gain advantage for the day when talking turned to killing, and the blood began to flow.

Granted, he didn't like the way tonight's initial meeting had been interrupted, but the violence troubled Baklanov far less than knowing he had been the target, rather than the instigator. It had set him back, damaged his reputation, and it would take forceful action to restore the image he had crafted for himself.

Beginning now.

"He's coming," Shurochka said. "My side."

The terse announcement was rewarded by a curse from Vladimir, and Baklanov could only shake his head in wonderment. How else could the pursuer try to pass them on a two-lane road? To go the other way, pass on the right, meant veering off the pavement into cultivated fields.

He frowned, considering if he should have his lieutenant dispose of Vladimir on general principle, because he was an idiot, and then decided that it made no difference, as long as he shot straight and followed orders instantly.

"Coming," Shurochka repeated, as if talking to himself, and then he cut loose with the AKSU, filling the passenger compartment of the limousine with noise, the reek of cordite and shiny brass that jingled at his feet.

Baklanov turned his head in time to see the Buick drawing up beside them, and then a muzzle-flash.

BOLAN WAS SWINGING out to pass the limo when the shooting started, automatic fire erupting from a gun port on the driver's side, but well back toward the rear end of the vehicle. The first few rounds went high and wide, a natural result of firing prematurely, when the gunner didn't have a decent opportunity to aim, but then a bullet struck the Skylark's hood a glancing blow and cracked into the windshield, pelting him with pebbles of glass.

He stamped on the accelerator and was instantly rewarded with another surge of speed, the Skylark's engine giving everything it had. The shooter in the limo, likewise, was unloading with a vengeance, peppering the Buick's starboard side, some of the rounds punching through to bury themselves in the dashboard and passenger's seat. The weapon's racket told Bolan it was some kind of Kalashnikov, but he was unconcerned with the specifics. One hit could be crippling, even fatal, and he needed time to make his shot, at least, before the Russian gunner took him out.

To buy that time, he goosed the Skylark forward, nosed the muzzle of his weapon through the open window and unleashed a burst of 5.56 mm rounds at point-blank range. He had no realistic hope of penetrating armor plate with the return fire— it would be a total fluke, almost a miracle, if one of Bolan's rounds slipped through the limo's gun port—but the fusillade apparently had some effect, as his assailant broke off firing for a moment. Maybe he was startled by the bullets that had etched faint patterns on his tinted window, or perhaps he had already spent a magazine. In any case, there was a momentary lull in gunfire from the limousine, and Bolan took the best advantage of it that he could.

He brought the CAR-15's stock to his shoulder, braced his right elbow against the backrest of the driver's seat and wrapped his other hand around the M-203's pistol grip. Another second, now, and—

The Executioner saw disaster coming in a heartbeat, recognizing his peril even as the trap slammed shut. Inside the limousine, his enemy unleashed another burst that raked the Sky-

lark with a fierce hailstorm of bullets, making Bolan duck
involuntarily before the CAR-15 was ripped out of his grasp.
It could have been a bullet or the rifle's stock that cracked
against his cheek and sent bright pinwheels spinning in the dark
behind his eyes. Bolan was reaching for the steering wheel,
already standing on the brake pedal, when his assailant shot
out both tires on the Buick's right-hand side and sent him
swerving across the blacktop toward an open field.

The Skylark clipped a barbed-wire fence as if it had been
made of flimsy thread and plunged on another sixty feet or so
until the bare rims on the right sank into soft, plowed earth.
The engine sputtered for a while, then died, pale wisps of
smoke or steam curling upward from the vents near the broken
windshield.

Bolan swiveled in his seat, shrugging off the pain, the Desert
Eagle in his hand before he had a conscious thought of drawing
it. Downrange, he saw the limo's taillights dwindling, fading
in the distance, and he knew his enemies wouldn't be coming
back to finish the job. They didn't care if he was dead or not,
as long as they got clear.

That was their first mistake.

He let another moment pass, working his jaw and dabbing
at his bloody cheek, before he cranked down the rearview mirror and switched on the dome light to check the damage. He
didn't appear to have a bullet wound, although his face was
swelling, and the blood drained from a ragged gash below his
eye. He checked the CAR-15 and found a bullet scar across
the plastic foregrip, and the butt was crimson-smeared from its
collision with his cheek.

A lucky break of sorts, then, even though it meant that he
had lost his shot at Rurik Baklanov. For now.

He didn't bother with the Skylark, knowing it was finished.
Climbing out to stretch, he looked around and saw the nearest
house was some three-quarters of a mile away, due west, in
the direction he had come from. Lights were on, but he had no
way of knowing whether anyone was home, if they had heard

the shooting, or whether they were on the phone right now to 911 and the authorities.

He had a long walk back to the point where he had left his car before he scaled Gino Gambola's fence. If luck was with him—better luck, that was—he might get there without patrolmen or a nervous, trigger-happy farmer spotting him. He'd lose time by hiking through the fields, but he needed cover now, not speed.

He slid the Desert Eagle back into its holster, took the CAR-15 and started walking back toward Gambola's hardsite and his ride. The good news was that he had only come about three miles from the Gambola killing ground before he lost it, and his car was just another quarter mile or so beyond the walled estate. Another hour, give or take, should see him on the road, provided that he met no opposition in the meantime.

Moving through the darkness, loose dirt lapping at his boots, he didn't brood about the way his probe had gone to hell. It was a gamble, going in, and if he hadn't taken home the jackpot, neither had he lost.

The losers for tonight were dead; the Executioner, in turn, would live to fight another day.

And Rurik Baklanov was very much mistaken if he thought that he was free and clear.

3

Two days prior to the Burlington blowout, Mack Bolan and Hal Brognola had strolled along The Mall, in Washington, D.C. They walked in daylight, rubbing shoulders with the tourists, within a stone's throw—or a pistol shot—of Brognola's office in the Justice Department building on Constitution Avenue. The day was bright and clear, unlike the tale Brognola had to tell.

"You knew old man Perrugia," he said, by way of introduction.

Bolan frowned. "By reputation, sure. Vinnie the Viper, out of Kansas City."

"Relocated as of seven weeks ago," Brognola said, "to maximum security at Leavenworth."

"It was a long time coming," Bolan said. "I would have liked to meet him."

The big Fed made no response to that. Their private history went back to the chaotic days when Bolan launched a one-man war against the Mafia from coast to coast, eliminating bosses and the soldiers who surrounded them like pop-up targets in a shooting gallery. The Executioner had been an outlaw in those days, with price tags on his head from both the Syndicate and U.S. government.

"He's history," Brognola said. "He'll die inside before they finish hashing over the appeals. That isn't why I asked you for the meet."

It was unusual for the big Fed to meet with Bolan one-on-one these days, and when they did meet, it was normally at

Stony Man Farm, the secret hardsite in the Blue Ridge Mountains of Virginia that had come as close to being "home" as anyplace a rootless soldier could expect, when he was caught up in a never-ending war.

"What, then?" asked the soldier, prodding Brognola enough to get him started down the dark road that would soon be Bolan's path, as well.

"We nailed Perrugia on a RICO beef," Brognola said, referring to the federal racketeering in corrupt organizations statute that had laid whole gangland Families to waste on sundry charges of conspiracy. "You knew that, right?"

"I heard," Bolan replied.

"Our main witness against him—hell, the keystone of the case, if you want to know the truth—was a Russian, Rurik Baklanov by name, who had a big deal working with Perrugia, between the States and Moscow. They were moving any damned thing you can think of—weapons, drugs, illegal immigrants—the whole nine yards. The DEA got hip to Baklanov and nailed him with a shipment from Colombia about a year ago. Turns out that he was wanted back in Russia, too, on a murder charge that could have put him in the ground."

"Unless he cut a deal," Bolan said.

"That's the ticket," Brognola admitted. "Baklanov rolled over on Perrugia and sent him up, along with half a dozen heirs apparent to the top job in KC. The outfit's decimated there. It might be years before they get reorganized—or never, if we stay on top of them."

"So far, so good," Bolan remarked.

"We thought so, too. Of course, there was a payoff for the Russian," the big Fed went on. "We had to ante up immunity, witness protection. You know how it goes."

"The problem being...?"

"That we lost the bastard," Brognola replied, his voice now tight with bitterness.

"You lost me, too. What, exactly, are you saying?"

"Jesus, this is rich," the man from Justice said, snorting derision at himself. "We gave this guy a total makeover, you follow me? Beginning with a whole new face. His mama wouldn't know him now, assuming that the bastard had one.''

"And?'' Bolan could see where Brognola was going, but he had to hear it from his old friend's lips, find out exactly what went wrong…and how he was supposed to make it right.

"And he was down to set up housekeeping in San Francisco,'' Brognola continued. "He was leaving with an escort on the next flight out, for Christ's sake.''

"Next flight out of where?'' Bolan asked.

"Jefferson City, Missouri,'' the big Fed said, "but that won't help you any. He's long gone, by now.''

"So, what happened?''

"The night before his move, a hit team swept the farm where he was hiding out. We lost six agents KIA, two of them friends of mine.''

"And Baklanov?''

"No sign of him,'' Brognola said. "At first, there was a notion that the shooters might have grabbed him, even though it didn't make much sense. I mean, why haul the guy off, even if you want to make his dying last awhile? They had the place all to themselves and could've done him on the spot. They could have dressed him out and tacked his hide up on the barn door as a warning if they wanted to.''

It didn't take a master strategist to play connect the dots. "He staged the hit himself,'' the soldier concluded.

"And he's gone,'' Brognola said.

But where? Bolan wasn't required to voice the question, as his friend seemed to read his mind.

"Of course, new face and all, the first thought was that he'd go home to Russia, maybe pick up with his old connections in the Chechen outfit over there,'' Brognola said. "It's what I'd do, I guess, if I was in his place.''

"But now, you don't think so.''

Brognola shook his head. "The guy's still here. We're getting rumbles off the street, odd comments from a wire tap, here and there. There's something in the works, big time, and Baklanov's behind it.''

"That's a little vague," Bolan suggested, trying not to make it any worse on Brognola, but needing more.

"It's nothing you can put a finger on," the gray-haired Fed replied. "Three weeks since Baklanov—or 'Rory Baker,' if you want to use his new name—pulled the fade, and all we've got are bits and pieces. The way it looks right now, this oily bastard set Perrugia up from the beginning. Hell, for all I know, he might have planned his own arrest last year. If not, he knew a good thing when he saw it, and he's swift at thinking on his feet. This way, he gets rid of the top boss in the country—and the strongest opposition any newbie had to deal with, coming in—plus, Uncle Sam picks up the tab for his new face."

"And now?" Bolan asked.

"With KC out of the equation, Baklanov apparently has managed to convince a handful of the other bosses, nationwide, to throw in with him on some kind of pipe dream for a New World Order. Maybe New Underworld Order's more like it."

"An international conglomerate?" asked Bolan.

"Looks like," Brognola replied. "I can't be sure of any details, understand, but what I'm hearing off the street, the Russian winds up with an equal vote on La Commissione—or, maybe he's the whole show, if he's got a few more capos in his pocket."

"How am I supposed to spot him?" Bolan asked, "with the new face?"

"That's a problem," the big Fed replied disgustedly. "The surgeon—one we've used before, a Dr. Louis Marx, out of Chicago—had before-and-after photos in his files."

"Had photos?" Bolan had a hunch where this was going, but he let Brognola lead the way.

"That's right. The morning after Baklanov went missing in Missouri, someone took out Marx's office in the Loop. Four dead up front, before the shooters used some kind of military-style incendiary on the files. There's nothing left."

"They nailed the doctor?" Bolan asked.

"He wasn't in the office. He's gone, though."

"Snatched?"

"It doesn't look that way," Brognola said. "He tapped a bank account the morning of the flameout at his office. How it looks, he's in the wind."

"But still alive."

"I'm hoping."

"And we're clueless, as to where he is."

"I've got people watching for him," Brognola said, "but he hasn't used his credit cards so far. He doesn't have the background or the skills for staying underground for long. The problem is, we're running short on time with Baklanov and his playmates."

"Which still leaves the question of how I find him," Bolan said. There was no doubt remaining in his mind that he would take the mission, but it wasn't clear, by any means, that he could track down his quarry in time to make a difference.

"I just might have a line on that," Brognola said. "We picked it off a wiretap in Manhattan, covering Ted Peredo."

Bolan knew "Terrible Ted" by reputation. He was the nearest thing to a "Boss of Bosses" remaining in New York, since Bolan's one-man blitz and years of relentless federal prosecution had stripped the historic Five Families of their most ruthless and talented leadership. Ted Peredo was an animal, no doubt about it, but he was strictly bantam-weight beside some of the capos Bolan had known—and killed.

"So, what's the word?" he asked.

"The big boys—some of them, at least—have got a sit-down on their calendar, two days from now. Gino Gambola's hosting in New Jersey, at his home. So far, besides Peredo, we've been able to confirm DeRicco, Donatelli and Fortini coming in."

Miami, Buffalo and Cleveland, plus the ruling capos of New Jersey and Manhattan. Bolan knew a summit meeting when he saw one, but he had to ask. "So, where does Baklanov come in?"

Brognola frowned, his eyebrows puckering. It was a long-familiar look, which meant that he was shooting craps, uncertain if the dice were straight or loaded.

"What we've heard," he answered, "is that the Sicilian

crowd is having company. They haven't dropped a name, per
se, but Peredo calls him 'Mr. Red,' and Gambola made a crack
about 'the Russki.'"

It was Bolan's turn to frown. "That's pretty thin. There must
be—what, five hundred Russian mobsters in the States, right
now?"

"I wish," Brognola said. "Smart money says it's double
that."

"So, why should we assume this 'Mr. Red' is Rurik
Baklanov?"

"Call it a hunch. My gut's been talking to me," the big Fed
replied. "We know he's got the savvy and the pull back home,
indictments notwithstanding, to command attention from the
big boys over here. On top of that, none of the delegates to
Gambola's little house party would ever be mistaken for friends
of Vinnie Perrugia. They'd all like a piece of his action, and
they might just be inclined to look with admiration on the man
who took him out of circulation."

"Even from the witness stand?"

"Even so," Brognola said. "Why not? It wouldn't be the
first time one boss fed his opposition to the courts, instead of
wasting him. Remember Luciano's move on Waxey Gordon in
the thirties?"

Bolan grinned at his friend and said, "That was before my
time."

"Nobody likes a smart-ass," Brognola responded, but his
frown was slipping. "Anyway, letting the government take
Perrugia out saved everyone the cost and casualties of a pro-
tracted turf war, and it left his rackets more or less intact—
except for someone to step in and run the show."

They had come to a halt, as if by mutual consent, within a
hundred yards of the Smithsonian. Bolan stood with his head
tilted backward, eyes closed, enjoying the warmth of the sun
on his face. When he next spoke, the vague reluctance that he
felt didn't come through in his tone.

"Looks like I need to crash a party."

There was no mistaking the relief in Hal Brognola's voice as he responded, "I was hoping you'd say that."

"Meanwhile," Bolan said, "we could use a line on Dr. Marx, ASAP, in case something goes wrong."

AND SO, IT HAD.

It took some thirty minutes longer than the Executioner had hoped, to reach his rented car. Three times along the way, he had been forced to duck and hide while squad cars, fire trucks and an ambulance sped past with flashing lights and sirens wailing, headed for Gino Gambola's estate. Someone had dropped a coin—more likely to have been a neighbor than the Don himself—and Bolan had to skirt the property at a distance, retracing the path to his ride. The whole estate was lit up like a football stadium at halftime, as he skirted the perimeter, taking advantage of the night.

Bolan wasn't concerned about Gambola's difficulties with the law. The New Jersey boss had managed to survive this long by bribing, frightening or killing off his opposition. This time, when he was in fact the victim of a criminal assault, there would be questions, but Gambola wouldn't be a suspect in the case. Assuming he had managed to dispose of any outlawed weapons by the time police arrived, the worst that lay in store for Gambola—at the moment, anyway—would be a game of twenty questions with the bulls from homicide.

No sweat.

Bolan, meanwhile, had come up with the short end of the stick. The Russian had eluded him, which meant the hunt would have to start again, from scratch. One of Gambola's VIPs, at least, had gone to his reward, but Bolan didn't know which one, since there had been no time to check inside the flaming ruin of the limousine. That still left three, besides Gambola…but would Baklanov be reaching out to any one of them after tonight's fiasco?

Bolan barely knew the Russian, from Brognola's dossier—still hadn't glimpsed his brand-new face, in fact—but he didn't see Rurik Baklanov as someone who surrendered easily, once he had fixed his sights on an intended goal. That meant that he would have to get in touch again—somewhere, somehow— but Bolan couldn't count on Brognola's wiretaps and snitches to record the contact, much less give him time to beat the clock and take out the Russian.

The Executioner would need an edge, and if he couldn't find it in the Russian mobster's present, or his future, he would have to seek it in the past. And that, in turn, meant finding Dr. Louis Marx.

But, where to start?

With Brognola.

The big Fed had been chasing leads on Marx from the moment Baklanov had disappeared, the doctor dropping out of sight mere hours later. Bolan hadn't checked back with Brognola since their meeting in Washington, preoccupied as he had been with setting up the Jersey strike, but now he had no other likely angle of attack.

He stopped in Medford, found a service station that had closed down for the night and parked his rental so that it provided cover while he used the public telephone. A land line was the safest way to go, and Bolan had his miniscrambler plugged into the box before he tapped out Brognola's private-and-restricted number from memory. Same time zone, for a change, and Brognola didn't sound sleepy as he picked up on the other end.

"Hello?"

"It's me," Bolan said, trusting his friend to recognize his voice. "We scrambled?"

"Just a second…there," Brognola said. "So, how'd it go?"

"Not well," the soldier admitted, serving up a condensed version of his probe and Rurik Baklanov's escape. "We're back to square one," Bolan said in closing. "Maybe worse."

Brognola didn't criticize or second-guess. The men had known each other far too long for that, and the big Fed couldn't imagine Bolan slipping up through negligence. Shit happened, sometimes, in the killing grounds. Sometimes you got the bear; sometimes the bear got you…or simply got away.

"I'm thinking that he won't go far," Brognola said. "If he was heading back to Russia, he'd be gone by now. He wants this deal, or maybe something bigger. I don't see him letting go of it this easily."

"I need the doctor, Hal."

"We caught a break there," Brognola informed him. "Maybe caught a break, I mean. Marx has a girlfriend who lives in Berwyn. That's a suburb of—"

"Chicago, right."

"Cheryl LeBlanc," Brognola forged ahead. "A former patient. Marx improved her outlook, shall we say, and they wound up together, going on the past two years or so. We got that off his home phone records, and I have a couple agents watching her. Phone cover, too."

"Results?"

"She got a call this evening," Brognola said. "It was Marx. We got a trace."

"You pick him up?"

"Not yet. I thought it might be better to give him some space, in case you had the need to get in touch with him."

"Good thinking," Bolan said. "Where is he?"

"Downstate Illinois," Brognola said. "Some kind of country place outside of Fairfield, in Wayne County." Then he gave Bolan the directions.

The soldier checked his watch and frowned.

"I'm on my way," he said, and hung up the receiver before moving swiftly toward his car.

4

Bolan flew into Evansville, Indiana, on a commuter flight out of Trenton, and found a Dodge Avenger waiting for him in the parking lot. The keys were underneath the left rear fender in a small magnetic box. A duffel bag in the Avenger's trunk contained the hardware Bolan had requested from Brognola, certain items that the airlines generally frowned upon as check-through luggage. The soldier made a hasty inventory, satisfied himself that everything was present and accounted for, then motored out of town on Highway 66, heading northwest.

He crossed the toll bridge into Illinois, at New Harmony, shortly after 3:30 p.m. He stopped for food and fuel in Burnt Prairie, then drove another seven miles to pick up Highway 45, northbound into Fairfield, the seat of Wayne County.

His quarry wasn't in Fairfield, of course, and the town of some six thousand residents interested Bolan only as a place where he could kill some time, waiting for night to fall. He bought some takeout coffee from a Stop-n-Go convenience store, downtown, and drank it in the parking lot of an IGA market, watching the locals come and go.

Bolan had become a self-taught expert, of sorts, on the subject of Dr. Louis Marx, reviewing Brognola's discussion of the plastic surgeon as he flew and drove from New Jersey to downstate Illinois. A graduate of Stanford Medical School, in the top five percent of his class, Marx had completed his internship and residency in the San Francisco area, moving on from there to specialize in plastic surgery. About eight years ago, already well-known in the Golden State, he had pulled up stakes and moved to Chicago—encouraged, Brognola said, by the promise of steady off-the-books work for Uncle Sam, constructing new faces for a list of clientele that included foreign defectors, protected witnesses and a handful of deep-cover agents operating both within the country and abroad. It was a sideline that padded Dr. Marx's income with an extra quarter-million dollars every year, on average, and since the Treasury Department also used him—Secret Service, ATF, even the IRS Criminal Investigative Division—that stipend fell through the cracks at tax time, his ''special'' bank account and safe-deposit box ignored by federal auditors.

Not bad.

It didn't bother Bolan in the least that Dr. Marx was making out like gangbusters, in league with Uncle Sam. Somebody had to do the work, and if he got results, so be it. Bolan's one and only interest in the doctor lay in his ability to finger Rurik Baklanov—aka Rory Baker—and hang a face on the Executioner's latest target.

Bolan only hoped that he wouldn't be forced to kill Marx in the process.

There was bound to be a fair degree of paranoia on the doctor's part, considering his background and the recent blowout at his office that had claimed the lives of two employees and two patients. Marx had known enough to run and hide—if not to break off contact with his lover—when the chips were down, and it wasn't unreasonable to suppose he might be armed, prepared to fight if unknown men came looking for him at his hideaway.

The soldier wasn't concerned about the issue of doctor-patient confidentiality. That rule was waived by law in the case of ongoing crimes, and the Baklanov makeover had been commissioned by government agents, in any case; a phone call to Washington would clear up that end of the deal if Marx proved stubborn.

The real trick, the Executioner thought, would be keeping the doctor alive long enough to raise the subject in the first place. If he came out shooting at first sight of Bolan, there

were only so many ways to disarm a violent adversary, short
of blowing him away. Even a bullet aimed to wound was capable of killing, and if Marx checked out before they had a
chance to talk, Bolan would find himself well up the stinky
creek without a paddle.

Then again, there was a chance that Marx might already be
dead.

If Rurik Baklanov was slick enough, well-connected enough,
to arrange the massacre of his own federal escorts while still
under guard in Missouri, wipe out Marx's records in Chicago
and fix a sit-down in New Jersey with six of the Mafia's top-
ranking capos, it was possible he might have known about the
surgeon's girlfriend, maybe had a set of ears piggybacking the
FBI wiretap upstate. And if that was the case, a hit team could
have easily been on its way to Fairfield, while Bolan was chasing Baklanov's limo through Burlington County.

Why not?

The thought made Bolan nervous, but he sat and waited out
the daylight, all the same. At sundown, he found a drive-in
restaurant and forced himself to eat. Afterward he retrieved his
nightsuit from the Avenger's trunk, locked himself in the one-
toilet men's room long enough to strip down, slip it on and
rearrange his street clothes.

He was ready to go.

Brognola had provided fair directions to the doctor's hideout,
supplemented by a road map Bolan purchased at a gas station,
heading out of town. The place where Marx had gone to ground
lay two miles west-southwest of Fairfield, in the midst of farm-
ing country, but he had no fear of any backup gunners loitering
around the house.

The plastic surgeon was alone and knew it, which would
make him double dangerous on the approach.

It was half-past seven and well after dark when Bolan drove
past the house, westbound, and kept going. He had glimpsed a
light on, shining through a window on the east side of the
house, together with the standard rural power pole that lit the
yard in front as bright as noonday. Half a mile beyond the

house, he turned onto an unpaved access road and killed his headlights, rolling another hundred yards or so until he was satisfied that no one passing on the highway would spot the Dodge.

Bolan switched off the dome light before he opened the driver's door, stepping out of the car into darkness. It was a moment's work to strip off his jacket and slacks, leaving them folded on the driver's seat. He switched his loafers for high-topped combat boots, then retrieved a combat harness from the trunk and shrugged it on, buckling the web belt at his waist. A weapons check confirmed that both side arms were fully loaded, live rounds in the chambers. Bolan chose an Uzi sub-machine gun from the mobile arsenal, then reconsidered and replaced it in the trunk, aware that if it went that far, his mission would have been a waste of time. In lieu of frag grenades, he chose two flash-bangs from another bag and clipped them to his webbing.

Ready.

The field beyond the access road wasn't fenced in. Bolan paused with the soft, crumbling earth underfoot, got a fix on the house and began his advance through the darkness, moving toward his unscheduled rendezvous with the one man who could help him finger Rurik Baklanov.

THE PISTOL LYING next to Dr. Louis Marx's Hungry Man TV dinner, on the cheap dining table, was a .45-caliber Colt automatic, the classic Model 1911A1. A Cook County judge, duly grateful for the breast enhancement, fanny tuck and other touch-ups Marx had wrought upon the judge's mistress, had supplied the doctor with a license that permitted him to pack the weapon anywhere he liked, within the state of Illinois.

He wondered, at the moment, whether it would be enough to save his life.

The TV dinner—Swiss steak, potatoes, corn and apple crisp, nuked in the microwave—was Marx's first choice on the rare occasions when he "cooked" at home, but at the moment, in his present state of mind, it tasted like a stew of mush and cardboard. Finally, distracted and disgusted, he leaned back and pushed the tray away from him.

To hell with it.

He wasn't hungry, anyway. His appetite had vanished when he heard the news about the slaughter at his office—Carol and Janice gunned down like stray dogs, along with two new clients Marx had never even had a chance to meet.

Four dead, and half a dozen U.S. marshals in Missouri made it ten, so far. Marx would have been made eleven, if the gunmen who had tried to take him out were more efficient, quicker on the uptake. If it hadn't been for Cheryl, Marx would have been totally cut off from contact with the outside world.

But, was he safe?

A bitter rasp of laughter managed to escape before Marx bit it off. He didn't know what safe meant anymore. For years on end, he had assumed the government was watching over him, somehow—the same Feds who protected those he operated on, who managed to ignore his special bank accounts—and now, they left him high and dry. He was afraid to call them, even try to get in touch, worried that if they couldn't help a client under constant guard, what could they do for Marx himself?

Nothing.

He took the pistol with him when he got up from the table, tucking it into the waistband of his slacks before he scraped his dinner into the garbage disposal, rinsed the tray and dropped it in the trash. That done, he walked back to the living room, switched off the kitchen light in passing and found the remote for the old Sony console TV. Poised above the armchair, Marx remembered to remove the big Colt from his belt before it gouged him in the groin.

Some gunfighter, he thought, and snorted out another laugh before he switched on the television. Marx spent a few distracted moments channel surfing—past *Green Acres*, local news, a noisy game show, bad news from the Middle East on CNN—before he switched off the TV again.

"Goddamn it!" he addressed the empty room. And, once again, "Goddamn it all to hell!"

It was amazing, when he thought about it, seeing how fast a well-ordered life could implode under unexpected pressure. In the space of a few short hours, he had gone from being Dr. Louis Marx, a well-respected physician with friends in high places, to fugitive Louis Marx, hunted like an animal by unknown enemies, afraid to show his face outside this rustic hideaway. He wondered what would happen when the stock of food on hand began to dwindle, and he had to go shopping in Fairfield.

And the thought occurred to him at once: No sweat. He could be dead by then.

But he wouldn't go down without a fight; that much he promised to himself. He had already dodged his would-be killers once, and if they found him here, Marx was determined to resist. He wouldn't be mistaken for a Rambo-type, by any means—indeed, he didn't even care for action movies, and had practiced with the big Colt automatic only twice, four years ago, before the qualifying test required for his carry permit. But he was cornered, and the lowest form of animal would fight with its last ounce of strength to stay alive.

So, that's what he'd become, he thought. A hunted animal.

What else? His university degrees were useless to him, now. His social and political connections might as well have been in Bosnia, for all the good they did him, at the moment. Cheryl had volunteered to come and join him, but he had persuaded her to stay at home, saying that it was for her own good, that she shouldn't place herself at risk.

All true, of course, but it wasn't the real reason why Marx wanted her to stay away. The bottom line was that he was afraid someone might be watching Cheryl, that she might be followed from Berwyn by a hunting party that would kill them both. This way, at least, if one of Marx's nameless enemies came knocking on her door, she couldn't give him up.

Because he hadn't told Cheryl where he was.

Marx wished he had a dog, the thought arriving out of nowhere. Not a German shepherd or a pit bull, necessarily, but some breed that would bark, at least, and give him warning if the hunters tried to creep up on him in the middle of the night.

Like now.

It wasn't all that late. At home, unless he had an early operation in the morning, Marx would frequently be wide-awake at 1:00 a.m. or later. He had always been a night owl, born and bred, but now he lay awake in brooding silence, barred from sleeping by the fear that someone he had never seen or heard of in his life would creep up on him while his eyes were closed and put a bullet in his head. Pills helped him stay awake, if not alert, but Marx was running low on his supply. That would pose another problem if he had to write himself a fresh prescription and go into town to have it filled.

Marx wondered how much longer he could stick it out, before exhaustion and the strain upon his nerves became too much and wore him down.

Marx had tried to put the scrambled pieces of the puzzle in some kind of order that would make sense in his mind. At first, the news out of Missouri seemed to indicate that his most recent client had been hunted down and killed, presumably by agents of the mobsters he had testified against. That much was logical, but it wouldn't explain the subsequent attempt on Marx's life, the slaughter at his office in Chicago.

No. His role in reconstructing faces for the government was known to certain Feds, and to the clients he had served. A mobster seeking vengeance on the man who sent him up would have no way of tracing Dr. Marx, nor would he care to try. The surgeon was irrelevant…except, perhaps, to someone with a brand-new face and a desire to keep his old identity a secret from the world at large.

In that case—

Marx couldn't have said exactly what alerted him to danger, possibly a sound that registered subconsciously. He simply knew, between one moment and the next, that there was someone lurking in the dark outside, and he wasn't expecting company.

He reached out for the nearby lamp, then stopped himself.

The draperies were closed, depriving any prowler of an inside view, but Marx would tip his hand if he switched off the lights. Instead, he palmed the big Colt automatic, rising from his chair and moving toward the kitchen, with its back-door exit to the yard.

Marx tried to keep it casual, as if he could be seen by watchful eyes, but he couldn't control the frantic throbbing of his pulse. The course he had elected for himself was dangerous, no doubt about it, but he had more fear of waiting in the house, while unknown enemies surrounded him and cut off all retreat. They could start pouring bullets through the windows any moment now, or even set the house on fire. The news reports about his office had referred to some kind of incendiary bomb. If they had one…

Marx reached the kitchen, thankful that the lights were off, giving his eyes a chance to partially adjust. He moved directly to the nearest window, peered out with the pistol ready in his hand, but saw no targets. With a bit of luck, he might still make it to his car.

A quick pat down confirmed that he had car keys, wallet and the roll of cash that he had carried since the last stop at his bank upstate. That roll was smaller than it had been on the day he fled Chicago, but still large enough to last him awhile longer, on the road.

Marx carefully unlatched the door, eased it open and stepped outside into the night. His right hand gripped the .45 pistol so tightly that his fingers had begun to lose their feeling, and he willed himself to take his time, relax as much as possible, before he made a clumsy error.

It was all of fifty paces to the car, his sleek Mercedes S-420 parked inside the barn that served him now as a garage. The distance was nothing to speak of—mere seconds if he ran flat out—but he would still be vulnerable to a bullet in the back. When he considered the alternative, however—seeking out his unknown enemies, engaging them deliberately—it made his blood ran cold.

Marx got his bearings, took a breath to steel himself against the coming rush and took off running toward the barn. He was no more than halfway there, when someone called his name in a commanding tone.

"Marx! Wait!"

Screw that, he thought, but something made him turn, breaking his stride, scanning for targets as he swung the heavy Colt around.

There! By the house, a tall man, dressed in black!

Marx jerked the automatic's trigger twice, a double crack of thunder in his ears, smelling the cordite and his own fear-sweat before he turned once more and bolted toward the barn.

MARX MIGHT BE slick with a scalpel, Bolan thought, but he could use some more practice with a handgun. The .45 slugs, fired in haste, missed him by at least six feet, off to his left. They also missed the house, zipping past the soldier like a pair of angry hornets on the wing.

In other circumstances, Bolan would have dropped the runner in his tracks, an easy shot before he reached the shadowed doorway of the hulking barn, but Louis Marx wasn't his enemy. Not yet, at any rate. The doctor was reacting out of fear, in self-defense, and Bolan knew that simply calling out to him would only bring another bullet in response. Before they could sit down to have a chat, the soldier needed to relieve the surgeon of his pistol and any other weapons he was carrying.

That meant he had to close within arm's length, and even Marx would be hard-pressed to miss at that range.

In moving toward the barn, he didn't make directly for the open door, where Marx would have a clear shot at him from the shadows. Rather, Bolan veered off course and ran around the north side of the barn, dodging another hasty bullet on his way.

It didn't take a genius to work out why Marx had left the house and risked his life—as he would view it—just to reach the drafty barn. There was no vehicle in sight, but Marx had plainly driven from Chicago to Fairfield. There was nowhere else close by for him to hide a car. And that, in turn, meant

Bolan's time was short, before his rabbit made a break and left him in the dust.

The doctor's fear would work against him now, dividing his attention between escape and defense. Marx was jumpy, having missed his target twice, and since he thought Bolan was gunning for him, he would be expecting some kind of counterattack, afraid to turn his back to the door, even for the brief time needed to climb inside his car and start the engine. As for fully opening the double doors, which stood ajar at the moment, Bolan guessed that Marx would let it slide, ram through the barrier and sacrifice his car's paint job in lieu of making himself an easy target.

Bolan cleared the north side of the barn and stopped short when he saw a ladder propped against the east wall, leading to the open hayloft. Scrambling deftly up the ladder, Bolan eased his way inside the loft and paused to test his footing on the wooden floor, drawing the sound suppressed Beretta 93-R from its shoulder rig.

He still had no desire to shoot the doctor, but if winging Marx turned out to be the only means of stopping him—or if a bullet was required to stop the surgeon's car—Bolan was ready to oblige.

He moved across the loft with long, swift strides, whatever sound he made in passing covered by a man's voice, cursing bitterly, below him. Poising at the drop, he peered down into darkness, saw the figure of his quarry beside the driver's door of a Mercedes-Benz, trying to fit a key inside the lock. He used his left hand, clinging to the bulky automatic with his right, and missed the narrow target twice as Bolan watched.

"Goddamn it!"

Bending lower, Marx was finally successful on his next attempt. The key fit snugly, and the car's dome light came on as Marx gave the key a twist. He had the door half open when a shadow launched itself from the loft.

Bolan landed atop the Mercedes, crouching, as Marx recoiled with a shout. He swung up the big Colt automatic to fire, but the Executioner was already moving once again, the muzzle-blast bright in his eyes as he dropped to the floor of the barn, lashing out with his empty left hand. The .45 slug struck the roof of the Mercedes-Benz a glancing blow and ricocheted, slapping the wall somewhere behind him, wasted.

The soldier's free hand gripped the doctor's gun arm, wrenching it aside as Marx kept firing, three more thunderclaps before the automatic's slide locked open on an empty chamber. Bolan gave that arm a twist and heard the pistol clatter at his feet. Marx let out a cry of mingled pain and rage, balling his left hand in a fist and swinging it toward Bolan's face.

The Executioner was quick enough to block the roundhouse with his gun hand, stepping close to Marx and bringing up his right knee with sufficient force to lift the doctor several inches off his feet. Marx wheezed a cry of pain, knees buckling, and collapsed when Bolan let go of his arm.

The surgeon curled into a fetal posture, covering his wounded genitals, as Bolan kicked aside the empty Colt and crouched in front of him. He stayed just out of reach, in case Marx found the wherewithal to make a sudden move.

The doctor's eyes were narrow slits of agony, but he could focus well enough to watch as the soldier holstered his Beretta, fastening the thumb-break strap that held it snug in place. Confusion mixed with pain and fear on Marx's face, but he didn't have strength to voice the question that was on his mind.

"Relax," Bolan suggested. "If I meant to kill you, you'd be dead already."

"Who...are...you?" Marx forced the words between clenched teeth, as if each of them weighed a ton.

"I just might be the only friend you've got," Bolan replied. "As soon as you can stand, we need to go back to the house and have a talk."

5

The shaken doctor took his coffee black, spiked with a double shot of bourbon, but it didn't seem to calm his nerves. Bolan had helped him to the sofa in the living room, and when he shifted in his seat, Marx grimaced from the pain Bolan had caused him with that knee shot to the groin.

"I'm still not clear on who you are," the surgeon said.

"You're not supposed to be," Bolan replied. "For now, the only thing you need to know is that I'm on your side... assuming you play straight with me."

"Play straight?" Marx tried to cross his legs, but winced and quickly gave it up, taking another shot of his high-octane coffee for the pain.

"I need your help to find one of your patients," Bolan said.

Marx seemed to have a measure of experience at playing dumb. He kept his face impassive as he said, "That's not the way referrals work. Patients may recommend physicians, but it doesn't go the other way. Assuming that you have a name, of course, there's still the telephone directory. You could—"

"One of your special patients," Bolan interrupted him. "The ones you handle for the government."

"Assuming that was true," Marx said, "you understand that any information would be covered by the laws concerning patient confidentiality. Revealing information from my files, to you or anybody else, would cost me my medical license."

"Only if the government decides to prosecute," Bolan said. "On the flip side, keeping quiet might cost you your life."

"Is that a threat?"

"Not even close," Bolan replied. "You obviously know about what happened to your office in Chicago. You've been hiding out since it went down."

"I'm on vacation."

"For your health," Bolan said. "Yeah, I heard. The problem is, that if I found you, someone else could find you, too. The men who blitzed your office, for example. Something tells me that they're not entirely satisfied with burning out your files."

Marx took another healthy slug of loaded coffee and considered his reply. "Assuming you're correct," he said at last, "I couldn't offer much in terms of help. All notes and photographs were in my files—which, as you've pointed out, have been destroyed. My contacts with the government—again, assuming such a link exists—wouldn't have trusted me with names or the location of a relocated patient. That much must be obvious."

"I'm not concerned with names," the Executioner replied. "I need a face."

"And as I've said, the photographs—"

"You don't strike me as the forgetful type," Bolan said, interrupting Marx again.

"I beg your pardon?"

"Plastic surgeons are a lot like artists, so I'm told. Creative. Some might say inspired."

Marx wasn't in the mood for flattery, but he couldn't help nodding slightly in agreement. "The comparison is not entirely inappropriate," he said.

"An artist knows his work on sight," Bolan pressed on. "Unless we're talking idiot savant, the odds are that he can describe it in detail from memory."

Marx saw where they were going now. He frowned before he spoke again. "There is some truth to what you say, of course. There should be no great difficulty picking out my work if, say, I met a former patient on the street. The problems in our present situation are self-evident, however. I would have to find the patient first before a sighting could occur. And frankly, I have no incentive whatsoever to pursue a man who obviously wants me dead."

"Survival is the best incentive I can think of," Bolan said. "And no one's asking you to join in the pursuit. That's my job."

Marx couldn't seem to shake his brooding frown. "And how am I supposed to recognize this person in absentia?" he asked.

"Up here," the Executioner replied, tapping his forehead with a fingertip. "You sketch your work beforehand, I assume?"

"It's mostly done on the computer, these days," Marx explained. "I'm not much of a freehand artist, truth be told."

"But you're familiar with Ident-I-Kits?" asked Bolan.

"Certainly," Marx said. "The mix-and-match technique employed by law-enforcement agencies."

"I need to get you with an artist," Bolan said. "Work out a likeness of the man who wants you dead, so I can spot him when we meet."

"Assuming I agree..." The surgeon hesitated, shrugged as if some heavy weight had settled on his shoulders, and he sought to throw it off. "You have to understand," he said. "I've worked with several dozen patients on referrals out of Washington. It could be any one of them."

"Not quite." Bolan decided it was time for him to drop the other shoe. "In fact, I know exactly who it is."

Marx blinked at that, clearly surprised. "You do? I mean, who is it?"

"Rurik Baklanov."

The name didn't appear to register with Marx. "I don't—"

"The Russian," Bolan said.

That did it. Marx blinked twice, lips narrowing into a bloodless slit. "I understood that he was dead. Some business in Missouri. It was on the news."

"I thought you didn't have his name," Bolan said.

"No, that's true. One of the agents on the case told me, in conversation, that the witness was involved with a specific case."

"Perrugia," Bolan said.

"Correct. I had assumed the individuals involved found out where this man was. Except—"

"That wouldn't lead them back to you," Bolan said. "And Perrugia's people wouldn't care about your business, either way."

"That had occurred to me."

"The way it looks right now," Bolan went on, "the Russian got a new face on the house, then set it up to kill his guards and go about his business. You're the one hole in his plan. He tried to plug it in Chicago, but his people didn't finish off the job. As long as he's alive and on the street, you're still at risk."

Marx thought about that for a moment, cupping his coffee mug in both hands, as if for warmth. "I see your point," he said at last. "What can I do to make this go away?"

BROGNOLA TOOK THE CALL at home. It rang through on his private line, the number known to fewer than two dozen people in the world. It was approaching midnight when he lifted the receiver, frowning in anticipation of bad news.

"Hello."

"It's me," the deep, familiar voice informed him. Bolan's voice. "I'm scrambling, here."

"Hang on," Brognola said, and tapped the button that engaged his compact scrambler. A click-and-whir response told him the mechanism was engaged. "Okay. We're set."

"I've got the doctor."

"He give you any problems?"

"Nothing to speak of," said the Executioner. "He's playing ball."

"So, can he do us any good?" Brognola asked.

"That's why I'm calling. I need to hook him up with someone who can handle an Ident-i-Kit and let me get my first look at the target."

"Not a problem," the big Fed replied. "The Bureau's got it all computerized, these days. It's like *Star Trek* or something. They can age him, put the weight on, take it off, whatever."

"How long will it take?"

"That normally depends on who the subject is, how well he can express himself, the memory, whatever. With the doc, it ought to be a breeze."

"I'll need to hand him off, then."

"Where are you now?"

"At his place," Bolan said, "outside of Fairfield."

When Brognola tried to picture southern Illinois, call up a map inside his head, he drew a blank. It was late, he told himself, or maybe he was just getting old.

"What's close, again, in terms of airports?" he asked Bolan.

"Evansville," the Executioner replied.

"Okay," Brognola said. "I'll wake up somebody and have him waiting at the airport, there. We need some kind of recognition signal. How about a Bible? Look for someone near the Northwest ticket counter, studying the Good Book. By the time you get there, I imagine you won't have that many choices, anyway."

"Sounds good to me," Bolan said.

"Once you hand him off, I'll have him brought back here to me. Chicago's closer, and they have the right equipment in the Bureau office there, but I don't like the feel. It's too damn close."

"Agreed."

"Anyway," Brognola said, "if he can do his sleeping on the flight, we'll put him right through to the techs and get him started on arrival in D.C. Whatever he comes up with, I can fax it to you once it's done. All right?"

"Suits me," Bolan replied. "We'll get a move on, then, as soon as he can throw some things together."

"Right," Brognola said. "I'll make that other call. What's up for you, meanwhile?"

"Well, I was thinking," Bolan said, "that while I'm in the neighborhood, I might head up to Cleveland for a visit with Don Vito. Maybe find out if he still thinks holding hands with Baklanov is such a hot idea."

Brognola had to smile at that. Two states away, and Bolan saw himself as being "in the neighborhood" of Don Vito Fortini's Cleveland Mafia Family. Two days of nonstop traveling and action, yet the soldier was prepared for more—as much as it would take, in fact, to see the mission through.

They didn't make them like that anymore, Brognola thought. Or, if they did, those kind of men were few and far between.

"Vito may be a little nervous after what went down in Jersey," the big Fed suggested.

He could almost see his old friend smiling, as the Executioner replied, "I'm counting on it."

"Nervous doesn't mean his boys will miss, you know," Brognola said. Almost before the words were out, he cursed himself for telling Bolan how to fight his war. The guy had done all right without Brognola's help—had done all right while the big Fed was hunting him, in fact—and nothing that had happened since suggested any lessening of his survival skills.

"I'll have a look around," Bolan said, ever casual. "Some course of action might suggest itself."

If Brognola was selling life insurance, he wouldn't have favored Don Fortini's odds of waking up the day after the next.

"You want to watch yourself up there," Brognola said against his own best judgment.

"That's the plan," Bolan replied. "I'd better hit the road."

"Okay."

Brognola cradled the receiver, automatically disconnecting the scrambler, and reached for his personal address book—the small one, bound in black imitation leather. His wife had chided him more than once, in her joking way, about his "little black book," but this one was reserved for business contacts, a catchall heading that included sundry Feds and several informants on the wrong side of the law. Right now, he needed the name and number of the FBI's chief resident agent in Evansville, Indiana.

Eleven digits for the call, long distance, and it didn't bother Brognola that he was more than likely waking someone up, certainly dragging his contact away from hearth and home in the middle of the night to run an emergency errand. That kind of duty came with the badge, and anyone who couldn't handle it should find another line of work.

Besides, he thought, if he didn't sleep, nobody slept.

His contact picked up on the third ring, and Brognola was a trifle disappointed that the G-man on the other end didn't sound sleepy. Even with the hour's difference in time zones, something nasty in his makeup had been hoping he would rout the agent out of bed. Next time, perhaps.

Brognola rapidly identified himself and issued his instructions, caught the brisk "Yes, sir!" and listened while the order was repeated. There was just a moment's hesitation when he told the fed in Evansville to take a Bible with him to the airport, but he got no argument. It made as much sense as a red carnation, say, and would be easier to come by at that hour of the night, assuming that the G-man didn't have to stop somewhere and borrow one.

When he was done, Brognola poured himself a double shot of whiskey and sipped it slowly, feeling the heat spread itself through his system, slowly relaxing muscles that had tightened during his brief conversation with Bolan.

They had the doctor, fine. That put them points ahead if he was able to provide them with a face for Rurik Baklanov. But then, what?

It was still a deadly game of hide-and-seek, with Bolan playing solo for the home team, while Baklanov presumably had gunners of his own, plus more on loan from his Sicilian allies. That made long odds in the Russian's favor, even after Bolan knew his face, even if the soldier could run the bastard down.

Long odds, but that was Bolan's game, in spades. In fact, it was the only way he knew to play the game.

The big Fed finished off his drink and opted for another, prior to turning in. With any luck, the alcohol would help him fall asleep and ward off any dreams involving the untimely, sudden death of trusted friends.

He didn't have that many of them left, these days, and every one he lost diminished him.

"Stay frosty, Striker," he told the silent room. "For God's sake, watch your ass."

THE WATCHER HAD BEEN baby-sitting Dr. Louis Marx for nineteen hours straight before the stranger showed up, all in black, and nearly blew the game. At first, it had been tempting to butt in, eliminate the prowler with a single well-placed shot, but something held the watcher back.

He had come close when Marx broke from the house and ran into the barn, pursued. The gunfire covered his advance, and he was skilled enough that neither of them—Marx nor the impressive stranger—noticed his approach. He had been poised outside the old barn, gun in hand, prepared to strike, when he had overheard the stranger's words.

"Relax," he had said. "If I meant to kill you, you'd be dead already."

The comment bought him time, prolonged his life. The watcher stood in darkness and observed the stranger, helping Marx back to the house. And he crept closer in the night to watch them through a lighted window, as they sat down in the living room and talked. He couldn't overhear them, then—lipreading wasn't among his many skills—but it was evident that Marx didn't feel threatened by the stranger once they had an opportunity to talk a while. Before they finished, Marx was nodding in agreement with whatever plan the stranger had suggested, then the tall man dressed in black made one short phone call, and the surgeon hobbled off to pack his clothes.

So, they were leaving, going who knew where, and Marx didn't appear to be a prisoner. That told the watcher that the man in black wasn't a soldier hired by Rurik Baklanov. If such had been the case, he would have killed Marx in the barn—or tried to, anyway—and then departed from the scene, assuming he was still alive.

But he wouldn't have been alive. The watcher would have seen to that.

Now, lurking in the midnight shadows as the two men left the farmhouse, turning off the lights and locking up, the watcher had a choice to make. He could reveal himself—take out the man in black by one means or another, never mind his true identity—and that would end the waiting game. Of course, such action, coming on the heels of Marx's evident agreement with the stranger, would present the watcher as an enemy, destroy whatever chance he had of using Marx himself.

The basic plan was simple, as initially conceived. He knew that Rurik Baklanov had tried to kill the surgeon once, and would most likely try again. The watcher meant to be there when it happened. He could interfere or not, depending on his mood. The point was to find out where Baklanov had made his lair, and he would trust his gut as to the proper method—whether he should let the shooters do their job and trail them home, or whether he should stop them, letting one survive, and grill the shooter forcefully until he broke and spilled his guts.

That was the plan…and it had gone to hell before his eyes.

The good news—if, indeed, it was good news—was that the duo didn't leave in Marx's car. Instead, they set off walking through the night, the black-clad stranger toting Marx's suitcase in his left hand, while the surgeon trudged along beside him, limping slightly, as if suffering some kind of pain. Perhaps he had been injured when they grappled in the barn.

The watcher gave them ample room, then fell in step behind them, using every trick at his disposal to prevent the tall man noticing the tail. They covered something like two hundred yards before the watcher realized that he would have to make a choice. Marx and his unknown escort were moving away from the point where the watcher had hidden his car. Presumably, the man in black had wheels nearby, but if the watcher trailed him that far, he would wind up eating dust while they drove off without him.

Dammit!

Swallowing the bitter knowledge that he might be doomed to fail, the watcher broke off his pursuit and turned back, moving cautiously until he was convinced the others wouldn't hear him when he broke into a run. His vehicle was hidden on a side road, some four hundred yards west of the house where

Marx had gone to ground. Running full-tilt, slowed a bit by the terrain, the watcher reached it in less than five minutes. He slid behind the steering wheel, fired up the engine and pulled out onto the blacktop without using his headlights.

It was a short drive back to the highway, turning east in the direction of the surgeon's hideout. As it was, the watcher found himself in time to catch a pair of taillights pulling onto the main road, some three-quarters of a mile in front of him.

It had to be the stranger, bearing Marx away. The odds against another vehicle appearing on this stretch of road, just now, were astronomical.

The watcher left his headlights dark, driving by moonlight, following the taillights eastward, back toward Fairfield. He let the point car gain a healthy lead, and switched on his own lights when it had passed around a curve, then stayed well back, so it wouldn't appear that he was following in hot pursuit. The last thing that he needed was to spook the black-clad stranger and precipitate a chase.

He had no clue where they were going, but it stood to reason that the stranger wasn't taking Marx to a hotel in town. Security would be no better there than at the farm, and if the doctor needed anything, his new protector could have brought the items with him.

No. The man in black was stealing Marx away, and there was nothing for the watcher to do except follow, keep track of the men if he could. Marx, as a sitting duck, had been his only hope of finding Rurik Baklanov. But now...

Another thought occurred to him as he drove on through midnight darkness, following the distant taillights. It was possible the game had changed, without his being conscious of the fact. Perhaps he didn't need the surgeon now if someone else— a warrior, by the look of him—had joined the play. If that turned out to be the case, then he might find his quarry by following the hunter, instead of staking out the bait.

It mattered little to him who finished Rurik Baklanov in the end. Of course, he would be pleased to do the job himself—it would be pleasant for him, back at home—but the result would be the same in any case. As long as Baklanov was dead, the watcher would be satisfied.

He drove on through the night, pursuing taillights that reminded him of incandescent drops of blood.

6

The Cleveland syndicate has fallen on hard times in recent years. There was a time when mafiosi in the self-proclaimed "Safest City in America" controlled vice and racketeering from Lake Erie through northern Kentucky and West Virginia, with outposts in Buffalo, Miami and Las Vegas. More recently, however, natural attrition at the top had been combined with mutiny in the ranks, civil war between the Irish and Sicilian mobs, and sweeping federal prosecutions that had decimated the remaining leadership.

And still, the worst was yet to come.

Don Vito Fortini, Cleveland's capo by default, had already sampled a taste of the Executioner's special fare in New Jersey; he simply didn't know it yet. Now, back at home, he felt secure, surrounded by his own handpicked troops.

That was about to change.

Fortini's hardsite was a twelve-acre estate in Shaker Heights, traditionally one of Cleveland's most exclusive and expensive neighborhoods. Since the turn of the century, Cleveland's movers and shakers had made their homes there.

Tonight, it was time for some moving and shaking of a very different sort.

The Executioner had been in Cleveland for approximately thirteen hours, but he knew the layout well enough from other visits in the past, and from the update information Brognola had faxed him, with the computer-generated likeness of Rurik Baklanov. Louis Marx had signed off on the picture, pronouncing it ninety percent accurate. Barring some double cross on the surgeon's part, Bolan was confident that he would recognize his man on sight.

But he wasn't expecting Baklanov in Shaker Heights.

Tonight was strictly shake-and-bake, an opportunity to test the limits of Baklanov's new alliance. It was time to raise the ante to find out how many of Baklanov's fair-weather friends stood beside him when lightning began to strike.

Dressed all in black, hands and face darkened with combat cosmetics, Bolan perched atop the eight-foot wall that circled Don Fortini's grounds. The place was always under guard, but in the absence of specific threats, it seemed that Vito had refrained from pulling out the stops. There were no dogs in evidence, no sentries prowling on the outskirts of the grounds, as far as he could see. There seemed to be no cameras or sensors, further validating Bolan's take on Don Fortini as a retro-Don who put his faith in men and guns, rather than high technology.

So much the better for a soldier coming at Fortini, unexpected and unseen.

He dropped into a crouch inside the wall, his CAR-15 ready to rock and roll. The harness Bolan wore supported side arms, frag and smoke grenades, spare magazines. The pockets of his blacksuit held stilettos and piano-wire garrotes, and first-aid supplies in case he took a hit along the way. His combat boots had steel-capped toes that could provide a lethal kick if it went hand-to-hand.

He made directly for the house, lights showing on the first and second floors. Was Don Fortini even home? It made no difference to the Executioner, since he didn't intend to take out the capo. His need was better served, in fact, by letting Fortini live and carry his complaint to Baklanov, spread fear among his fellow mafiosi.

But getting in was only half the battle. If he meant to pull it off, Bolan would also have to make it out alive.

He was fifty yards from Casa Fortini when it blew up in his face. A bank of floodlights blazed to life, momentarily blinding him, as a shout went up from somewhere on his right. The soldier spun in that direction, dropping to a crouch as someone cut loose with an automatic weapon.

It sounded like an SMG to Bolan, probably 9 mm, but it made no difference as he answered with a short burst of his own, the 5.56 mm tumblers streaming downrange.

Too late to second-guess what he had missed, if anything, as he was closing in. The challenge, now, would simply be surviving, taking out as many of the enemy as possible while getting out alive.

VITO FORTINI FLINCHED at the first sound of gunfire, slopping wine from his long-stemmed glass across the front of his silk shirt and jacket.

"Goddamn it!" he blurted. "What's this shit?" He swiped at the stains on his clothing, frightened and angry, all at once.

"It's what we've been expecting," said the Russian, rising from his chair with easy grace, as if he had to use the john, instead of rushing off to battle.

"Maybe you," Don Vito snapped, and flung his glass in the direction of the marble fireplace. "Me, I don't expect bastards coming after me at home. This kind of shit went out with Danny Flynn and the Umberto brothers twenty years ago!"

"It's why I'm here," the Russian told Fortini in his stilted English.

"Yeah?" The capo fairly sneered. "So, maybe you should get out there and do your fucking job!"

The Russian's smile was like a razor slash across his face. Fortini knew the shooter's name, but he couldn't pronounce it worth a damn and settled for "Hey, you," if he had anything to say.

Which wasn't often, granted, since the dustup in New Jersey. He had been all set to pull out of the deal with Baklanov, the shooter's boss, but he had let himself be talked into a compromise. The Russian would provide Fortini with beefed-up security. No insult to it, Baklanov explained, since the problem was likely his fault and his soldiers were supposed to have some kind of special military training.

All right, then. If they were so damned tough, Fortini would leave them to it. Seven men, with what's-his-name in charge, and God knew they were packing iron enough to stop an army in its tracks.

It still boiled down to trouble, though, in Don Fortini's own backyard. The cops would have a thing or two to say about this kind of fireworks show, despite the envelopes of cash his people passed around each Friday afternoon. Those payoffs bought smooth sailing during normal times, business as usual, but they wouldn't be adequate to cover up a shooting war.

So be it.

Money was the least of Fortini's problems at the moment. It sounded like all hell was breaking loose outside, and he couldn't forget about New Jersey, the fiasco at Gambola's place. The morning after, there were headlines telling him that Jules DeRicco had been toasted in his car—an armor-plated limousine at that, for Christ's sake. If he wasn't safe in a tank, what made Fortini think he would be safe inside a house? Because some Russian said so?

Bullshit.

He was all for bailing out, a reflex that had served him in the past, but then the Cleveland capo thought about poor Jules DeRicco, blown up as he tried to get away. Gino Gambola, meanwhile, stuck it out and managed to survive, although his house got wasted in the process, and he had to answer umpteen questions from the cops.

Still, even talking to the law beat lying on a metal slab in a refrigerated drawer. Fortini had built this house from scratch, and it was customized with some surprises, just in case some uninvited guests dropped by with mayhem on their minds. There was a "closet" in his den, for instance, that was bullet-, fire- and bombproof, with a special ventilation system built to filter smoke and poison gas. He kept it stocked with food and bottled water, had some weapons and a toilet in there. They could burn the house down, and Don Vito would be sitting pretty on his throne.

With any luck, though, it would never get that far.

Fortini was counting on the Russians—and his own boys, too, of course—to clean up the mess swiftly and efficiently. It wouldn't bother him tremendously if something happened to the Russians in the meantime, maybe wipe that smug expression off their boss's face and let Fortini's soldiers claim the victory. Why not?

But, one way or another, Fortini planned on coming out of it alive and in one piece. Whatever happened, he could smooth it with the cops…but not if he was dead.

He watched the Russian go to join his men outside, then Fortini crossed the room and found the hidden switch beside the fireplace, pressing it, watching the hidden door swing open on his private, air-conditioned hideaway. He stepped inside and closed the door behind him, starting to relax the moment that he heard the solid bolts slide home.

Much better.

Now, all Don Fortini had to do was bide his time, wait for the smoke to clear, when it was safe for him to reemerge. He took a riot shotgun from its rack beside the door, and sat on the toilet with the gun across his lap.

"Let's get this over with," he said aloud. "I haven't got all fucking night."

HEDEON CHAPAEV WAS exhilarated as he stepped out of the house, his nostrils picking up the first sharp tang of gun smoke on the breeze. Unlike the fat Sicilian he had been assigned to baby-sit, Chapaev was delighted by the prospect of engaging the unknown enemy. He relished the thought of settling the issue once and for all.

There was no doubt in Chapaev's mind that he and his soldiers—a dozen crack troops, all ex-Spetsnaz—would emerge victorious from the present contest. He didn't care who the adversary was, how numerous they were. His soldiers were the finest in the world.

Chapaev cocked his AKSU assault rifle, leaving the skeleton stock folded as he moved across the porch of the Fortini house and out into the yard. He had donned sunglasses before leaving the house, prepared for the bright glare of floodlights that bathed the grounds, and the light reflected from the mirrored lenses made Chapaev look as if his eyes themselves were glowing coals of fire.

His soldiers were moving away from the house in a pincers formation, closing on the point where scattered trees concealed their target, firing as they went. A group of stragglers—Don Fortini's men—were close behind them, squeezing off a stray shot here and there, most of them being careful not to jeopardize the Russians in the leading rank.

Chapaev couldn't see the man or men they were pursuing, but it hardly mattered. He would see the corpses soon enough if all went well. Whether he managed to identify them was another matter, but again, it made no difference.

Chapaev's orders were specific. Cover the Sicilian and destroy whomever sought to harm him. Other teams had been assigned to guard Gino Gambola and Ted Peredo, while Gaetano Donatelli had declined protection in Buffalo, insisting that he could defend himself. Despite the recent shootout in New Jersey, Chapaev had believed it was unlikely that another raid would follow. He had been inclined to think the first attack had sprung from fratricidal tensions in the U.S. Mafia, some foolish war between the goombahs.

He might still turn out to be correct, but at the moment, Chapaev was required to carry out his master's orders. He had to stop the raiders cold and do his best to guarantee that they couldn't repeat the interference with a scheme beyond their reckoning.

His men were armed with silenced weapons, telling him that it was one of Don Fortini's men who fired the first rounds. That meant police would soon be on their way, an inconvenience, but he had no fear of officers arriving on the scene before his soldiers finished off the enemy.

Chapaev anxiously picked up his pace, closing the gap between himself and the Sicilians who were following his men. A couple of them glanced back toward him, showing off their natural aversion to a stranger in their midst with scowls and glares. Chapaev cared no more for their opinion of him than he would have for a homeless beggar on the street. They had no meaning to him, unless one of them was fool enough to meddle in Chapaev's business and disrupt his plan.

In which case, it would be his pleasure to exterminate the idiots without a moment's hesitation.

Chapaev picked out muzzle-flashes in the woods ahead of him—one automatic weapon firing toward the house, joined seconds later by another—and he heard the angry snap of bullets passing somewhere to his left. A wet smack told Chapaev that at least one of the shots had been well placed, a member of Fortini's muscle squad collapsing facedown in a heap.

Chapaev shrugged it off, indifferent to the dead or wounded man. His full attention focused on his first glimpse of the adversary, as he broke into a jog, passing the rest of the Sicilians, closing with his own crack troops. The AKSU rifle, close to eight pounds with its 30-round box magazine, felt featherlight, toylike, in Chapaev's hands.

His skirmish line was within thirty yards of the trees, closing fast, when a burst of smoke erupted in front of them, spreading rapidly across the path of their advance. The clever bastards! They had come prepared. Chapaev barked orders at his men when they appeared to hesitate before the smoke screen.

"Hurry up!" he snapped at them in Russian. "Go! Get after them!"

The soldiers did as they were told, more frightened of Chapaev than they were of anything that might be waiting for them in the smoky darkness up ahead. It was a wise choice on their part, since he wouldn't have hesitated for a heartbeat when it came to executing rebellious subordinates.

Given a choice, he'd prefer to kill the enemy, but he was determined to kill someone before the night was through. And the sooner the better.

Chapaev smiled in grim anticipation.

He could hardly wait.

THE RUSH HAD TAKEN Bolan by surprise. He had been lulled by the appearance of relaxed security around Vito Fortini's house, and still had no clear fix on how the enemy had spotted him. The first short bursts of automatic fire were merely the precursor to a fusillade from better than a dozen weapons ranged across the line of his advance.

He ducked back toward the shelter of the tree line, feeling like an insect on a kitchen floor, trapped when the lights come on, and Bolan had no doubt that he would be exterminated with the same dispassion as a cockroach if he gave his adversaries half a chance.

One thing that struck him, even in his rush for cover, was that most of the weapons ranged against him were fitted with suppressers. Bullets swarmed around him, rippling through the air, slapping at trees behind him, but the muzzle-flashes came without a sound, except for one submachine gun—the first that had fired—away to his right. He fanned another burst in that direction from his CAR-15 and caught a fleeting image of the shooter as he staggered, going down.

It was a start, but Bolan knew that he'd be a fool to stand his ground and make a battle of it. He was not dismayed by odds alone—indeed, he had faced longer odds, not once, but many times before. Rather, it was the notion that his adversaries had been waiting for him, that there might be something else in store, that told him it was time to disengage.

And that, in turn, wasn't as simple as it seemed.

The hostile gunners were advancing in a double skirmish line, the silent weapons up in front, a second rank of shooters ranged behind the first who mostly held their fire. There were enough of them to pin him down if Bolan tried to dodge them in the patchy woods that covered this part of Fortini's property.

He needed time, some combat stretch, and he could only pull that off if he became invisible.

The GI smoke grenade was in his hand almost before he thought about it, instinct taking over in a rush. He yanked the safety pin and pitched the canister away from him, toward the advancing line of troops. An instant later, the first white plume of smoke burst forth and swiftly turned into a rolling cloud.

He raked the smoke screen with a long burst from his automatic carbine, just to slow the shooters, retreating toward the point where he had scaled the outer wall.

Bolan had barely traveled fifty feet before he heard a shout in Russian from beyond the rising wall of smoke that hid him from his enemies. He knew, then, that the trap was something more than old Don Vito simply covering his backside. Rurik Baklanov was here in spirit, represented by a flying squad of gunmen who were clearly skilled professionals, and that made all the difference in the world.

For one thing, it told Bolan that his first strike, in New Jersey, hadn't toppled the alliance with the Sicilian team Baklanov was working on. It also let him know that he might not have seen the last of preparations laid for the defense of Don Fortini's property.

There had been no one waiting for him when he climbed the wall, but it was possible, he realized, that mobile flying squads were stationed elsewhere in the neighborhood—disguised, perhaps, to suit the mood of Shaker Heights, but ready to respond and intercept intruders fleeing from the grounds.

Under the circumstances, Bolan did the only thing that still made sense.

He ran.

It was another hundred paces to the wall, and he could hear the sound of his pursuers closing from behind him. It would take only one lucky shot to drop him, even slow him enough for them to close and finish it. If he could reach the wall before one of the hunters took that lucky shot...

Ahead of him, he saw a bulky shadow heave itself across the wall, immediately followed by a second, then a third. Bolan didn't require ID to know that they were hostile. Simply being present at this moment told him that, all doubt erased when one of them cut loose on Bolan with a sound suppressed automatic weapon.

He hit the deck, feeling grass against his cheek, the bullets snapping overhead, around waist-level for his normal height. A second's hesitation, and the gunner would have nailed him, cutting him in two.

Bolan was grappling with his carbine, wrenching it toward target acquisition, when another automatic weapon opened up behind him, firing short, repeated bursts, its jarring racket unrestrained by any type of suppresser.

He waited for the searing impact that would end his life...but nothing happened. In a flash, he realized this gunfire was directed toward the wall and toward his enemies. He saw the man shapes jerking, twitching, tumbling with the impacts of bullets from what sounded like an AK-47, one of the originals, before the newer models were converted to the smaller 5.45 mm round.

Someone had intervened to save his life.

Now, all he had to figure out was who, and why.

THE WATCHER HAD BEEN faced with an unpleasant choice after he trailed his quarry into Evansville and shadowed them inside the airport. They were met by someone—probably a lawman, he decided, from the cheap suit and the regulation haircut—and he loitered close enough to learn that Dr. Marx was on his way to Washington. A write-off, then. The watcher was relieved that he had chosen to pursue the man in black.

But he had not been pleased at learning he would have to catch the red-eye flight to Cleveland. It had meant the unexpected purchase of an airline ticket—thankfully, the flight was nowhere near capacity, at that time of the night. Then he had been forced to backtrack, fetch his luggage from the car, remove his shoulder holster with the German P-9 automatic pistol, pack it with his clothing and the folding-stock AKM rifle, before he hurried back inside.

It was an oddity of U.S. airline regulations that, while weapons were clearly forbidden in carryon luggage, nearly any type of firearm could be checked through to fly in the luggage compartment. Federal laws required that guns transported in that manner be unloaded and declared to airline personnel before they were accepted, but there were normally no baggage checks, no X rays or other screening procedures to prevent undeclared weapons—or bombs, for that matter—from slipping past a harried ticket clerk.

The watcher, therefore, was well armed when he arrived in Cleveland, and he didn't hesitate in trailing his new quarry around the city in a rented car, observing each stop, maintaining sufficient distance to avoid recognition. In that respect, he was assisted by the fact that his new mark clearly didn't expect a tail. The tall man was a hunter, and no doubt would have some skill in self-defense, but he didn't anticipate whomever he was hunting in Ohio to be hunting him.

The watcher knew that they were getting down to business after nightfall when the tall man drove to Shaker Heights and found a place to stash his car. It wasn't easy, trailing him that far unseen, but once again, the city traffic helped. Even the wealthy suburbs had their share of vehicles in transit after dark, and there was nothing to suggest the watcher had been seen before his quarry parked behind a service station that had shut down for the night, emerged in combat gear and moved away on foot. The watcher was behind him, keeping pace, when the man in black approached the outer wall of what appeared to be a rich man's home, climbed over it and vanished from his sight.

He could have waited there, until the man in black returned, but then he started wondering if Rurik Baklanov was beyond that wall.

And that eliminated any choice he might have had.

He trailed his quarry at a distance, over lightly wooded grounds, in the direction of a large but unattractive house. He had been well back from the tree line when the floodlights framed his mark in silhouette. The shooting started almost simultaneously—the first rounds from a standard submachine gun, answered by his quarry, while the bulk of the defenders carried weapons that were sound suppressed.

Professionals.

The watcher had no plan to intervene at first. In fact, he was retreating, recognizing hopeless odds, determined to stand watch and wait for Baklanov to show himself another day, when it occurred to him that he might not be wise to let the stranger die. For one thing, he still had no guarantee that Rurik Baklanov was there, and with the tall man dead, his best—perhaps his last—hope of finding the elusive Russian would be lost. And for another, when—not if—the firefight drew police, the principals would either flee or face arrest. In either case, it stood to reason he would miss his shot at Baklanov, whether his prey was here or not.

The watcher hadn't come this far to stand aside and let the American establishment deal with Rurik Baklanov. The law had tried and failed, with the result that Baklanov was now more powerful and more dangerous than ever.

So, he kept retreating toward the wall, but only when he saw the man in black had also started to withdraw, laying down a smoke screen to cover his escape. The watcher let him pass, staying behind to cover him should the armed defenders of the house draw near.

Both of them were nearly at the wall when he saw more troops scrambling over, cutting off their one clear path to freedom and survival.

When the new arrivals opened fire and pinned down his quarry, the watcher knew what he had to do. It happened almost without conscious thought, his AKM unslung and hammering away at those who barred his path. There was a danger that the man in black might turn and fire on him, but he would deal with that risk if and when it happened.

In the meantime, he was busy fighting for his life.

THE MAN CAME OUT of nowhere, brushing past him, firing one more burst in the direction of the crumpling figures at the wall. The last of them was crumpling now, his automatic weapon spitting wasted rounds into the turf before a lifeless finger lost its purchase on the trigger.

Bolan could have dropped his savior where he stood, a clear shot from behind, and while he had no prejudice against back shooting in the proper circumstances, he was curious to know the stranger's name, find out what he was doing here and why he had decided to pitch in on Bolan's side. There was no time for questions at the moment, though, with some two dozen gunners closing rapidly behind him, thrashing through his smoke screen, drawn inexorably to the sounds of combat near the wall.

"We should go now," the stranger said, glancing at Bolan for a heartbeat, then in the direction of the angry voices that were growing closer by the second. The abbreviated sample of his accent pegged his origin somewhere in Eastern Europe.

Russia?

Bolan trusted his suspicion as a finely tuned survival mechanism, but he couldn't picture Rurik Baklanov devising such a scheme as this—one of the Russian mobsters' gunmen killing three of his own troops, and all for...what? To make a friend of Bolan? Why, when he could just as easily have finished off the Executioner instead of saving him?

The soldier was on his feet before the train of thought had run its course. "I need to slow them down," he said.

"As long as it doesn't slow us down," the watcher replied, and flashed a grin.

"It won't. You can go ahead without me if you want."

The stranger shrugged and said, "I wait."

"Okay." Bolan unclipped two frag grenades and gave them to the stranger, palming two more for himself. He hooked the pins free with his thumbs and nodded to his nameless ally. "Any time you're ready."

With another smile, the stranger lobbed his first grenade toward the approaching voices. Bolan followed suit, switching the second to his right hand for a better pitch, clasping the spoon in place until he let it fly. Without discussing it, the two of them had thrown their grenades at slightly different angles, so that they were spread along a front of fifty yards or so. Of course, precision was impossible, allowing for the darkness and the trees and—

The first grenade went off, immediately followed by the second, third and fourth. They sounded like a string of giant firecrackers, their flashes lighting up the night like lightning strikes. In one flash, Bolan thought he caught a glimpse of tumbling bodies, but he wasn't sure. The screams and curses that he heard immediately afterward were no illusion, though. Someone was wounded out there, maybe dying, and Bolan didn't have the luxury of lingering to make a body count.

"You ready?" the soldier asked the stranger.

"After you." The same smile was hanging in there, like the killing was a part of normal life.

Who was he? Bolan thought, then reckoned he would find out soon enough.

Without a backward glance, he turned and started for the wall.

7

The stranger had a rental car parked half a block from Bolan's ride. When the soldier dropped him off, he waited for the other man to start his engine, make a U-turn in the middle of the residential street and follow him away from Don Fortini's neighborhood. The Executioner drove on until he found an all-night coffee shop in Garfield Heights and pulled into the parking lot, watching the second set of headlights trail him. When the stranger got out of his car, a black windbreaker hid the semiauto pistol that had been in his shoulder rig.

The place was nearly empty when they entered, one old man hunched at the counter, working on a bowl of stew or chili— Bolan couldn't tell for sure, and didn't care. By silent, mutual agreement, they proceeded to a corner booth, the horseshoe kind that let both of them place their backs against the wall and watch the doorway. Nothing passed between them until a waitress brought them coffee, took their orders—ham and eggs for Bolan; waffles for the stranger—and retreated to the kitchen once again.

"You want to start?" Bolan asked, when they had the corner to themselves.

"You wonder why I saved your life," the stranger said.

"It crossed my mind."

"My name is Dima Petrov," he began. "I'm—how should I say?—a visitor to your United States."

"I figured that much out," the Executioner replied. "From Russia?"

"I have come from Moscow, yes."

"That's quite a trip to watch a total stranger's back."

Petrov graced Bolan with another smile. In different circumstances, the soldier thought, the man could pass for charming. With a little effort, he'd have the ladies back home eating out of his hand.

"You're right, of course," Petrov replied. "And while I'm happy that I could assist you, it's not the purpose of my visit. Still, I find it advantageous for you to remain alive."

"How's that?" Bolan felt the suspicion coming back. He didn't care for being used without his knowledge, or against his will, in pursuit of some goal that he didn't even recognize.

"Because we have, I think, a mutual acquaintance." Holding Bolan's eyes, the Russian dropped his smile. He wasn't frowning yet, just passive, waiting.

"Baklanov," Bolan said, knowing he was right before the nod acknowledged it.

"The very same," Petrov replied. "Important men in Moscow are concerned that he has overstepped his bounds. There is, as you might know, a good deal of corruption in my government—throughout society in fact." The Russian shrugged. "Such is the life we lead, a legacy of communism, when the masses meant to rule the state were forced to bow and scrape—or bribe and steal—for every favor they received. Today, we have a different party in control, the people have their civil rights, but it's still the same. Between the poverty and shortages on one hand, and the sudden affluence in certain quarters on the other...well, I'm sure you understand. Bargains are made, sins go unpunished for a price. It keeps the big machines from breaking down."

Petrov fell silent as the waitress brought their food, then moved away. When she was out of earshot, he continued. "Now, with Rurik Baklanov, we have a man who doesn't recognize his limits. He ignores the rules, you understand?"

"I'm starting to."

"We had thought the problem remedied," Petrov went on, "when Baklanov came to America. Of course, we understood it was a business trip, as you might say, but there was hope that your police and FBI might deal with him. He was arrested, after all.''

"And cut himself a deal," Bolan replied.

"That is regrettably the case. With Baklanov, however, deals are made to be broken. It was foreseeable that he'd violate the terms of his agreement with your government and strike off on his own."

"The new face helps."

"Exactly so. It has slowed me from finding him, as well."

"I'm still not clear on who you are, exactly," Bolan said.

Petrov was silent for a moment, as he thought about the best way to respond. At last, he said, "I'm what might be called in English a repairman…no, a troubleshooter."

"With the emphasis on shooter," Bolan said.

"When necessary." Petrov didn't seem offended by the comment. "You're in the same line, I believe. Clearly, you don't represent the Federal Bureau of Investigation or related agencies. One man, without a warrant, armed as you are, it's not—how should I say it? Constitutional?"

The Russian had him there, but Bolan stopped short of admitting anything. "You're ex-KGB?" he asked.

"I was never part of it. There are, as you Americans might say, more ways than one to skin a rat."

"And you were sent for Baklanov."

"As you were," Petrov said.

"But he could walk in here right now," the Executioner suggested, "and you wouldn't know him, right? I mean, new face and all."

"Again, you are correct," Petrov replied. "I hope you may be able to assist me with that minor difficulty."

"Why should I do that?" Bolan asked.

"We desire the same result, I think," the Russian said. "Rurik has broken your rules, too. He is your problem, at the moment, but I have good reason to believe that he'll come back home, someday, when he has finished with his business here. By then, if he hasn't been stopped, it might well be too late."

"You take him seriously, then," Bolan said.

"But of course," Petrov replied. "I wasn't sent halfway around the world to play some childish game. My people are extremely serious about removing Baklanov from circulation."

"So, let's hear it," Bolan said.

"Hear what?" The Russian frowned, seeming confused.

"You've got a deal in mind, something you want from me, or else you would have let me die back there."

"Perhaps I'm a Good Samaritan," Petrov said, smiling once again.

"And I'm the Easter Bunny," Bolan answered. "What's the deal?"

"I'm correct in thinking that you might have found a way to recognize our common target, yes? The surgeon told you something, did he not?"

"It's possible," Bolan replied.

"While I, in turn, have something that might help us both to find the man who wears that face."

"Such as?"

"A name," Petrov said. "More specifically, a woman's name. The name of Rurik's lover. An American."

"If you have that, why aren't you camped out on her doorstep," Bolan asked, "instead of trailing me around?"

"Because I don't know where that doorstep is," the Russian grudgingly admitted. "My contacts in the United States are limited, to say the least. And unlike Dr. Marx, this lady doesn't advertise her services."

Now it was Bolan's turn to smile, as he replied, "Let's hear the rest."

"ANOTHER MISS," Rurik Baklanov said. "I'm starting to believe that you have hired incompetents."

Semyon Shurochka bit his tongue. He wouldn't take the bait and launch into an argument, not when his master was in such a wretched mood. Provoking Baklanov at such a moment was a good way to get killed. Shurochka knew that much from personal experience.

"We lost five men," he said. "Chapaev says they did their best, under the circumstances."

"You accept that?"

Shurochka thought about it for a moment, finally nodding. "The attackers came with automatic weapons and grenades," he said. "They were professionals."

"Or lucky?"

"No. Chapaev and his men are all ex-Spetsnaz. Luck wouldn't be enough."

The news from Cleveland had been bad, but Shurochka knew it could have been much worse. If men were to be lost, he much preferred that they be killed, rather than taken into custody. They couldn't question corpses; dead men couldn't lose their nerve and let some bit of secret information slip while they were being grilled by the authorities. A bullet to the head eliminated any risk of second thoughts. More to the point, Chapaev and the rest of his commandos had escaped before police arrived. Vito Fortini liked to boast of his influence with the local law. He had an opportunity to prove it, now.

Baklanov was silent for a moment, as he poured himself another shot of vodka, downed it in one swallow, and then set the glass aside. "We still don't have an answer to the most important question, Semyon," he remarked.

Shurochka didn't have to ask what question that would be. It had been on his mind since the disruption of their meeting with the five Sicilians in New Jersey. Baklanov still hadn't discovered whether the attacks were aimed at him, or if they simply represented some unrest within the local Mafia. Until that question had been answered, there could be no peace of mind, no progress toward the culmination of their grand design.

"I think it must be the Italians fighting with each other," Shurochka said, although he had no evidence for that conclusion. Still, he had to offer something. "If the strike team had been seeking you, why go to Cleveland? It makes no sense, Rurik."

"Perhaps not," Baklanov allowed. "And yet..."

"We need to draw them out," the lieutenant offered, keen

enough on the idea to take the risk of interrupting. "So far, they have chosen when and where to strike. If we could bait a proper trap, then the advantage would be ours. If they ignore it, then we know it's a domestic problem. We let Donatelli and the others work it out themselves."

"I see one problem with your plan," said Baklanov, reaching for the vodka bottle once again.

"Which is?"

"The bait, you idiot!" he snapped. "They won't come after you or Chapaev, much less his soldiers. Would you put me on the hook and wait to see who comes to snap me up?"

"I didn't mean—"

"Then tell me what you meant!" Baklanov's gray eyes had darkened almost to a charcoal shade, reflecting fury. He downed another shot of vodka, topping off his glass before he set the bottle down. "This is no time for games."

"We need something," Shurochka said, "which will suggest your presence. Something that will make the strike team think they have you. That is all I meant, Rurik. Of course, I wouldn't risk—"

"Something?" Baklanov asked. "Or, better yet, why not someone?"

Shurochka blinked at that. He was a childhood friend of Baklanov's and believed he knew the other's mind as well as anyone alive, but there were still times when he couldn't follow his boss's train of thought, his quantum leaps between one notion and the next.

"Of course," he said uncertainly, "if there was someone to impersonate you, we could—"

Baklanov's laughter stopped him cold. Shurochka shut his mouth and waited for the explanation that he knew would be forthcoming, in due time.

"Impersonate me!" the Russian mobster shook his head, still laughing. "What would be the use of that, Semyon, when no one knows my face?"

That wasn't wholly accurate, of course. They still hadn't located Dr. Marx, the surgeon, and while he survived, Baklanov's new face might yet be compromised. And then, the various Sicilians were familiar with his look, as were the members of their own team, and—

A flash of sudden understanding made Shurochka smile. He felt the corners of his mouth begin to levitate, against his own best judgment, but he couldn't help himself. At once, he knew what Baklanov had in mind and understood the beauty of the plan. He spoke the name at last, with something close to reverence.

"Justine."

"Why not?" Baklanov replied. "She's good in bed, of course, but she can also serve in other ways."

No sooner had Shurochka solved the riddle than he saw its glaring flaw. "But your relationship—"

"Has been kept secret," Baklanov said, anticipating him. "What of it? Secrets are revealed from time to time, sometimes deliberately."

Shurochka was already thinking through the details, planning how to do it subtly. It wouldn't do for him to advertise the plan, leave tracks that anyone could recognize. Still, there were ways to get it done. A whisper here, a rumor there.

"She would be placed at risk," he cautiously reminded Baklanov.

"A pity, granted," the Russian boss said. "We must protect her, by all means. That is the whole point of the exercise. But if misfortune should befall her...well, we may find solace in the knowledge that she served a greater good."

"I'll see to it at once, Rurik."

"And send Chapaev to see me here, as soon as he arrives," Baklanov commanded.

"Certainly."

"He needs a bit of an incentive to succeed next time."

Shurochka was immediately and intensely grateful that he didn't stand in Hedeon Chapaev's shoes. First, he had missed the plastic surgeon in Chicago; now, he had the mess in Cleveland to explain. Baklanov would probably allow him to survive, because they had no better man on staff just now, but Chapaev wouldn't enjoy the interview by any means.

Meanwhile, Shurochka had a trap to bait. And if it failed, the Russian knew he would have problems of his own.

"I DON'T BELIEVE IT," Hal Brognola said on recognizing Bolan's voice. "A call in daylight, during office hours. What's this old world coming to?"

A chuckle on the other end was cut short as Bolan said, "You heard about the snag in Cleveland?"

"Courtesy of CNN," Brognola said. "It didn't go as planned, I take it."

"Not exactly," Bolan answered. "They were waiting for me, and it didn't feel like Fortini's people. Too professional by half."

"Russians?" Brognola asked.

"I wouldn't be surprised," Bolan said. "And there's something else."

"I'm listening."

"I had an unexpected helping hand at Don Vito's, getting out. A helping hand from Moscow."

"Say again?" Brognola didn't have to feign surprise.

"Moscow has someone tracking Baklanov. He calls himself a troubleshooter."

"Is he any good at it?"

"Not bad," the Executioner replied.

"This troubleshooter have a name?" Brognola asked, as he was reaching for a pen and notepad.

"Dima Petrov, if it's not an alias," Bolan replied. "Of course, he thinks I'm Mike Belasko."

"Gotcha. I can try to check it out, but Moscow...it's a long shot," Brognola declared, "and then some."

"Understood. I'm leaning toward provisional cooperation, even though we probably can't check him out."

"Your call," Brognola said. And he couldn't resist appending, "If you think it's wise."

"I may be vague on who he's working for," Bolan said,

"but I'm sure it isn't Baklanov. He had me cold last night and helped me out of Fortini's place instead of dropping me. He also capped three of the housemen in the process."

"Well..."

"I know, it doesn't prove he's straight," Bolan acknowledged, "but the guy we're after doesn't play that kind of subtle game. He would've killed me while he had the chance—or bagged me for interrogation at the very least."

"I hope you're right," Brognola said.

"There's something else," Bolan said.

"Geez. Again, with something else." The big Fed frowned. "Go on."

"Petrov gave me a name. Are you familiar with a Justine Palmer?"

"Should I be?" Brognola jotted down the name, immediately followed by a question mark.

"If Petrov has it straight, she's Baklanov's main squeeze here in the States—or was, before he cut his deal with Uncle Sam."

"It doesn't ring a bell," Brognola said, "but if he's right, there ought to be a record with the Bureau or the U.S. Marshal's office. I can check it out."

"ASAP," the Executioner replied. "We're thinking she might know a way to get in touch with Baklanov."

We're thinking. Brognola wasn't entirely sure he liked the sound of that, the notion of his oldest friend accepting aid—however marginal—from someone who might prove to be a ringer, maybe turn around and stab him in the back. Still, he had been correct in saying it was Bolan's call.

"The Bureau or the marshals should have checked that out," Brognola said.

"Maybe they did," Bolan replied. "It might be nothing. Hell, for all I know, the lady's just a rumor. Still, it's all I've got right now. The other way to go is slugging through the Families until something breaks."

Brognola didn't like the sound of that plan, either.

"I'll start making calls," he said. "It might take a couple hours. Can you call me back at, say, ten o'clock?"

"Will do," Bolan said. "Thanks."

"No sweat," Brognola told him. "And no promises."

"Just touching all the bases," the soldiers said. "Good luck."

You, too, the big Fed thought. But what he said was, "Right. I'll talk to you at ten."

The thing with wishing someone luck, he thought, was that it often seemed to blow up in his face, as if the spoken words could somehow jinx an operation in the works. That was ridiculous, he knew…but why take chances, all the same? Most cops would ardently deny it, but in his own experience, they nursed more superstitions in their daily lives than any other segment of the population.

Brognola was uneasy with the thought of Bolan teaming up, on short acquaintance, with a man who might in fact be working for a rival Russian syndicate, instead of for the government in Moscow. Even if the wild card in the game was straight, though, there were still all kinds of legal, diplomatic and strategic problems to consider, with a foreign stranger on the team.

And what about the woman? Justine Palmer. Brognola would make his calls and hope for something he could pass along to Bolan, but he wondered whether it would come to anything. Their quarry, Rurik Baklanov, had shed his face and walked out of his old life with plans that no one in authority had managed to divine, until it was too late. Why would he risk the whole thing for a woman—any woman, much less an American—who, judging from her taste in men, had to be the next thing to a whore?

Still, one could never tell. Sometimes, the whole game hinged upon an adversary's hidden weakness. More than one impressive player had been brought down by a skirt.

Brognola reached out for the telephone again and started making calls.

8

The good news was that Brognola found Justine Palmer on his second call. The bad news was that she lived in Manhattan. Bolan swallowed the report like he would any bitter medicine, trying his best to block the taste and concentrate on the desired results.

The problem with Manhattan wasn't the unfamiliar territory. Bolan had engaged his adversaries there on more than one occasion, dating back to the days of his private war against the Mafia, and he could find his way around the Big Apple as well as any native. The problem, simply stated, was Manhattan's density of population. If their plan went sour, and it came to shooting in the streets, it would be difficult to avoid civilian casualties.

And yet, he seemed to have no choice.

Petrov agreed, and while his personal concern for strange Americans was marginal, at best, he still didn't strike Bolan as the type who would deliberately provoke a firefight in the streets. And if he was, if that assessment proved to be in error…well, the Executioner would handle it.

The address Brognola produced for Justine Palmer put her right downtown, a luxury apartment building at the corner of Columbus Avenue and West 68th Street. She was a long block west of Central Park, three blocks north of Lincoln Center and the Metropolitan Opera House. It was prime real estate, and nothing in her slim case file revealed a source of income that would touch the price she had to be paying for the digs alone. Toss in the clothes and other goodies necessary to preserve appearances in such a ritzy neighborhood, and it left a monthly income well beyond the range of a self-described unemployed actress.

Bolan was willing to bet, sight unseen, that the lady did most of her acting these days in the bedroom, probably to standing ovations. The question in his mind, right now, didn't concern diversity in Palmer's audience, but whether she was still in touch at all with Rurik Baklanov. If she wasn't, if he had cut her loose when he went underground, the whole damned trip would be a waste of time.

And he would have to start from scratch.

Bolan and Petrov hit the street in business suits, each with his favored side arm in a shoulder rig and compact automatic weapons hidden under lightweight raincoats. There were smoke grenades beneath the rented Chevy's driver's seat, inside a plastic shopping bag.

It was impractical for them to park the car and watch Palmer's apartment building, as the trackers in a Hollywood production might have done. There were no spaces at the curb, for one thing, and if something opened up, a meter maid would be along to ticket them if they remained in any one place longer than an hour. As it was, they didn't even know if Justine Palmer was at home. Two calls from pay phones had been picked up by her answering machine, which could mean anything, or nothing.

One of them would have to check it out on foot.

It was a toss-up, regarding who should drive around the block and who should go inside to see if there was anybody at home. Beyond that point, the plan got vague—interrogation or abduction, both of them agreed that simply staking out the flat would be a monumental waste of time. They ultimately flipped a coin, and Bolan won the toss. It was his turn to be the infantry.

They had a photograph of Justine Palmer in the rented Chevy, courtesy of Hal Brognola. It revealed a blond, attractive woman in her early thirties, definitely see-worthy, but there was nothing to be learned about the subject from a photo. Bolan couldn't see beyond the eyes into her soul.

For that, he needed contact, and the effort to establish contact came with risks attached.

The doorman was his first obstacle, a fortyish hulk of a man in a tailored uniform that made him resemble an old-time railroad conductor. Bolan showed him a gold detective's shield and said, "NYPD, official business," while the doorman checked it out. The badge was genuine, or nearly so. A call to One Police Plaza would be required to determine that the specific number stamped on the shield had never been assigned to any living officer.

"Sure thing, Detective," said the doorman, making up his mind. "If you'll just tell me the apartment number, I can—"

"You can open up, and never mind the call," said Bolan. "If I wanted to be chasing him around the block, I would've called ahead myself."

"Oh, right." The doorman bobbed his head and ushered Bolan into the lobby proper. "Anything that I can do…"

"I'll let you know," Bolan replied, thinking twice about the elevator, finally deciding on the stairs.

A little exercise never killed anybody. On the other hand, an elevator could become a death trap in an instant if the play went sour.

Six floors, twelve flights. He took a breath and started up.

THE CALL HAD COME at 3:30 a.m. Four months of waiting—not quite sitting by the telephone, of course, but close enough—and then the bastard called while she was sleeping. Not to ask how she was doing, mind you, but to tell Justine Palmer he needed help.

She lit another cigarette and moved to stand before the window, facing east across Columbus Avenue, toward Central Park. She wasn't really close enough to see the park, of course, but if she stared up 68th Street on a good day, with the sun just right, there was a hint of greenery. It was enough to boost her rent another five bills every month and keep her always on the lookout for some ready cash.

It wasn't only money that she saw in Rory Baker, of course. There was a certain chemistry, an animal attraction—something close to love, perhaps, although Palmer still wasn't sure that she would recognize the real thing if she saw it served up on a silver platter. In any case, she didn't care about the phony name, the fact that he had changed his face. If forced to tell the truth, which she had done from time to time, the mystery and the excitement added something to their strange relationship. Money aside, Palmer was looking forward to the day when she could see Baker again, and get her hands on him. The day when he could get his hands on her.

But none of that explained the presence of gorillas in her living room.

Make that gorilla, singular, since only one of them remained in her apartment, sipping coffee and ignoring Palmer as she paced the room or stood and stared through the glass. She knew gorillas when she saw them. Not the zoo variety—leg breakers, triggermen, torpedoes. Palmer had serviced mobsters in her time and knew the type.

These weren't homegrown gorillas, though. She knew that from the accents, picking up the taste of borsch. They were like Baker, only less refined. Less powerful. Still, they were frightening enough: hard faces, slicked-back hair, the jackets worn a size too large as cover for the hardware underneath. These were the kind of men who worked for Baker, handling the dirty chores he left to other, coarser hands.

And they were watching her, so Baker said, because some other hardmen might come looking for her, using her to get at him. She hadn't questioned Baker, for it made sense in a loopy kind of way. She knew about his dealings with the government and understood that he had pulled a fast one on the Feds somehow—slipped out before Perrugia's men could find him, so he said—and if the Mob was looking for him with a score to settle, they might ultimately try to squeeze her. Palmer didn't understand why that idea had only just occurred to Baker, in the wee small hours of the morning, but at least she knew that he was thinking of her.

There had been the monthly checks, of course, to tide her over in his absence, but Palmer had been expecting them to stop one day. The longer he was out of touch, the less incentive any man would have for keeping up the rent. But now, with any luck, she thought things might work out all right.

Assuming she survived the next few hours.

If there was trouble in the building, she would be out on her ass. That much was cut and dried, a firm clause in the lease, and she would lose her full deposit, too. Granted, the money had been Baker's to begin with, but she didn't relish the embarrassment, knowing that one black mark would make it harder when she tried to relocate.

Palmer was thinking of a life in Queens or Brooklyn, when a hiss of static drew her full attention back to the gorilla on her couch. She turned to find him reaching underneath his coat, extracting what appeared to be a compact two-way radio. A small, metallic voice came out of it, speaking Russian, and the team leader answered in kind. To Palmer, it sounded as if he were clearing his throat.

"It's time," the hardman informed her, rising to his feet. "You'll stay here and wait."

With that, he pocketed the radio and turned his back on her, moving directly to the door and out. The door latched automatically behind him, a safety feature she had appreciated about the department from day one. It meant she had to take her key along each time she stepped outside, but no one could slip in behind her, either.

She stared after the shooter for a moment, hearing his last words again. "You will stay here and wait."

Like hell she would, Palmer answered to herself.

THE SECOND TIME he drove around the block, Dima Petrov picked out the same two men he had seen on the first pass, standing together on the sidewalk directly opposite the mark's apartment building. They both wore suits, and one carried a briefcase in his right hand, while the other had a folded news-paper clutched beneath his left arm.

There was no reason they should not be standing there, de-spite the fact that it had taken him nearly ten minutes to circle the block. They were two businessmen, perhaps, on a break from the office or coming in late. Who knew the customs of Americans in New York City in this day and age?

It was the way they stood and watched the building opposite, not even speaking to each other as he passed, that set the Rus-sian's nerves on edge. That, and the fact that on his second pass, the taller of the two—the man who held the briefcase—had begun to smoke a cigarette. The way he held it pinched between his thumb and forefinger, "backward" for an Amer-ican, told Petrov he was looking at a fellow countryman.

And that meant trouble.

Slowing as he approached the traffic light, Petrov dismissed the two men for a moment, glancing left and right around him toward the other corners of the intersection. Two more watch-ers stood on the northeast corner—one gray suit with a brief-case, and one in navy blue, his hands clasped behind his back, a soldier at ease. In Petrov's right-hand mirror, two more came up the sidewalk on the north side of the street.

The side toward the apartment building.

He couldn't be sure about the final pair, since they were moving, both men empty-handed, but they had the look about them—close-cropped hair and faces molded out of leather. The jackets that they wore seemed just a bit too large, which could suggest armed soldiers or a simple lack of style.

He made it six, for safety's sake, and if they had six gunners on the street, logic dictated that there would be more inside the building, where Belasko was. For all he knew, the tall Amer-ican might already be dead. If he was still alive, the soldiers down below were in position now to cut off his retreat.

It was an oddity, Petrov thought, that the soldiers didn't seem to notice him as he drove past. Of course, he hadn't let Belasko out in front of the apartment building, but rather on the next block down, before he started circling. They could have missed him easily and only noted the American once he had made his way inside.

What should he do?

The choices were distinctly limited. He couldn't go inside to help Belasko, since there was nowhere for him to park the car, and leaving it would sacrifice their only method of escape. That left two options. Petrov could assume the worst and leave Belasko to his fate, or he could stay the course, keep circling the block until he knew for sure.

And when would that be? If his comrade of the moment was already dead inside the luxury apartment building, it could be hours—even days—before police were summoned to the site. Indeed, if the assassins found another exit and some way to hide the corpse as it was carried out, there was no reason why police should ever be involved. Belasko had no contacts in New York that Petrov knew of. The Russian couldn't even alert the tall man's friends in Washington, since he had no idea which agency Belasko represented, who to call, or what to say.

And he wouldn't have jeopardized himself by making such a call if he *had* known.

His instinct told him to get out of there while there was time, but something held him back. Not yet, the small voice said, and he had learned to trust it in the past from grim experience.

Not yet.

The light turned green in front of him, and Petrov checked the watchers one more time before he made his left-hand turn and started on another circuit of the block. Before the gunmen on the northeast corner vanished from his sight, he had drawn the P-9 automatic from his shoulder holster, wedging it between the console and the driver's seat, where it was readily available. Next, he reached down to fetch the shopping bag, the smoke grenades inside it clanking softly as he placed them on the vacant seat beside him.

Ready.

Now, all Petrov had to do was drive around the block once more, or maybe twice, and pray that he wasn't too late.

BOLAN WAS HALFWAY up the final flight of stairs, almost to the sixth floor, before he paused, catching his breath, and eased his raincoat back to clear the compact MP-5 K submachine gun slung beneath his right arm on a swivel rig. The piece was cocked already, with a live round in the chamber, and he eased the safety off as he continued up the stairs.

He paused again on the landing before he risked a glance around the corner, down the hall. Justine Palmer lived in apartment 6D, midway down on his left, and he started in that direction, checking out the doors on either side. A stereo was playing in 6B, the rest of the apartments silent as he passed. Bolan was twenty paces from his destination when a stocky figure in a black trench coat appeared at the far end of the hall, a pistol in his right hand, walkie-talkie in his left, the radio held to his lips.

Bolan glanced back toward the stairwell he had come from, quick enough to catch the shadows of two figures on the landing, just about to show themselves. He had a heartbeat to decide a course of action, and the shooter at the west end of the hallway, with the walkie-talkie, made his mind up for him as he raised the automatic, sighting down its slide.

The Executioner was faster, squeezing off a short burst from his SMG almost before the weapon cleared his coat. Downrange, the gunman staggered, reeling as a line of Parabellum bullets stitched across his chest. The gunner got off two shots as he fell, but both of them went wide, one punching through the ceiling tiles, the other taking out a light fixture adjacent to the door of 6E.

Bolan turned away before the dead man hit the carpet, doubling back toward the stairs. Justine Palmer could wait—assuming she was even here at all, with shooters covering the flat—and any hope of speaking to her in the present circumstances had evaporated when the soldier with the walkie-talkie showed himself.

Now, all that mattered was survival, getting out of there alive and in one piece. He wondered what was happening downstairs, if there were more guns waiting for him on the street, and what had become of Petrov.

Never mind.

The way to live through combat was to take it one step at a time and deal with adversaries as they came.

Bolan was halfway back to the stairs when the first gunner stepped into view, an Uzi submachine gun leveled from his hip. The gunfire from the hallway had alerted him, and he was ready now, squeezing the trigger as he caught his first glimpse of the Executioner.

Bolan reacted automatically, dodging to his left and dropping to a crouch as he returned fire with his SMG. For an instant, while the two guns fired together, their staccato sound reverberated in the hallway like the noise of jackhammers. A startled cry behind a nearby door alerted him to neighbors who would soon be on the telephone, spilling their panic to the 911 dispatcher.

The Executioner hosed the shooter with another burst of Parabellum slugs as he dived toward a prone position on the floor. He scored this time, the gunner doubling over, clutching at his gut with one hand, while the muzzle of his weapon dipped, still firing. Bullets from his own gun ripped into the shooter's feet and ankles, dropping him as if he had been cut down by a scythe.

And that left one that Bolan knew of.

Springing to his feet, the soldier rushed the landing and the stairs before the fallen gunman's sidekick could recuperate from his surprise. He got there as the shooter raised a sawed-off shotgun, triggering a hasty blast. Bolan recoiled as buckshot pellets sprayed the wall and ceiling, plaster spilling from a dozen ragged holes.

The gunner shouted something unintelligible in Russian before he pumped the action on his 12-gauge and squeezed off a second blast. A corner of the wall across from Bolan vaporized, leaving a hole he could have put his head through, with an inch or so to spare.

Before his adversary had a chance to pump the shotgun's

slide again, Bolan stepped out and hit him with a rising burst of automatic fire, strafing the Russian with a dozen rounds that slammed him backward into a clumsy somersault. The soldier pursued him as he tumbled down the stairs, barely a yard behind the shooter as he hit the midfloor landing in a boneless sprawl.

He stepped across the body, craned his neck to scan the next flight down, expecting reinforcements. If the enemy was covering Justine Palmer, would they be satisfied with three men on the job? Had they been watching on the street, when he arrived? Were others drawing down on Petrov, even now?

Bolan hit the stairs running, reloading his MP-5 K on the move. No matter how he tried to calm himself, a voice inside his head repeated that it might already be too late.

JUSTINE PALMER HAD BEEN so upset when Baker called and spilled his plan to her, giving the orders, that she started packing then and there, as soon as she was off the telephone. Before his three gorillas rang the bell—and God knew how they made it past the doorman; probably some kind of bribe—her suitcase and an overnight bag were ready, waiting in the bedroom closet.

Palmer had made one mistake. She should have bailed out then, before the hardmen showed and placed her under house arrest. The problem was a lack of nerve; she could admit that to herself. Palmer was frightened that the heavies would arrive as she was leaving, catch her in the act and drag her back— tell Baker she was bailing on him, maybe even rough her up, just for the hell of it.

So, she had waited, thinking she could see it through, no problem. All she had to do was sit around and wait for some guy she had never seen—would never see—to show up in the building, and the hardmen would take care of it. Palmer wasn't involved. She would have been there anyway, regardless, even if the predawn call had never come.

Bullshit.

The fear had started nagging at her big-time, once the head

gorilla sent his people out to do whatever shooters do when they weren't shooting. When the main man got his call and left her flat, she was prepared to take the chance and make a break for it. Whatever. Anything to get away.

And then, all hell broke loose outside.

She was familiar with the sound of guns, as anybody was who watched TV these days, or saw a movie more than once a year. Still, it was different in real life, up close and personal. It sounded like a pitched battle was raging just outside her door, and Palmer caught herself moving toward the telephone, her first instinct to call for help.

Screw that!

She waited for the sound of automatic fire to fade or move downstairs before bolting for the bedroom and her bags when it was quiet in the hall outside for sixty seconds straight. She still might run into the hardmen, but it was a chance Palmer felt she would have to take under the circumstances. There was simply no good way out of the present situation, now that guns had gone off in the building. She was finished as a tenant here, whatever happened next, and it would mean a trip downtown if she was there when the police arrived.

More to the point, Baker's gorillas might decide she ought to tag along with them when they withdrew, assuming they were even still alive. She had been looking forward to reunion with her lover—if they were still lovers—but she didn't trust the hardmen to deliver her intact.

And, truth be told, she wasn't sure how much she even trusted Baker, anymore. If he could use her as bait in a trap where shooting was involved, what else was he capable of doing?

Her bags felt heavy when Palmer picked them up, but she attributed that to the tremors she felt as she moved toward the door.

Outside, the hallway smelled like fireworks, but she guessed it had to be gun smoke. There was a light out—broken—down the hall to Palmer's left, and beyond it, on the landing to the west, she saw a crumpled heap of clothes that had to be a body.

Pockmarks on the wall above the supine form showed where the bullets had flown past or through him, as he fell.

Palmer didn't know who he was, or whether he was dead, nor did she care. The dark suit looked familiar—could it be the leader of the team?—but there were thousands, maybe millions, like it in Manhattan.

Turning to the right, she moved with long, determined strides toward the stairs on her right, to the east. Palmer had thought about the elevator, but it made her queasy, fearing that Baker's gorillas might be waiting for her in the lobby. This way, she could always drop her bags and make a run for it, if necessary. They would catch her, maybe shoot her in the back and leave her where she fell, but at least she would have made the effort.

There was another body on this landing. No question of this one surviving, with so much blood everywhere, the awkward, twisted attitude his body had adopted when he fell.

Palmer could feel her breakfast croissant coming back on her, and swallowed hard to keep it down. She stepped around the corpse and started down the stairwell, with the reek of cordite stronger here, and caught her breath at the sight of a third crumpled form down below. She scuttled down the steps and dodged the corpse, feeling the suitcase bump against her leg. She almost let it go. The cash and credit cards were in her shoulder bag, enough to get her by, but Palmer felt that dropping it would almost be a gesture of defeat.

And she wasn't a woman to surrender when her life was riding on it.

No damned way at all.

IT WAS A BRISK twelve paces from the stairwell to the street. The doorman had retreated to a corner at the sound of gunfire from upstairs, and he watched Bolan, wide-eyed, as the Executioner moved toward the exit, making no attempt to stop him, no move toward the nearby telephone. The SMG in Bolan's hand was all he had to see, enough to freeze him in his tracks and make him pray that he wouldn't be next to feel the weapon's bite.

Bolan was halfway to the door when two men stepped in front of it. They were outside, both aiming semiautomatic pistols through the glass, and Bolan didn't wait for them to fire. The MP-5 K hammered at them, shattering the plate glass of the double doors, spent brass catching the glare of the fluorescent fixtures overhead, as empty cartridge casings fell around his feet.

One of the shooters raised an arm, as if to shield his face from flying glass, but it was no protection from the bullets ripping through his chest. He went down in a heap, his partner half turned from the door, as if to flee, his pistol blazing as he pumped rounds blindly through the door into the lobby. Bolan felt a couple of them sizzle past him, but he held his ground and stroked another burst out of his SMG, the second gunner lurching as he took the hits, collapsing like a puppet with its strings slashed.

Stepping through the ruins of the shattered double doors, Bolan ignored the bodies on the sidewalk, glancing left and right in search of other enemies, in search of Petrov and the rental car. He came up empty on the latter, but at least four other gunmen had him covered, staked out on opposing corners to the east and south. The flow of morning traffic gave him cover of a sort, but those grim-faced assassins had a job to do, and they weren't afraid of racking up civilian casualties if that was what it took to make the score.

One of them proved the point by stepping into the crosswalk, rubber squealing as he went against the traffic light, horns blaring outrage. He was carrying an imitation-leather briefcase, and he made no move to drop or open it as he advanced on Bolan, scowling with a face that might have been rough cut from clay. Three strides toward Bolan, and the briefcase started spitting fire, 9 mm bullets knocking divots in the wall beside him, tracking toward the Executioner in a rapid zigzag pattern.

Bolan hunched behind a mailbox on the corner, and he could feel it taking hits, as the shooter found his mark. The briefcase was an item he had seen before in sundry variations. There would be a compact submachine gun braced inside—perhaps an Ingram, or a mini-Uzi—a trigger mechanism built into the briefcase handle, while a gun port the size of a dime at one end was aligned with the muzzle. Such weapons were short on accuracy and long on close-range firepower, designed as "room brooms" or "street sweepers" for special occasions.

Like this one.

The down side, for his adversary, was that any weapon that would fit inside the briefcase also had a rate of fire that would exhaust its magazine within two or three seconds, maximum, of sustained fire. Bolan stayed where he was, hunkered down, knowing the other gunmen had to be circling around to cut him off, but he could only deal with one threat at a time.

A heartbeat later, after half a dozen more rounds clanged against the mailbox, followed by a sudden lull in firing, Bolan knew the time had come for him to make his move. The others would be watching, waiting for him, but he had no choice. He lunged around one corner of the mailbox, keeping its bulk between him and the shooters on the corner to the east. A pistol blasted at him from across the street—the briefcase gunner's sidekick—but he had his nearest adversary cold, halfway across the street and fumbling with a side arm underneath his jacket.

Bolan hit him with a short burst to the chest and saw his target stagger, dropping to his knees, before he ducked back out of sight behind the mailbox. Three more left to go, at least, and by the time he dealt with them—assuming he could tag them all—police could well be on the scene. In that case, there was nothing he could do but cut and run. Unless—

Traffic had stalled on 68th Street, since his enemies had started firing over and around the passing cars. Most drivers ducked out of sight, trusting their vehicles for cover, but a few had bailed out and were running for their lives, adding further confusion to the scene. Gunfire aside, a kind of hush had fallen on the busy intersection—all except for one excited driver who was leaning on his horn, trying to clear the path of other vehicles that blocked his way.

Afraid to hope, Bolan still glanced in the direction of the blaring sound and recognized the rental Chevrolet, with Dima

Petrov at the wheel. As the soldier watched, his Russian ally of the moment swung the car hard left, onto the sidewalk, shearing off two parking meters in the process, scattering pedestrians as he pursued the only clear path still available.

Bolan was ready for him as the Chevrolet approached. He sprang into the open, laying down a screen of cover fire to south and east. Petrov had the passenger's door open as he drew near, and it missed Bolan by inches, striking the mailbox as Petrov stood on the brakes. The soldier slid into the empty seat and slammed the door behind him, Petrov accelerating almost before he was seated.

Across the street, two of the Russian gunners were unloading in rapid fire with semiauto pistols, a couple of their bullets chipping at the Chevy's windshield. Bolan stuck his SMG out the window and returned the fire one-handed, holding the stuttergun steady and tracking as Petrov hit the accelerator, bouncing over the curb and back onto blacktop, northbound on Columbus Avenue.

"Use this!" the Russian said, and passed a smoke grenade to Bolan, steering with his left hand. He was grinning, checking out the rearview mirror, seeming to enjoy himself.

The smoke grenade wasn't a bad idea. Bolan released the safety pin and chucked the canister through his open window, watching in his mirror as it started spewing clouds of smoke. They could expect some fender-benders, but free-for-all gunfire and Petrov's slick driving maneuvers had already slowed traffic at the intersection to a crawl, and no one was likely to be seriously injured. Meanwhile, the smoke screen would prevent their enemies from sighting on the car, as they retreated out of range.

"The woman?" Petrov asked when they had covered half a dozen blocks.

"I never saw her," Bolan answered. "They were waiting for me."

"Baklanov," the Russian said with venom in his tone.

Who else? Bolan thought. And the certainty did nothing to improve his mood. It was the third time that he had been outmaneuvered by an adversary he had yet to see. It galled him, made him even more determined to proceed.

And it told Bolan that they could be running out of time.

Whatever Rurik Baklanov was planning, he had thus far been at liberty to go about his business, more or less unhindered. Bolan might have thinned his ranks—more recently, with Dima Petrov's help—but he hadn't done anything, as yet, to seriously stall the Russian's scheme.

That had to change, and if it took a shooting war against the Mafia to shift the balance in his favor, Bolan was prepared to go that route, as well.

Been there, done that, he thought, and nearly smiled.

Who said you couldn't go home again?

At times—increasingly, of late—it seemed to Rurik Baklanov
that if he didn't find a way to vent his anger and frustration,
he would start to swell up like some kind of cartoon character,
until he finally exploded. That was how he felt that morning,
listening to news of the pathetic screwup in New York.

"Another six men dead," he said, repeating what Semyon
Shurochka had just told him. "One arrested by New York
police."

"Yes, sir." Shurochka's tone was glum, and rightly so.

"What charges have they booked him on?" the Russian
mobster asked.

"He had a pistol, which is not permitted in New York, without a special license from authorities," Shurochka said.

"He must not be allowed to talk," Baklanov stated. "If bail
isn't permitted, you must silence him."

"In custody?" Shurochka was frowning at him now.

"Such things aren't unheard-of," Baklanov replied. "If necessary, you may call on Comrade Donatelli for assistance. It'll
be in his best interest, also, for the matter to be tidily resolved."

"I'll see to it," Shurochka said.

Six dead, Rurik repeated to himself. That made eleven soldiers lost within two days, an even dozen if he had to kill the
one locked up in jail. And all for what? He still had no idea
who was stalking him, what motive drove them on. The only
thing he had learned, from the latest incident, was that the
hunters wanted him. If it had been a feud among the various
Sicilian Families, Justine Palmer wouldn't have been involved.

The trap had worked to that extent, but it had told him nothing else.

And now, it seemed, Palmer was gone, as well.

"How did she get away?" Baklanov asked.

"Justine?"

"Who else?" He made no effort to conceal the biting sarcasm.

"I thought…" Shurochka reconsidered whatever it was he planned to say. "We can't be sure what happened, Rurik. It appears that she slipped out in the confusion, while the fight was going on downstairs."

"And no one saw her go." It was a statement, not a question, but Shurochka felt obliged to answer anyway.

"The men inside died quickly. The others had their hands full, trying to contain the enemy. And then, of course, there were police."

"One man," Baklanov said bitterly. "One man, to do all this."

"There was the driver, too," Shurochka reminded him. "Two men, that is."

"But one did all the shooting that we know of, yes?"

"The two of ours who got away—"

"Two out of nine."

"Yes, sir. They only saw one man come out of the apartment building. That doesn't mean he was alone, of course. There might well have been others who went out the back, for instance, or—"

"One man!" Baklanov snapped. He bolted upright from his chair, Shurochka retreating, as if fearing physical attack. "How is it that this bastard makes such fools of us?"

"I don't know, Rurik." What else could he say, without provoking an explosive outburst?

"You don't know." The sneer was audible in Baklanov's voice. "There is a great deal you don't know these days, Semyon. I'm more concerned with what you do know. Anything at all, my friend?"

The last two words exuded bitter mockery, but Shurochka

refused to take offense. For one thing, it would do no good; and for another, it could get him killed.

"We know they drove a Chevrolet Lumina, but the license number…" Shurochka left the sentence hanging, shook his head and shrugged. "It would be useless, anyway. The car was struck by several bullets and has no doubt been discarded by this time. When it is found, there may be fingerprints, or—"

"Fingerprints!" Baklanov glared at his second in command with something like amazement. "Are we part of the police, now?"

"Of course not, Rurik, but I thought…that is, if the police identified the gunmen, one of Donatelli's contacts might inform us who they are."

It was the first time Rurik Baklanov had smiled in days. "You might have something there," he said, "but I'll be very much surprised if any fingerprints are found. They might not even find the car. These are professionals we're dealing with."

And, then again, the Russian mobster thought, his unknown enemies might even be in league with the police. Such things were not unknown, in Russia or in the United States. All governments had operatives and agencies assigned to deal with "special" problems out of court and off the record. Anything was possible, which made it all the more difficult for Baklanov to base future plans on the basis of such fragmentary evidence.

"We can afford no more delays," he said at last. "Our plans have been unduly sidetracked, as it is. We cannot count on the respect of the Sicilians if we show ourselves as weaklings. You agree, Semyon?"

"Of course, Rurik." What more could Shurochka say? He knew how critical their deal with the Sicilians was to Baklanov—indeed, to all of them. If they were held up now…

A telephone rang somewhere in the house. A moment later, both men were distracted by a rapping on the door, with Baklanov growling, "Yes?" The door was opened by his houseman, carrying a cordless phone in one hand, with a frown etched on his long, thin face.

"A call for you, sir," he declared.

"Who is it?" the Russian mobster asked. The answer made him smile and snap his fingers as he reached out for the telephone. Baklanov was beaming as he spoke into the mouthpiece. "Ah, Justine, my love!"

THE CALL HAD BEEN a gamble. Justine Palmer had to talk herself into it after she had managed to evade the gunmen and police surrounding her apartment building, flagging down a taxi two blocks west, on Amsterdam. She named a hotel for the cabbie—one she had used on business several times, a mid-priced setup in the lower eighties—and paid the clerk in cash when she checked in. She knew enough to skip the credit cards to avoid leaving a trail that could be followed by computer, just in case someone was looking for her.

Someone like the shooters Baker had been watching for when he sent his gorillas over to her flat. Or, someone like Baker, himself?

The latter possibility chilled Palmer to the marrow of her bones. It made her feel alone, abandoned. Not so much because she loved him—thinking back, now, she could hardly say that it had gone that far; she wasn't even sure what "loving" someone meant, in concrete terms—but rather, thinking of the power Baker wielded, on his own and through his friends in the Italian Mob. If all of them came looking for her, Palmer knew she couldn't hide.

Nobody could.

First thing, she had considered getting out of town. It hardly mattered where she went, as long as it was far away from the Manhattan killing ground. Los Angeles was nice and warm, the whole year round. And there was always Vegas, too; an easy town to get lost in, with no state income tax.

On second thought, though, Palmer had to wonder if a panicked evacuation was the smartest way to go. If Baker's men—or the Italians, for that matter—caught up to her later, running put a guilty spin on everything she said or did. And, Palmer told herself, the last thing she wanted to do, at the moment, was to anger her boyfriend.

So, she picked up the telephone. Granted, it took her a couple of drinks from the minibar—straight vodka from those tiny airline bottles—to work up the nerve. That done, she flubbed the dialing twice, punching the wrong damned buttons with her trembling hand.

But when she got it right at last, she recognized the gravel voice that answered. Palmer didn't know the houseman's name, although she would have recognized him on the street: long face and thinning hair, a prison-gray complexion, shoulders slumped from years of carrying his guilt around. She asked for Baker, gave her name when asked and waited while the houseman went to fetch his boss. It took the best part of a minute, listening to dead air, feeling like an idiot, before another voice came on the line.

"Ah," Baker said, "Justine, my love!"

"What was all that, Rory?" she asked him, cutting through the crap to the bottom line. "You almost got me killed, goddamn you!"

"Now, Justine—"

"I had to walk on dead men getting out of there," she said, exaggerating slightly for effect. "The guns were going off all over, Rory! I—"

"Justine," he interrupted her, "this line—"

"What were you thinking of, to put me in the middle of all that?" she challenged him.

"I need to bring you in, honey," he said.

"In where?" She felt the short hairs bristling on her nape, a danger signal. She was working overtime to trust this man who sometimes shared her body and her bed, but Palmer knew he was a killer, and survival still took top priority.

"I don't want you in danger," he replied.

Oh, right, she thought. That's why he stuck her in the middle of a goddamned shooting gallery. And what she said was, "I don't know."

"You don't know what, Justine?" He sounded reasonable now, but somewhat on the tense side, like his nerves were tightly strung. And why not? After all the shit that had gone down that morning, Palmer had to be impressed that Baker wasn't bouncing off the walls, like some kind of demented maniac.

"I don't like being used for bait," she said at last.

"That was a poor decision on my part," Baker admitted, sounding almost penitent. "I'll make it up to you. Let me protect you, now."

She wouldn't need protecting if he hadn't set her up, she thought. Palmer delayed her answer for another moment, biting on her lower lip.

"I'll have to think about it," she replied.

"Justine, Justine." He sounded weary now, as if from pleading with a headstrong child. "The longer you delay, the more you place yourself at risk. I really must insist—"

"I said I'll think about it, Rory. And I'll call you back."

She cut off his protest by hanging up the telephone. Too late, she wondered whether Baker had one of those little boxes at his house—caller ID, she thought it was—that would have told her where she called from. Damn! She should have gone down to the lobby and used the pay phone. She could have saved some money in the process, with the dollar charge the hotel pinned on each outgoing call.

So much for being smart and cautious.

Angry and disgusted with herself, Palmer fired up a cigarette and smoked it down to the filter in half a dozen long, fierce drags. She lit another from the first one's butt and paced the hotel room, arms crossed below her ample breasts, trying to figure out what she could do to save herself.

There were a few friends she could call—all men, of course, from prior relationships—and while she reckoned they would all be glad to hear from her, the fact was that she hesitated to involve them in her present difficulty. They had all been good to Palmer, generous and caring in their way, and it would be a rotten trick for her to put the shooters on their scent.

The bottom line appeared to be a choice of evils. She could cut and run today, tomorrow at the latest, or she could forget about the massacre at her apartment building and give Baker another chance. The question was, would she be safer on her own, or in his hands?

The second time she called, the houseman put her through in something close to record time. Baker was almost cheerful when he answered, never mind the fact that she had cut him off, short moments earlier.

"All right," she said without preamble. "When and where?"

"Now, there's a question," Baker said. It sounded like he might be smiling. "Let me think."

THE HOTEL SEARCH hadn't been easy, and it could have been a waste of time, but it had paid off in the end. Petrov had followed a suggestion from Belasko, pocketing a phony badge and ID card for the New York Police Department, plus a wad of cash to tide him over if he ran into "forgetful" clerks. Next thing, he drew a circle on a large map of Manhattan, guessing—accurately, as it turned out—that Justine Palmer wouldn't run to the outer boroughs yet, much less desert the city.

She might leave in time, Petrov decided, but she still had things to do around New York. If nothing else, there would be bank accounts to close, perhaps a safe-deposit box to empty out and transportation to arrange. She owned no car, according to a check Belasko's people had completed with the state Bureau of Motor Vehicles. Petrov couldn't imagine Palmer on the subway, rubbing shoulders with a crowd of common peasants, which would mean that she was using taxicabs—unless, of course, she summoned Baklanov to pick her up.

That was a possibility, Petrov acknowledged, but his gut told him that she would be cautious—for a time, at least—after the killing in her luxury apartment building. It was fifty-fifty that she might abandon Baklanov entirely, angry over being used as bait, and if she called him for assistance, Petrov reckoned she would think about it first, for several hours, anyway.

Which gave him time, but maybe not enough.

He started off with the Manhattan Yellow Pages, let his fingers do the walking through the section on hotels. Petrov was lost if Palmer ran to hide with friends, or checked into a women's shelter, but he counted both as being long shots. She wouldn't enjoy the company of "losers," battered housewives and the like, nor did the Russian think Palmer would trust her friends—assuming she had any in Manhattan—to resist the lure of Baklanov's money, if the mobster started looking for her. That left several hundred small and large hotels that he would have to check before he started on another angle of attack.

Or, maybe he could narrow down the list and save himself some time.

Petrov began by concentrating on Manhattan, striking out the names of those hotels within ten blocks of her apartment building—too obvious, if she had fled on foot—and then deleting more that sounded too expensive or high profile. Justine Palmer liked her comfort, granted, but she didn't have a fortune at her fingertips, and Rurik Baklanov could easily reach out to New York's finer hostelries, persuade a greedy clerk or bellman to report on any new arrivals who conformed to his blond mistress's description.

No, Petrov decided, she would seek a smaller hotel, something in the midprice range and off the beaten track where paparazzi stalked celebrities and foreign diplomats. She would seek distance from her apartment building, but wouldn't run too far. The trick in hiding out was to rely upon deception, rather than to place your faith solely in speed and mileage.

After he had thought it through, Petrov inscribed a second circle on his map, extending some two dozen blocks beyond the first, so that he had two zones of search—uptown, between 78th and 90th streets, and downtown, between 48th and 36th. He chose to search the uptown section first, based on a hunch that Palmer wouldn't flee in the direction of Manhattan's southern tip, but rather northward, where her fallback choices weren't limited to Brooklyn, Jersey City and the sea.

It was a stroke of pure dumb luck that Petrov caught a break on the fourth hotel. He could have searched through the night, in vain, but here, on 82nd Street, he found a clerk who readily identified his photograph of Justine Palmer as the likeness of a woman who had checked in shortly after ten o'clock that morning. The young clerk remembered her because she was attractive and because she had been "frazzled-looking" when she walked into the lobby, carrying a suitcase and an overnight bag, paying cash for a seventh-floor room, to the rear. About three hours after checking in, the blonde had made a phone call, followed shortly by another one. A C-note, split between the desk clerk and the switchboard operator, bought Petrov the number she had dialed—same one, both times—together with the operator's word that it was somewhere out in Queens.

Petrov decided it was time to press his luck. He had already flashed his NYPD badge, and now he muttered something vague about obtaining search warrants, perhaps a court order to monitor the hotel's telephones. It was a gamble, but judged—once more, correctly—that the management would rather not have business stalled and guests unsettled by a uniformed parade. Petrov sweetened the deal with another hundred dollars and received the all-clear to park his car in the hotel's subterranean garage, then went back upstairs to stake out the office and monitor any foot traffic, along with phone calls in or out of Palmer's room. When he came back to the office, Petrov wore a Model 61 Skorpion machine pistol slung beneath his right arm, balancing the P-9 automatic on his left.

There was no point in taking chances, after all.

While Petrov waited, he considered calling Mike Belasko, but the tall American was on the move, having informed Petrov that he was off to rattle cages. Rather than distract him, Petrov found a public telephone and fed it coins until a small metallic voice approved his call to Queens. The number that Palmer had dialed rang twice before a gruff male voice responded.

"Da?"

The Russian yes. Petrov hung on the line until it was repeated, then he cradled the receiver, smiling to himself. If he hadn't found Rurik Baklanov, Petrov was reasonably sure he had the next best thing. A contact he could trace—and squeeze, if necessary—to discovery where his prey had gone to ground.

That would come later, though. For now, he was content to

watch and wait awhile, find out if Justine Palmer was expecting guests, or if she suddenly bailed out of the hotel. With luck, he thought, his quarry might yet come to him.

In either case, it was the closest he had come to Rurik Baklanov since landing in America, and he wasn't about to let that lead slip through his hands.

Not even if he had to sit and wait all night.

10

Mount Vernon lies adjacent to the Bronx, due north, a bedroom community of greater New York. It was approaching noon when Bolan crossed the line, following White Plains Road to Lincoln Avenue. His target was a high-rent neighborhood adjoining Pelham Manor, on the east, where Don Ted Peredo made his home and pulled the strings on his Big Apple empire from a distance.

That buffer zone had served Peredo in the past, but it wouldn't protect him from the Executioner.

Bolan had opted to go hunting, while his Russian ally of the moment combed Manhattan, seeking Justine Palmer. Petrov might get lucky—the soldier hoped he would—but it was still no better odds than fifty-fifty that the woman could direct them to the current lair of Rurik Baklanov. Meanwhile, it seemed to Bolan that the best thing he could do was keep the pressure on his target's homegrown allies, rattling the Italian Mob until he either forced a major confrontation, or the capos had enough and cut their ties to Baklanov. Whichever way it went, the Mafia was fair game to Bolan on general principles, his first and oldest enemy in a long war against the human savages who preyed on civilized society.

A daylight strike was doubly risky, and for that reason, Bolan had switched from his rented sedan to a Ford Econoline van, magnetic logos on each side proclaiming him an employee of Ace Pest Control. He wore denim coveralls with the name Sal stitched above his heart, its baggy fit sufficient to conceal his shoulder rig and the Beretta underneath his arm. Behind him, on the corrugated metal floor, an OD duffel bag contained his chosen weapon for the strike, a Galil sniper rifle.

Bolan found the street he was looking for and cruised until he saw the address painted on the curb. It was a stylish home, not quite a palace, but he knew the risks involved in plunking down too much money on real estate, when Uncle Sam might want to know where all the cash had come from. It made better sense to stash the bulk of one's illicit wealth in offshore banks and spend a wad of cash from time to time on artwork, diamonds for the wife or mistress, foreign travel and similar "extras." In fact, Bolan wasn't even sure if the Don was home.

It made no difference to him, either way.

He drove around the block and nosed the van into an alleyway that ran behind the houses there, primarily for garbage pickups, meter readers and the like. He drove two houses past Casa Peredo, left the van and walked back with the duffel slung across his shoulder, no great burden even with the rifle and its extra magazines inside. One house short of the mafioso's manse, he climbed a fence and scrambled up into the overhanging branches of a shade tree in the next-door neighbor's yard. From his position on one of the lower limbs, Bolan could watch two sides of Don Peredo's house, while covering the pool, the backyard and a portion of the front.

Perfect.

When he was settled on his perch, Bolan unzipped the duffel bag and took out the Galil. The sniper version had been modeled on the Israeli assault rifle, which in turn was a descendant of the tough Kalashnikov design. The semiautomatic weapon had a 20-round box magazine in place, loaded with 7.62 mm NATO rounds, and it was fitted with the standard Nimrod six-power telescopic sight. The fat suppressor mounted on the rifle made it muzzle heavy and would slow the bullets a trifle from their normal muzzle velocity of 2,615 feet per second, but it would hardly matter at a range below one hundred yards.

Unfolding its stock, Bolan shouldered the rifle and peered through the scope at Peredo's back door. The yard was empty, no one visible through any of the windows he could see. He didn't want to cut loose on the house in case Peredo had civilian family or help inside, and he had planned for this contingency before he made connections for the van.

A pocket on the hip of Bolan's coveralls held a compact cordless telephone. He palmed it now, tapped out the private number for Peredo's house and waited for a gruff male voice to answer on the third ring.

"Yeah?"

"This Joe?" asked Bolan, reaching for a name out of thin air.

"Nah, he ain't here right now," the deep voice said. "Whose this?"

Bolan ignored the question, saying, "Maybe you should take a look out back. I think somebody dumped him in the pool. What's left of him, that is."

He severed the connection, pocketed the phone and hoisted the Galil back to his shoulder, with its sight fixed on the back door.

Any minute now...

IT RANKLED HEDEON CHAPAEV, being sent out like an errand boy to fetch a common prostitute, but he couldn't complain about it in the present circumstances. After all, his soldiers had failed twice in their efforts to destroy the gunmen who were stalking Rurik Baklanov. In fact, his men were dying like flies, and all he had to show for it was a battered ego, most recently smarting from his present assignment.

Still, there was little Chapaev could do except make the best of it. Any show of defiance, whether real or imagined, would be taken as treason by Baklanov, and there was simply no future in defying the chief warlord of the Russian Mafia.

No future at all.

Chapaev took seven of his soldiers with him for the journey to Manhattan, splitting them between two vehicles. He rode behind the driver in a black Lexus LS 400, with another of his gunmen in the shotgun seat. The other five followed in a navy blue Lincoln TownCar, keeping the Lexus in sight without crowding its bumper. Palmer would ride back with Chapaev, in the lap of luxury, to meet whatever fate awaited her at Baklanov's hands.

Chapaev wasn't sure what his boss wanted with the woman, and he didn't care. It was his job to follow orders, as he had with Spetsnaz, in the old days, and it made no difference whether he approved. He was a soldier, paid—and rather handsomely, unlike his years in uniform—to deal with problems, root them out and make them go away.

Or, in this case, to bring them safely home.

The ambush at Palmer's apartment had been well thought out and organized. It had gone sour through no fault of Chapaev's, but the stigma still attached to him, as if he had been present, had done something foolish that left half a dozen of his soldiers sprawled in blood and another held by the New York Police Department, under questioning. That was another problem he would have to deal with if the lawyers couldn't handle it discreetly. Now, he had been sent to fetch the very woman who—for all he knew—had spoiled the trap to start with.

He was hoping Rurik Baklanov might have a fitting punishment in mind for her, and that he would let Chapaev lend a hand, but it was just as likely that the boss would take her back. Men could be funny that way, sometimes, over women. For his own part, Chapaev was immune to love. Warm feelings found no purchase on his heart; they shriveled up and died like seedlings strewed on barren rock, beneath a blazing desert sun. When he desired a woman, for the physical release, he rented one, did what he liked with her, then sent her on her way.

It was too bad, Chapaev thought, that certain others didn't adopt his attitude and keep their passions under firm control.

Palmer had given Baklanov the name and address of her hiding place. Before he left the house, Chapaev checked his New York guidebook and found the block where the hotel was situated: 85th Street, west of Amsterdam. The drive from Queens consumed the best part of an hour, crossing into Manhattan via the Queensboro Bridge, maneuvering around the

southern end of Central Park in midday traffic to catch Amsterdam Avenue, northbound from 57th Street. Twenty-eight
blocks remained from there, traveling through the snail's-pace
crush of cars and delivery trucks, his soldiers stoic and silent
in the front seat, while Chapaev scanned the sidewalks through
his tinted windows.

Palmer would be waiting for them, packed and ready. They
would call up from the lobby and wait for her to come down
on her own. Chapaev might be sent to fetch a whore for Rurik
Baklanov, but he was damned if he would run upstairs and
carry down her bags.

"When we arrive," he told the soldier in the shotgun seat,
"you go inside. Take Piotr and Vasili with you, just in case."

The soldier nodded his acknowledgment, not speaking. It
would take perhaps five seconds to retrieve Piotr and Vasili
from the Lincoln, ten or fifteen more to make their way inside.
The call upstairs and waiting for Palmer to ride the elevator
down—five minutes, tops. Another minute, give or take, to
walk her back outside. With any luck, they should be back in
Queens by half-past one o'clock.

Assuming she was there.

If she had skipped again, Chapaev would report to Baklanov—a land line, not the cellular—and do as he was told.
Betrayal would mean death, and for a moment there, Chapaev
almost hoped the woman would be gone when they arrived. At
least, that way, he would be hunting for a target he could recognize, instead of chasing shadows in the dark.

He spotted the hotel the same time as his driver did, the
Lexus braking, slowing to double-park. The Lincoln pulled in
close behind, an invitation to the first policeman passing by,
but Chapaev didn't care. He needed six or seven minutes, maximum, to do his job, and he would do as he was ordered, one
way or another.

Satisfaction guaranteed, at any cost.

THE FIRST SIGN of response to Bolan's call was just a flicker
at the window, ground floor, probably the kitchen. Bolan sat

and waited, peering through the scope, until a beefy gunner stepped outside and scanned the yard, a full-sized Uzi looking almost toylike in his hands. From where he stood, the shooter couldn't see into the swimming pool and verify if "Joe" was floating there, or not.

As Bolan's target moved in the direction of the swimming pool, some distance to his right, a second button man emerged from Don Peredo's house. This one carried a shotgun, a 12-gauge pump, and studied the wall of cinder blocks that screened the property from rubbernecking passersby. He glanced toward Bolan, in his tree, but failed to spot the Executioner, as Bolan fixed the scope's cross hairs on the second target's face.

From eighty yards, it was as good as point-blank range with the Galil. He stroked the trigger once and sent a round hurtling downrange toward explosive collision with the torpedo's forehead. Riding the recoil, eye fixed on his target, Bolan witnessed the result—a splash of crimson as the guy went over backward, out of frame.

Bolan swung to his left, tracking the first man out, and found him standing by the pool. The button man stood with his shoulders hunched, eyes focused on the flat expanse of chlorinated water, peering into its depths. There was no body to be seen, of course, and as that registered, the shooter turned back toward the house.

"Hey, man, it's bullshi—"

Through the eyepiece of the scope, Bolan saw him blink, surprise catching up with him as he saw his comrade down for the count. The shooter's jaw kept working, but he couldn't seem to find his voice. Or, maybe he was praying, as he started back in the direction of the house.

He never made it.

Bolan put his second round between the gunner's open lips, an easy shot at such close range. The impact slammed his target over backward, briefly airborne, splashing down into the deep end of the swimming pool.

He could have cut and run, but Bolan waited, knowing these

two weren't the brains behind the household, even in their master's absence. There was always someone paid to call the shots, and sergeants of the guard didn't go out themselves to check for bodies in the pool. They sent a flunky out to do it for them, maybe two, while they hung back and waited for a sitrep from the grunts.

Another moment passed before a gruff voice called out through the open doorway leading to the kitchen. "Tommy? Jake? What's going on out there?"

Bolan was ready, with the door framed in his telescopic sight, before the next face showed itself. This one was older, square cut, with a pile of wavy hair on top, the mouth etched in a scowl. Its owner took one look at Jake or Tommy, stretched out half a dozen paces from the door, and started to recoil, a turtle pulling in its head.

He almost made it.

Bolan gave him credit for the swift reaction time, but it wasn't quite good enough. The third round out of his Galil flew arrow straight and clipped the mafioso's chin before it disappeared around the doorjamb. Bolan heard a strangled kind of howl, uncertain whether he had made another kill or not, but positive that he had scored a hit.

Inside the house, at least two more defenders had been standing by, waiting for orders. Now, their crew chief lying dead or wounded on the floor in front of them, they showed commendable initiative. As if synchronized, two windows on the back side of the house were shattered simultaneously, automatic weapons cutting loose to spray the yard.

It was the best defense they could present without a target visible, and Bolan took advantage of the moment, sighting on the nearer of the windows first. His cross hairs moved along the barrel of an MP-5, the standard model, past a lean, white-knuckled hand, to find the shadowed outline of a face. He squeezed off three quick rounds, already pivoting to bring the second sniper under fire, before his latest mark collapsed into the room.

The other gunman had a window of perhaps two seconds

wherein he could save himself, but that would have required him to be watching as his comrade fell, reacting instantly, almost before the conscious thought could take shape in his mind. In fact, the guy was focused on his own attempt to save Casa Peredo from invaders whom he couldn't even see, strafing the wall out back, his bullets chipping abstract patterns on the cinder blocks.

And that gave Bolan all the time he needed for another kill.

The shooter had a lean, mean face, dark hair slicked back with enough oil to dress a salad. He was peering though his Uzi's sights with one eye closed, the other narrowed to a shiny slit, and Bolan closed it for him with a NATO round that snapped the gunner's head back, even as he lost his balance and his chin came down to strike the windowframe. Bolan shot him once more, punching him out of the windowframe like a tin silhouette in a carnival shooting gallery.

Enough.

He flicked on the Galil's safety and folded the stock, slipped the weapon back inside his duffel bag and zipped it shut, slinging the kit across one shoulder as he jumped down from his perch. It was a short run to the van, and Bolan had his keys in hand before he got there, ready when he slid into the driver's seat. He had already reached the far end of the alley, and was pulling out into the street, as a human figure cleared the back gate of Peredo's yard and waved an arm, as if in a bizarre attempt to flag him down.

Fat chance.

The shooter couldn't read his license plate from that far off, and it would make no difference if he did. A trace would lead them nowhere, and unless he missed his guess, Ted Peredo's men—those still alive—weren't the kind to file police reports.

Bolan drove on, smelling the cordite on his hands, obeying posted speed limits, and wondered how Petrov was faring on his woman hunt.

JUSTINE PALMER JUMPED when the phone rang, even though she was expecting it. The shrill sound set her teeth on edge, and for a moment she considered just ignoring it, but what good would it do? If she pretended to be out, the hardmen Baker sent would come up anyway to check the room, and they would be pissed off at her for playing games. They might not harm her—emphasis on might—but they would certainly report her odd behavior to Baker, and Palmer knew she was skating on thin ice, already, where the Russian was concerned.

She picked up as the third ring sounded, trying to act casual. "Hello?"

"Miss Palmer?" That was one of Baker's goons, all right. The accent was a giveaway; plus, she had plucked the name "Ruth Chadwick" out of thin air when she registered.

"Yes, that's right," she said. The three words tasted sour on her tongue, and Palmer instantly regretted speaking them.

"We wait for you," the hardman said.

"I'll be right down," she told him, and hung up before he had a chance to speak again.

There was no way around it, now. Whatever Baker had in mind for her, her fate was sealed. Palmer was tempted to by-pass the elevator, take the service stairs and see if she could slip out through the back, but where else could she go to hide? Baker already knew she hadn't left the city, and if she tried running out on him at this stage of the game, he could have people watching for her at Grand Central, in the airports, at the bus station, well before she got her act together and cleared out of town.

If Palmer tried an end run now, she was as good as dead.

Next time, she promised herself, she would think it through before she called on a potential enemy for help, regardless of how good he was in bed, despite the size and number of his bank accounts.

Next time. Assuming that there was a next time.

Palmer took her bags, closed the hotel room's door behind her and walked fifteen paces to the elevator. While she waited for the door to open, she was busy lighting up a cigarette.

The elevator seemed to take forever, but she understood that was her nerves at work, making the seconds feel like hours, creeping by. At last, the door slid open with a noise like rusty armor clanking, not at all a reassuring sound, but Palmer calculated that the ride would be the safest portion of her day from that point on. She stepped into the elevator with her bags and hesitated for another beat before she punched the Lobby button, standing back and waiting for the door to close.

Four men were waiting for her in the lobby, when the door opened again. Three stood before the elevator, like some kind of grim-faced not-so-welcoming committee, while a fourth was just emerging from behind the hotel registration desk. None of the faces struck her as familiar, but there was no reason why they should. Baker had people working for him she had never met, and never hoped to. These four were the kind she could have passed on meeting for another hundred years or so, and felt no loss at all.

As she was about to step out of the elevator, her eyes were drawn back to the fourth man, farthest from her, coming up behind the other three. The color drained from Palmer's face as she spotted the weapon in his hand, some kind of wicked-looking pistol with a long, curved magazine and stubby barrel. For an instant, she believed he was about to shoot her where she stood, but then she realized his friends were in the way. In fact, now that she thought of it, the fourth man wasn't really watching her at all.

He spoke in Russian, and Palmer saw the other three turn quickly, facing him. Two of the three immediately raised their hands to shoulder height, but then the odd man out, on her left, made a grab for something underneath his jacket.

That was all it took, the fourth man pumping several shots into the other's chest from ten feet out. Palmer bit off the scream that came unbidden to her lips, reached out to find a button—any button—that would close the elevator door again and take her up, away from there.

Too late.

The dead-or-dying hardman toppled backward, sprawling half inside the elevator car, his eyes locked open, staring up and under Palmer's skirt. The elevator door tried to close, but it jammed against his body, and the automatic safety held it open.

Trapped, Justine Palmer edged back into the farthest corner of the car before all hell broke loose.

IT WAS A DISAPPOINTMENT that the shooter tried to draw his weapon, but it wasn't unexpected. Dima Petrov shot him without thinking twice, the recoil of his Skorpion absorbed and covered as he eased off the trigger, pivoting to watch the other two. He saw death in their eyes, knew pride or something else would force them to defend their "honor" now, and waited for the first of them to make his move. Meanwhile, the dead man's body kept the elevator door from closing, trapping Justine Palmer where she was, and Petrov hoped she wouldn't find the nerve to kick it free.

The two surviving Russians stepped apart, as if they had rehearsed the move, dividing his attention. Both were reaching for their weapons, but Petrov blinked, surprised, as one of them turned toward the open elevator car, as if prepared to shoot the woman.

Petrov took the other man first, self-preservation winning out. Another short burst from his Skorpion ripped bloody tracks across the hardman's chest and slammed him back into the wall, smearing the faded floral-pattern paper with a daub of crimson as he fell, the automatic pistol still inside his jacket.

From the office, sounding miles away, the switchboard operator screamed, but Petrov had no time to think about her, as he swung around to find the last of three armed adversaries leveling his weapon at Palmer. There was no time for fancy shooting, much less verbal warnings, so he stepped in close and pressed the Skorpion against the gunner's skull, squeezing off a 3-round burst that spattered both of them with blood and brains.

The sight of him let Justine Palmer find her voice, a high-pitched squeal emerging, winding up and up until he thought it could have shattered glass. Petrov stepped past the corpses, grabbed her by one arm with his left hand and dragged her from the elevator as the scream died, and she tried to catch her breath.

"You come with me," he said, the combination of his tone and the smoking weapon in his hand permitting no debate.

And still, she asked, "Go where?"

It was a decent question, since they couldn't use the front door to the street. These three wouldn't have come alone, he realized. If nothing else, they would have left a driver in the car, most likely double-parked out front. More likely, there were reinforcements waiting, possibly responding to the sounds of gunfire even now.

Petrov had scouted the hotel's exterior as he returned from parking in the underground garage. There was a back door, though he didn't know exactly how to get there from the lobby, that would let them out into an alley, by the garbage containers. From that point, it was an easy walk around the corner, something like a hundred feet, to reach the exit ramp of the garage.

An easy walk, that was, unless he found the alley under guard.

Petrov drew Palmer after him, away from the doors facing onto the street, toward the kitchen and out the rear. She briefly resisted him, putting on the brakes.

"My bags!" she said.

"You want to die for underwear and lipstick?" Petrov asked her. "There are no porters here. We have our hands full, just staying alive."

She followed him, then, keeping pace. He had already noted her shoes, relieved to see that she was wearing flats instead of high heels. If they were forced to run, he didn't want to carry her or drag her like a sack of grain behind him.

Passing the kitchen door, they were confronted by a multi-hued bouquet of faces. The man in the chef's hat was slender and black; his flankers included a woman of Asian extraction and two young Latinos in hair nets, wearing full-length aprons. Petrov showed them all the Skorpion and was relieved when the chef slammed the door in his face.

The last thing that he needed, at the moment, was a hero getting in his way.

Arriving at the back door of the small hotel, Petrov released his hold on Palmer's arm and stepped in front of her. "Don't follow me until I say," he ordered her. And then, because he recognized the possibility that she might break and run, he added, "You're with me, now. If you go back to the others, you'll be shot on sight."

"He wouldn't do that," she responded, clearly meaning Rurik Baklanov.

Petrov dismissed her with a shrug. "So, test him, then. Be my guest. I have a better chance without you, anyway."

He counted on the frightened woman not to grasp the glaring contradiction in that statement, that he would have risked so much to capture her, then set her free without a second thought as if she were a burden to him. Whether Palmer recognized the ruse or not, she made no move to flee as Petrov tried the door.

It was unlocked, of course; the New York fire code saw to that. He opened it a foot or so and poked his head outside, holding the Skorpion against his leg, so that it would be hidden from a sentry standing in the alley. Petrov didn't think the gunfire from the lobby would be audible out back, and he was hoping any watchdogs in the alley could be taken by surprise.

In fact, the passageway was empty, save for one stray cat that bounded from a nearby garbage bin at the sound of Petrov opening the door. It fled without a backward glance and left him all alone. He turned and found Palmer still waiting, watching him.

"This way," he said, pushing the door wide open and stepping back to let her pass. He didn't take her arm again, content to have her follow of her own volition, just as long as she kept pace with him.

For they were running out of time.

He pictured Baklanov's backup gunners swarming through the hotel lobby, showing weapons to the clerk and switchboard operator, one or both of the employees pointing down the corridor where Petrov and Palmer had disappeared from view. The enemy might catch up to them at any moment, might be doubling back to watch the street and cut off access to the subterranean garage.

But once again, his fears were premature. Petrov and Palmer made it to the corner, where he risked another glance around the corner, half expecting to receive a bullet in the face. A steady stream of traffic passed by, but the pedestrians he saw were all unarmed, indifferent to a stranger standing in the alley's mouth. Some fifty feet away, the ramp that served the hotel's underground garage was open and unguarded.

"Come!" he ordered, securing the Skorpion beneath his jacket as he stepped out of the alley, Palmer close beside him. Things were looking better now, he thought. If they could only make it to his car, then clear the underground garage without a fight, traffic and daylight would be working on their side.

Petrov could feel the drop in temperature, as they proceeded down the ramp. He led Palmer back to the corner where his rental car was parked, opened the door on her side first, then closed it after her. So much for those who thought that chivalry was dead. Behind the wheel, he felt his spirits rising, took fresh courage from the engine's throat rumble, as he twisted the ignition key.

Another moment…

And he saw the shooters waiting for them, as he started up the ramp.

"Get down!" he snapped, Palmer already ducking in her seat, below the dashboard, as the first of Baklanov's gunners opened fire. Petrov had no time to unsling the Skorpion. Instead, he stood on the accelerator, hurtling up the exit ramp toward daylight and the human targets ranged before him, cursing all the way.

11

"Get after them, goddammit!"

Hedeon Chapaev had been raised from infancy without belief in any deity, a lifetime of experience persuading him that there was no supreme intelligence that guided man on earth—no afterlife with punishment for "evil" and rewards for "good"—but the profanity came easily, a habit he had picked up in his dealings with Americans.

His driver jammed the Lexus into gear and whipped the steering wheel around, putting it through a squealing U-turn, heedless of the blaring horns and traffic bearing down on them from either side. The gunners in the Lincoln would keep pace as best they could—the two who still survived, that was.

Chapaev had set out from Queens with six armed men to fetch Palmer. Now, three of them were dead, gunned down inside the hotel lobby by another of the faceless strangers who had plagued him for the past few days, and Baklanov's woman had escaped or been abducted by the same gunman. Worse, the two of them had made it out of the hotel, downstairs to the garage, where Baklanov's enemy had stashed a car. Despite a last-ditch effort to confine them there, they had brushed past two more of his gunners, nearly crushing Boris in the process.

Damn! Damn! Damn!

A broad-daylight chase through the heart of Manhattan was the worst possible folly, but what were his options? Chapaev couldn't simply go back to Queens, leaving three soldiers dead, and report that the woman had slipped through his fingers again. It might be all his life was worth to drop that bit of news in Baklanov's lap, today of all days, when the Russian mobster was already smarting from their previous defeats. At least, if he retrieved Palmer, he would have something to show for the debacle. And if he could bag the gunman who had killed his soldiers, it would be the first step toward a well-deserved revenge.

The speeding Lexus clipped one of those couriers who wound through New York traffic on their ten-speed bicycles, delivering whatever for a price, and sent him vaulting right across the hood and windshield of a Yellow Cab. Chapaev didn't give a second thought to whether the young man would live or die. He was a cipher in the Russian's mind, devoid of all significance.

One of his soldiers—lucky Boris—had described the fleeing car in breathless tones, while he was sprinting for the Lincoln. It was a Chevrolet, perhaps a Cavalier or Malibu, metallic green. The license number had escaped him, but it didn't matter. They were close enough to catch the bastard, run him down and finish it this time. If Justine Palmer stopped a bullet in the process, well, Chapaev was prepared to take the heat, and he would shed no tears over the passing of a whore.

There was a small compartment hidden underneath the back seat of the Lexus, virtually invisible to naked eyes, which opened with the application of specific pressure to the upper left-hand corner of its rectangular hatch. Chapaev reached between his knees to open it and brought out a micro-Uzi, cocking the little submachine gun as he placed it on the seat beside him.

Ready.

He would let his soldiers do the killing when the time came, but Chapaev was prepared to lend a hand if they hit any snags. He hadn't come up through the ranks by watching others do the dirty work, either in Spetsnaz or the Russian *mafyia*. In fact, if he was honest with himself, he still enjoyed a spot of killing now and then. It perked him up and made him feel alive.

Today wasn't for sport, though. He had work to do, with more than simple satisfaction riding on the outcome. If he failed, some drastic penance would be mandatory at the very least.

No failure, then. It was unthinkable.

Ahead of them, peering around the driver's head, he saw a sleek, metallic-green sedan swing out to pass a panel truck. A Chevrolet? Chapaev couldn't say, but told himself that it had to be his quarry. Even in Manhattan, legendary for its reckless drivers, he wouldn't expect to see two green sedans careering through the streets at break-neck speed, within a few blocks of the hotel shooting scene.

"Speed up!" he shouted at the driver. "Lose him, and I'll have your balls for cuff links!"

Instantly, the Lexus seemed to find more power, surging forward with a fierce snarl from the engine. As Chapaev rocked back in his seat, he took a firm grip on the micro-Uzi, cradling the little SMG in his big hands.

It wouldn't be long, he thought. Not long, at all.

PALMER CLUTCHED at her shoulder harness with her right hand, as if hanging from a subway strap, and kept her left palm braced against the cushion of her seat, stiff-armed, to keep herself from rocking as the Chevy swerved through traffic with a madman at the wheel.

She had convinced herself the Russian had to be crazy, shooting three men in the hotel lobby as he had, trying to run a fourth man down as they emerged from the garage. But, then again, the gunners on the sidewalk had been shooting at them, one round glancing off the Chevy's hood to knock a perfect divot in the windshield, six or seven inches to the left of Palmer's face. She was amazed the windshield hadn't shattered from the impact, and she couldn't stop herself from yelping as the slug drilled through and smashed the dome light, to her left.

At first, as they charged into traffic, nearly taking out a station wagon in the process, Palmer told herself it was a natural reaction, Baker's people firing on the man who had already killed three of their friends in the hotel. But then, she thought about what her abductor—rescuer?—had said before they made their run to the garage.

"You're with me, now." No threat apparent in his tone; a simple statement. "If you go back to the others, you'll be shot on sight."

She had denied it, felt the need to contradict him, but she hadn't run away. Why not? Was it because she doubted Baker, his intentions? Had her passion for him—always spiced with greed; she could admit that to herself—been transformed into fear?

All Palmer knew for sure was that a pair of her boyfriend's men had fired into the Chevrolet despite her presence in the car. She wouldn't let herself believe they meant to kill her—not yet, anyway—but it came down to a choice between complete disinterest in her safety and a plan to rub her out, what difference did it really make?

Not much, she told herself, twisting in her seat to see if they were being followed. She was just in time to see a black Lexus swing across the double line in hot pursuit, the silhouettes of two men visible inside it as the other traffic yielded grudgingly, horns blaring angry protest.

If there were only two, she thought, they might still have a chance. The Chevy's driver, her abductor-savior, had already proved that he was capable in combat, and his driving skills—while nerve-racking—seemed on par with his proficient marksmanship. Again, she wondered who he was, where he was taking her and why, but it wasn't the time for questions. She didn't wish to distract him from his driving, when the smallest slip could turn the Chevrolet into a twisted, smoking hulk.

Palmer had already faced forward when one of the Russians in the Lexus started shooting at them. When the bullet struck the Chevy's trunk, it sounded like a hammer blow, delivered with the full force of a strong man's arm. She jumped, too late to bottle up the startled squeal of panic.

If the driver noticed her reaction, he didn't hold it against her. Glancing briefly at the rearview mirror, he bore down on the accelerator, squeezed a few more rpm out of the Chevy's straining power plant and swung the steering wheel hard right. He veered between a white stretch limo and a hulking city bus, cutting the diesel monster off and gaining precious yardage as he passed the limo on the right.

Not bad, she thought, and would have smiled if she hadn't been scared out of her mind.

Whatever motive she attributed to Baker's men back at the hotel, the men behind them now were plainly bent on stopping them at any cost. And that in turn could mean one of two things: either the hardmen had been sent to kill her in the first place, or they now believed she had betrayed them, somehow helped her captor-rescuer devise the ambush that had left three of their number dead. In either case, the bottom line was that they meant to take her out. From this point on, her life depended on the man behind the wheel, a nameless stranger she had never seen before the moment he stepped up and killed three men in front of her.

Oddly enough, she found his violence comforting. If he could kill three men, she told herself, why not two more? He wanted her alive; that much was obvious. He had already risked his life to keep her out of Baker's hands. If he could only keep it up, prevent the gunmen on their tail from overtaking them, she might survive to see another day.

Where there was life, the saying went, there was hope. Palmer couldn't have said what she was hoping for, beyond survival, but it hardly mattered.

When a team of killers from the far side of the world were bent on blowing out your brains, she thought, survival just might be enough.

THE SECOND HIT took Bolan back into the Bronx. There was a little numbers bank on Gun Hill Road he had his eye on—nothing much to look at, with a newsstand and tobacco shop out front, but he had reason to believe it cleared a hundred thousand dollars on a slow week, when the bets were down. That kind of money would be missed by Don Peredo where it counted—in the pocketbook.

That kind of money would be guarded, too, and not by amateurs. Peredo bribed police to let the operation run without a legal hitch, his reputation warning off the punks with sense enough to recognize his name, but there would still be guns around the place, prepared to rock and roll in the event of unforeseen emergencies. By now, he realized, the soldiers might have been alerted to the blowup at Peredo's house.

Too bad for them. The Executioner already had his mind made up.

He made a drive-by, found a place for the van around the corner in a loading zone and slipped into the back to change. He swapped the coveralls for a gray Armani suit, gave the sound-suppressed Beretta in his shoulder rig a double check before he left the van and locked it behind him. Even if a meter maid came by to ticket him, Bolan would be back long before a city tow truck could be summoned to the scene.

Assuming he was still alive.

He walked back to the bank with long, determined strides, viewing the world through mirrored shades. The guy behind the counter eyed him as he entered, putting on a frown and slipping one hand underneath the countertop as Bolan said, "I'm here to get the money."

"Yeah? And who would you be?"

Bolan moved in close, uncertain if the guy was reaching for a weapon or a panic button, thinking one could be as deadly as the other if he let his guard down. For the moment, though, he would rely on sheer audacity, holding the fireworks in reserve.

"They didn't call ahead and tell you? Jesus Christ!" He shook his head in feigned amazement. "Hey, you must've heard what happened there at the Don's, in Mount Vernon. Right?"

"Mount Vernon? I don't know...."

"You don't know? Man, I can't believe this."

As he spoke, a drab Employees Only door swung open to his right, a twenty-something hulk in navy gabardine emerging, no attempt to hide the pistol tucked into his waistband.

"What's the trouble, Jackie?" asked the hulk.

Bolan beat Jackie to the punch line. "What's the trouble? Try this on for size, why don't ya. Half an hour ago, somebody shot the hell out of the old man's place up in Mount Vernon. Smoked a bunch of guys. They told me five or six. Now, here I am, on Ted's orders, to collect the cash, in case they show up here, and Jackie hasn't got a frigging clue what's happening."

"We got no call about a hit," the man behind the counter said defensively.

"Then, I suggest you make a call right now and bring your operation up to speed," Bolan said. "Crazy bastards. They could show up any minute, and you got me playing patty-cake. Get on the phone and you tell Ted why you won't release his money on demand. I wanna hear this for myself."

"I better do that," Jackie told the younger man. "Ya never know."

"Hold on a sec," said the man in gabardine, turning to Bolan. "Ted sent you for the cash?"

"Is there an echo in here? Take the frigging telephone and—"

"Never mind," the soldier interjected. "I don't wanna bother him. You need to count the cash?"

"Nobody told me that," Bolan replied. "Man just said sack it up and bring it home. You got some kind of bag here, I can use?"

"No sweat," the hulk replied, ducking back through the doorway, out of sight.

This was the moment, Bolan knew, when it could all go straight to hell. If the hardman was stalling him, dialing the capo in Mount Vernon or wherever, Bolan's bluff would fall apart in seconds flat. The gray Armani jacket was unbuttoned, showing off his vest—and granting easy access to the pistol in his armpit holster if the hulk came back with anything but money in his hand.

The anxious seconds stretched into a minute, and a minute into two, before the soldier reappeared, a fat gym bag dangling from one fist. He handed it to Bolan, telling him, "You got a little over sixty grand in there. Don't spend it all in one place, huh?"

They both laughed at the joke, and Bolan headed for the door, the gym bag in his left hand in case one of the mafiosi changed his mind and Bolan had to use his weapon. On the sidewalk, moving briskly back toward the van, he started to relax.

Not bad.

Let Jackie and the hulk explain their generosity to Don Peredo when the time came. Chances were that one or both of them had seen his last sunrise, and Bolan wished them luck.

All bad.

PETROV WAS RACING north on Amsterdam when his pursuers started shooting at him. They were plainly more concerned with keeping Justine Palmer out of hostile hands than bringing her to Rurik Baklanov alive. He voiced the notion, even as he concentrated on his driving, weaving in and out of traffic on the busy avenue.

"Somebody wants you quiet," he remarked, "whether you stay alive or not."

He felt the woman glaring at him, as she hunched in her seat, trying to make herself a smaller target. "Rory wouldn't do that," she replied with something less than full conviction.

"I suppose his men don't follow orders, then," the Russian said. "Has that been your experience?"

She offered no reply to that, and he expected none. Another burst of automatic fire from the pursuing Lexus rattled off the Chevy's trunk, one bullet blowing out a fist-sized portion of the broad rear window, flattening itself against the dash above the radio. Palmer yelped and hunched even lower in her seat, her short skirt riding up around her hips. In other circumstances, Petrov would have slowed to appreciate the view, but at the moment, he was more concerned with living through the next five minutes than he was with Palmer's near-transparent panties.

Turning left on red instead of stopping for the light, he swung onto West 95th Street, away from Central Park. Despite his fragmentary knowledge of Manhattan geography, he knew that he was heading for the Hudson River, and only two more major streets remained between him and the water. If he didn't choose West End Avenue, the only choice remaining to him would be Riverside Drive—that, or a headlong plunge into the polluted water that separated Manhattan from New Jersey.

Glancing at his rearview mirror, Petrov was in time to see the Lexus coming after him with yet another vehicle—this one a larger model, unidentified—veering through the light and snarled traffic to make it a three-car parade. How many adversaries altogether? There were two men in the Lexus, and he calculated two or three in the second chase car. Five guns, at least, and he would have to deal with all of them.

Unless…

New Yorkers liked to say that there was never a police officer present when one was needed. The same was often true in Moscow, where he came from, although the authorities were more pervasive there, and he was one of them.

Today, however, in the lunchtime rush hour, he caught a break. There was a cop, and Petrov saw him closing in behind the second chase car, lights flashing, siren wailing as he joined in the pursuit. No sooner had he recognized the blue-and-white than one of his pursuers in the second chase car leaned out of a window on the driver's side and started firing at the cops with what appeared to be an AK-47. Petrov had to focus on his driving, but he saw enough to know the squad car had been hit. A couple of its flashing lights were shot out, the windshield starred with cracks.

That tore it. If the officers survived the next few moments, they would broadcast an alert, and half the bluesuits in Manhattan would be racing toward the scene, hell-bent on helping out their comrades. Whether there would be enough of them, at first, to stop three cars, Petrov couldn't have said. He knew only that he had no desire to test their mettle or their marksmanship.

There was a chance for him to break the deadlock, though, if he was swift and skilled enough. It was a gamble, granted—nothing short of life or death—but he was bound to try it out.

Reaching inside his jacket as he drove, Petrov released the Skorpion machine pistol from its shoulder sling and placed the weapon in his lap. He wasn't sure how many rounds the magazine contained, but any effort at reloading was beyond him now, and he couldn't trust Palmer with the gun. However many shots remained, it had to be enough.

Next step, he found the button for the driver's window with his left hand, held it down and listened to the wind howl, felt it whipping at his face and close-cropped hair. The blaring horns and sharp, staccato sounds of gunfire from behind him echoed that much louder now.

"What are you doing?" Palmer asked, staring up at him, wide-eyed.

"Hang on to something," Petrov said, in lieu of a direct reply. "Be ready for a jolt."

"Oh, God!" She cringed and reached out for the dashboard with her right hand, while the fingers of her left clutched at the seat. Her legs were braced, after a fashion, with the skirt nearly around her waist.

Another time, another place, he thought, and then they had arrived at West End Avenue. He cranked the steering wheel hard left, accelerating through the turn against a yellow light—small favors—and kept on cranking the wheel as he lifted his foot off the gas, slamming down on the brakes. The Chevrolet whipped through a tight 180-degree turn, restrained from going farther when Palmer's side banged against a UPS delivery van. She screamed, and Petrov managed to ignore her, facing back in the direction of the chase cars, the Skorpion in his left hand extended through the open driver's window.

He was ready when the Lexus came around the corner, swerving, with a squeal of rubber on the pavement. Petrov framed the driver in his sights and squeezed the trigger, elbow braced against the sill to hold down the muzzle. He saw his bullets strike the glass and watched the windshield turn to frost before it all blew inward with a crash.

The driver brought up his hands, splashed with crimson, before the Lexus spun out of control. A second man, in the back seat, flailed his arms in passing, curses drowned out by the crunch of metal as the Lexus struck a Cadillac and came to a rest. Petrov could see him clearly, but the Skorpion was well and truly empty now, no way to finish it.

Petrov bore down on the accelerator and shot through the intersection, more brakes squealing as he charged across. A quick glance to his right showed him the second chase car, stuck in traffic with a pair of squad cars closing from behind it, armed men bailing out to try their luck on foot.

He left them to it, slowing after two blocks, turning back toward Central Park as soon as he was able. He would have to ditch the Chevrolet, now bullet scarred and battered, but they needed distance first, an opportunity to leave the shooters and police behind. When they had cleared the killing ground, there would be time enough for him to find new wheels.

And time for him to have a conversation with Justine Palmer.

HEDEON CHAPAEV RAN the first block south, on West End Avenue, then ducked into the entryway of a department store and took a moment to compose himself. He wiped the perspiration from his face with a silk handkerchief, then reached underneath his jacket to adjust the micro-Uzi, where it pulled his slacks down in the back. It was uncomfortable, but he still felt better with the SMG in his possession than he would have, wandering the New York streets unarmed.

A simple job had gone to hell on him, and now he would have to explain to Baklanov—once again—why he had failed. It was becoming tiresome, and it crossed his mind for just a moment, there and gone, that maybe he should pass on going back to Queens this time, forget the whole damned thing and cut his losses. Four men dead today, on top of all the rest, and three more maybe on their way to jail, if they weren't gunned down by the police.

It had become ridiculous, a comedy of errors, but Chapaev knew he couldn't simply walk away. He had a reputation to protect, whatever might be left of it at this point, and he also knew that if he ran, Baklanov would spare no effort or expense to track him down.

The first thing Chapaev had to do, now, was to touch base with his soldiers back in Queens and make arrangements for a car to pick him up. That meant another hour, minimum, of waiting in Manhattan, while Baklanov fumed over his latest failure, building up a head of steam, but there was nothing to be done about that. Chapaev had been trained to deal with situations that existed and to forget about what might have been. He couldn't dwell on fantasy and still hope to survive the afternoon.

Chapaev left the store and started walking south on West End Avenue. The one thing he had going for him, at the moment, was his average appearance and the fact that he was wearing an expensive suit, with no bloodstains that he could see. If the police came this far, looking for a nameless, faceless suspect, there would be no cause for them to pick him out among the hundreds of New Yorkers passing by on both sides of the street.

Next thing, he had to find a telephone.

Chapaev found it two blocks farther south outside a bank. He made the call, identified the voice that answered him in Queens and issued curt instructions in his native tongue, receiving an affirmative response.

The meeting was arranged.

Now, all Chapaev had to do was wait…and plot revenge.

12

Bolan drove past the safe house in North Bergen, where Petrov had gone to ground. He didn't recognize the car out front, except to note the Avis sticker in its window, reckoning that Petrov had acquired another rental to replace the Chevrolet. The shopping bag he carried, as he walked up to the house, contained an MP-5 K submachine gun, cocked and loaded. Any watchful neighbors might have questioned why the tall, well-dressed man kept one hand inside the bag, but that was his affair, as long as he didn't disturb the peace and quiet of their street.

Petrov was there ahead of Bolan, opening the door as the soldier reached toward the bell. He saw the Russian glance both ways along the sidewalk before stepping back to let him pass. In Petrov's hand, concealed behind the door, was a Skorpion machine pistol, its safety off.

"You're on the radio," Bolan remarked, as Petrov closed and double locked the door behind him. "Sounds like it was close."

The Russian shrugged and said, "We made it."

Bolan thought of asking him about the house, but then decided it would be bad form. The KGB had theoretically ceased to exist—at least by that name—with the collapse of communism, and Russia was America's ally these days, more or less. All things considered, Bolan didn't think it was the proper time or place to raise the issue of secret hideouts on American soil, purchased in advance of need with Russian cash.

He was more concerned, at the moment, with meeting Justine Palmer.

The woman was waiting for them in the living room, smoking a cigarette, pacing the floor. A small TV was playing in one corner, but the volume had been muted, making it a kind of silent window to replace those screened by heavy draperies to keep the outside world at bay. Palmer glanced at the screen from time to time, in passing, then forgot about it as Petrov returned, with Bolan following.

"So, who are you?" she challenged him, taking the initiative. "This whole thing is illegal, just in case you didn't know."

Defiance. Bolan wondered whether he could work with that, or if retrieving her had been a costly waste of time. "Illegal, like your boyfriend moving drugs and guns, you mean?" he asked.

"I wouldn't know about—"

"Illegal like mass murder?" Bolan interrupted her.

"Look, I—"

"Illegal like attempted murder…as in yours?"

That stopped Palmer long enough for her to stub out her cigarette in an ashtray that resembled something lifted from a cheap motel. She glared at Bolan, as if thinking he might crumble in the face of her accumulated wrath. Looks couldn't kill, however, and a moment holding Bolan's gaze was all it took to make her blink and turn away.

"That's not what happened," she replied, unable to conceal the tremor in her voice. "Your comrade there barged into my hotel and started shooting, killed three men right in the lobby."

"And your friends were so concerned about your welfare," Petrov said, "that they tried to kill both of us."

"Not me!" she snapped. "They wouldn't do that. Rory wouldn't let them do that."

"No doubt he would devise some fitting punishment for their mistake," the Russian answered, fairly sneering at her now.

"I wouldn't be at all surprised," Palmer retorted.

"On the other hand," Bolan said, "there's a fair chance

Baklanov—or Rory Baker, as you call him—might have had a change of heart about your whole relationship. That's twice you've broken dates with him and gotten people killed.''

"Oh, no, you don't!" She rounded on him, angry color rising in her cheeks. "I'm not responsible for this. None of it! Just because—"

"Hey, you don't have to sell me," Bolan interrupted her again. "I'm not the one who's lost—what is it, now, ten soldiers?—just trying to give you a lift.''

"It's not my fault!"

"There's still a way you might come out of this alive, though," Bolan said, as if she hadn't spoken.

"Let me guess," Palmer replied. "You need a Judas, and you figure I'm the type. That was your first mistake."

"Could be," the Executioner replied. "But, then, we're not discussing my mistakes, right now. You've made enough to keep us busy for the next few lifetimes, starting with your choice of men."

"I don't know anything," she told him, reaching for another cigarette.

"So, let me fill you in," Bolan said. "Rurik Baklanov— your Rory Baker—wore out his welcome back in Mother Russia, facing murder charges that could put him in the ground. He caught a lucky break and made it to the States. On this side of the water, he's arranged connections with the Mafia for drug deals, weapons, this and that. The first try blew up in his face and he got busted, but he's good at landing on his feet. Give credit where credit's due. He conned the Feds into a whole new look, gave up his partner—there's a Judas for you—then arranged to have his watchers murdered in cold blood, so he could slip away and start from scratch."

"Sounds like a fairy tale to me," Palmer replied through drifting smoke.

"No happy endings, though," Bolan said. "That's one problem when you burn your bridges. Pretty soon, you've got nowhere to go."

"You'd better stop," she said. "Sad stories make me cry."

"The thing is, now your boyfriend has two countries full of federal agents looking for him, plus the soldiers of the capo he sold out, and maybe certain other friends who have begun to doubt his honesty."

"And you," the woman said. "You save the worst for last?"

"And me," the Executioner replied. "You are exactly right."

"So, since I'm still alive and not in jail," the sassy blonde shot back at him, "does somebody want to fill me in? I mean, like, what's the deal?"

GAETANO DONATELLI made his home in Buffalo, New York. The Family he ruled had been established nearly seven decades earlier, when Lucky Luciano and the other young Turks of the Mafia had pulled a fast one on the old, archaic Mustache Petes and seized control. Stefano Maggadino was the don of Buffalo, in those days, and while times had changed since then, with federal prosecutions every time one turned around, the Family still did all right financially. Buffalo was far enough from New York City that the Five Families—or, rather, their shrunken remnants—left Donatelli alone, while he maintained traditional good relations with the bosses of Detroit and Cleveland, the proximity to Canada granting a world of possibilities for illicit commerce.

Donatelli had his manicured fingers in every major pie between Syracuse and Erie, plus liaisons with the outfits in Toronto, Ottawa and Montreal. He shuttled dope both ways—exporting coke and grass; importing Turkish heroin from Marseilles, through Quebec, and China white from Southeast Asia, through Toronto—while a steady flow of guns went north to circumvent Canadian firearms laws. Prostitution and gambling were also hot properties in cities and resorts on both sides of the line, the income fattening Donatelli's war chest to the point that he was actually bigger than most of the Big Apple Dons.

He had intended for the deal with Rurik Baklanov to take him all the way, opening new markets in Russia and Eastern

Europe, while cementing his alliance with the man who meant
to overhaul—and dominate—the stateside syndicate. He had
considered standing in the Russian's way, opposing him, but
only for a moment. When he caught his breath and thought
about it, Donatelli saw that it would work to his advantage,
having someone else—a foreigner, no less—out front, in case
something went wrong.

And now it had, before they even put the goddamned deal
to bed.

Donatelli was having second, third and fourth thoughts, now,
about his deal with Rurik Baklanov. For one thing, there had
been too damned much killing in the past few days. Not that
Gaetano Donatelli was a squeamish man; far from it. He enjoyed a little rough stuff, every now and then, but these were
killings in the headlines, some of them involving federal agents
and civilian bystanders. The blowout in New Jersey, meanwhile, had been just a trifle close to home for Donatelli's taste.

He had begun to wonder if the time had come for him to
tell the Russian ciao—or *dosvedanya,* as the case might be—
and cut his losses while he had the chance. New Jersey had
been one thing, but his fellow Dons were taking hits in Cleveland and in New York—Fortini and Peredo, both of whom had
joined him at the sit-down hosted by Gino Gambola. Jules
DeRicco was already dead. Poor bastard never even made it
home from Jersey.

Long story short, it wasn't working out the way he had en-
visioned it, when Baklanov was sketching bright tomorrows,
tempting him with numbers that, while not beyond Donatelli's
wildest dreams, came pretty freaking close. There was no men-
tion in those pipe dreams of a shooting war against some unknown enemy. One minute, Donatelli had been smelling roses,
and the next, the whole thing turned to shit.

He wanted out, all right, but that wasn't so simple, either.
Rurik Baklanov wasn't some street punk who had come to him
with plans to rob a warehouse, maybe fly some shit in from
the Keys. He was a seasoned pro who claimed to have the full
weight of the Russian syndicate behind him—and if that was

bullshit, well, he still had an impressive team of shooters right there in the states, despite their recent losses.

No. Donatelli couldn't simply change his mind and pull the plug. The Russian would go crazy on him, maybe even try to take him out, and that would mean another shooting war when they had one to fight already.

What it called for, getting out from under Baklanov and all his baggage, was a fair amount of stealth. Gaetano Donatelli knew his way around that game board, having learned from masters in the good old days, before La Casa Nostra started to unravel at the seams. There were some differences, okay, in dealing with the Russians, but he reckoned greedy men were all alike under the skin.

In the present case, all he might have to do was make a show of standing fast with Baklanov against their unknown enemy. It helped to have an adversary close at hand when warming up to stab him in the back.

The trick was to get the knife in first and made it count before the other sneaky bastard had a chance to make his move.

The thing Donatelli had to do was play his cards just right, make sure the Russian wasn't peeking at his hole card in advance. And he would have to take care of the bastard's troops, especially his bodyguard.

When he was ready with the knockout punch, Donatelli thought it might be nice to throw some kind of banquet for the Russian and his men, get all of them together in a single room—feeding their faces, maybe swilling down some booze—then open up with everything he had. Like in the good old days, damn right.

Donatelli felt better just thinking about it. He imagined the look on Baklanov's face—stunned surprise, with a brief flash of impotent fury, knowing he was outmaneuvered and outgunned. It would be worth the risk simply to wipe the smug grin off his face.

As for the rest of it—negotiations with the other capos toward a new, rejuvenated syndicate—there still might be a way for him to profit on the back end of the deal. Gambola, Fortini and Peredo had been weakened by the recent hits, and Jules DeRicco was a write-off. If the new alliance wasn't shot to hell beyond repair, who else besides Gaetano Donatelli was in any shape to lead the pack?

The prospect made him smile, the first time since he had been forced to flee New Jersey with his tail between his legs. It felt good for a change. He could begin to see the silver lining on the storm clouds that had dogged him for the past few days.

It had the makings of a bright new day.

No MATTER HOW the Russian and his tall American companion tried to hammer home their point, Palmer refused to let herself believe that Rory Baker had sent his men to murder her. Alone now, in a bedroom of the small New Jersey house where they were holding her, she wondered if they might not have a point.

There had been shooting, after all, without regard to her safety in the car. It was dumb luck—or, possibly, a product of the Russian's skill—that she was still alive.

And yet...

The whole thing had been his fault in the first place, dammit! She was safe and sound at the hotel, ready to take a ride with Baker's men, when this total stranger had come out of nowhere, killing three of them before her very eyes.

And then she remembered that one of them was aiming right at her.

That stopped her for a moment, staring at the floor and feeling tears spring to her eyes, but Palmer blinked them back and focused on the facts. She didn't know the young man who had aimed his pistol at her in the hotel lobby, but Palmer thought she understood how he might have felt, walking into a simple pickup and seeing two friends shot down in their tracks. Heat of the moment, literally under fire, what would be so irrational about the stranger thinking he had been betrayed? As for the other men in Baker's entourage, once bullets started flying, they had simply done what hardmen do.

None of it proved a thing, as far as her boyfriend was concerned. It clearly didn't mean that he had sent his men to kill her. On the other hand, she had to wonder what he might be thinking now. A number of his men were dead, and now it looked as if Palmer had run off with the man responsible for killing them. If she allowed that thought to put down roots and fester in his mind, the next time Baker sent his men to look for her, it was a safe bet that they would have orders not to bring her back.

She had already checked the windows in her room and found them barred from the outside. She could open the sash and cry out to the neighbors for help, but what good would it do her? One or the other of her baby-sitters would come in to silence her, and for what? Judging the locals by Manhattan standards, it was even money they would let her scream her head off and ignore the noise. The flip side of that coin would be a call to 911, and while she wanted out, Palmer had no illusions that her lot would be improved in any way by talking to police. For one thing, they would want to know what she was doing there, and that would lead them into a discussion of her link to Rory Baker, plus his status as a fugitive from justice.

Shit!

The only person she could count on to bail her out, at the moment, was Baker himself—assuming it wasn't too late, and he would even speak to her. There was a fifty-fifty chance that he would slam down the telephone receiver the moment that he heard her voice. Or, then again, he might decide to punish her for what appeared to be a flagrant case of sleeping with the enemy.

But what else could she do?

Palmer had faith in her ability to handle men. It was a skill she had acquired in puberty and cultivated all her life, but there were risks involved in dealing with a man like Rory Baker, who could rub you out like stepping on a bug. If she was careless, said the wrong thing to him, Palmer knew that asking for his help could be the worst mistake—the last mistake—she ever made.

Her bags were gone, left back at the hotel, but Palmer had her purse, and nestled at the bottom of it, underneath her wallet, compact, lipstick, cigarettes and lighter, was a pocket-sized cellular phone. It was a gift from Baker, in fact. The Russian hadn't searched her handbag when they reached the safehouse, and his companion didn't even see it, since she had already been assigned a sleeping room and left it there, parked on the nightstand. Now, she opened it and rummaged through her other things until she had the compact folding telephone in hand.

Could she even reach the New York number Baker used these days from where they had her stashed in Jersey? Palmer punched the buttons, listened to a high-pitched beeping sound and heard a prerecorded voice inform her that the number she had dialed was out of range.

Her first impulse was to haul off and fling the telephone across the room, smash it against the nearest wall, but Palmer was the master of her temper. Most times, anyway. She thought about the problem and decided there was one more number she could try. It was a cutout in Manhattan, nothing more than an answering service, as far as she knew, but she had used it once or twice before. Sometimes a woman answered, other times, a man. She left a message, and the faceless operator passed it on to Baker. Later, when he had the time, Baker would call her back.

But not this time.

If his number was out range for Palmer's cellular phone, that meant he couldn't call her back. Nor did she want him to, since any unexpected noise—the ringing of a telephone, for instance—would attract immediate attention from her keepers. Palmer didn't know if both of them were still on hand, but one was bad enough. She wouldn't have a chance to speak, convey her message properly, if one or both of them came barging in on her.

And how could she convey her message to a total stranger, get her point across in terms that would bring Baker to her aid without further enraging him, making him think she had switched sides to join his enemies? The operator was a drone, a middleman she would never meet, indifferent to Palmer's emotions, to her needs.

She had to keep it simple, then—but also cryptic—something that would tell Baker she needed him and wanted him, assure him that there was no trap, no backstabbing involved. Something to bring him on the run.

And tell him where she was, of course.

That part was simple, thanks to the distraction of her Russian baby-sitter. He hadn't blindfolded her, so she had seen the street signs and the number of the house where she was held. She knew that they were in North Bergen, and while she had never visited the town before, she trusted Baker and his men to find her, once they knew that much.

Rehearsing what she meant to say, Palmer tapped out a second number, waiting, praying that she wouldn't hear the beeping and recorded voice again. She felt herself relaxing slightly, as a distant telephone began to ring.

THE BEST THING about power, Rurik Baklanov sometimes reflected, was the fact that one could always opt not to display it. There was no hard rule demanding that specific situations had to be handled in some predetermined way. Sometimes, when he was furious—like now—it pleased the Russian to adopt a casual demeanor and pretend that he was unaffected by bad news. Sometimes, it was the lull before a deadly storm, his fury taking adversaries by surprise once they let down their guard.

He hadn't quite decided what to do with Hedeon Chapaev, yet. It was infuriating that the former Spetsnaz officer had let him down again, but there had also been extenuating circumstances, as Chapaev said. At least one gunman had been waiting for them when they went to fetch Palmer from the hotel, and he had taken three of his hit man's best soldiers by surprise. It crossed his mind to ask how they could be the best and yet be taken by surprise so easily, but Baklanov let it go. His first concern was tracking down Palmer, determining what role she played in the betrayal, and identifying those responsible. Once that was done, he could decide upon a fitting punishment for Chapaev and the soldiers who had let him down.

But for the moment, he was satisfied to watch his chief enforcer sweat and squirm.

"You didn't recognize the man responsible for this embarrassment?" he asked, frowning slightly to suggest that the embarrassment was Chapaev's, and not his own.

"I only glimpsed him for a moment in the car when he—"

"Yes, I remember," Baklanov interrupted. "When he killed your driver and escaped."

"That's right," Chapaev answered stiffly.

"And your men? Do any of them know this man?"

"The three who saw him clearly in the hotel lobby can no longer help us," Chapaev said. "Two others might have seen him briefly through the windshield of his car."

"Might have?" The Russian mobster knew where this was going, but he dragged the game out, playing cat-and-mouse.

"As I've already told you, sir—"

"Ah, yes. Your men are somewhere in Manhattan. Missing, yes? Perhaps locked up in jail by now."

"We would have heard if that was true," Chapaev said.

He had a point, of course. The soldiers each had memorized a sanitary number they could call in the event of an emergency. No calls, so far, told Rurik Baklanov that no one else had gone to jail. If he had been a praying man, he would have offered up a word of thanks.

Instead, he turned to his lieutenant, seated on his left beside the massive teakwood desk, and said, "Semyon, I'm growing weary of these childish games. Justine might have betrayed us. It's time we knew for certain, one way or another."

"Agreed," Semyon Shurochka said. "Of course, we have to find her, first."

"Of course," Baklanov said, making no effort to disguise his sarcasm. "I trust you have devised some plan in that regard."

"I thought, perhaps…that is, it seems to me, considering the circumstances—"

"Out with it!" the Russian snapped. He saw a smile begin to form on Chapaev's face and killed it with a glare.

"I thought we might solicit help from the Sicilians," Shurochka answered. "They have more experience, more contacts in New York than we do. If they help us, I believe Justine might soon be found."

The plan made sense to Baklanov, and yet he hated running to the Mafia for help on what was still, essentially, a personal concern. The other side of that coin, though, was the considerable loss his would-be colleagues in the Mob had already sustained, presumably inflicted by the same men who were bent on making Baklanov's life a kind of hell on Earth. Why shouldn't the Sicilians help him solve the problem when they stood to gain almost as much as he did in the end?

He let them think so, anyway, as long as the deception served his purposes.

"All right, then," he said, making up his mind. "Speak to Peredo, first. He should be pleased to help us. If he hesitates for any reason, talk to Donatelli."

"Yes, sir."

Shurochka had already risen from his chair, was turning toward the study door when it swung open to admit the sour-faced houseman. "Sir," he said, and then stood waiting for permission to proceed.

"What is it, Nikolai?" the master of the house inquired.

"A message from the service in Manhattan, sir," the houseman said. "They have received a phone call. From the woman, sir."

"Justine?" It came as a profound surprise, but Baklanov covered most of that, responding in what sounded—to his own ears—like a normal tone of voice. "Why did she call the service, rather than direct?"

A shrug from Nikolai. "They didn't say. I didn't ask. She left a message, sir."

"I'm waiting, Nikolai."

It was a source of constant wonderment to Baklanov, the way his houseman could speak without cracking his perpetual frown. "She gave an address in New Jersey," Nikolai informed him. "Someplace in North Bergen. Said she couldn't get away without some help."

A smile came instantly, unbidden, to the Russian mobster's lips. "So, Justine needs our help again," he said to no one in particular. "By all means, let us give it to her, then. And Hedeon…?"

"Yes, sir?"

"Don't fail this time. My patience is exhausted. If you can't return Justine to me, let no one come back here alive."

13

Before he hit the streets again and took the war back to his adversaries, Bolan thought he owed it to himself to try communicating with the woman one last time. If all else failed, he was prepared to let Brognola have her, keep her safe out of the line of fire, while Bolan picked up with his blitz against the mafiosi who had cast their lot with Rurik Baklanov. It was a slower method than the more direct approach, of course, but he believed that it would ultimately bring results. Sooner or later, if he kept the pressure on, someone would crack and lead him back to his primary target.

But first, the woman.

"One more try," he told Petrov, and saw the Russian shrug as Bolan started down the hallway toward her room at the rear of the house. He knocked on the door, then stepped through, uninvited, when Palmer didn't respond.

He found her seated on the bed, legs crossed, smoking a cigarette. Her purse lay beside her, Palmer's left hand resting lightly on top of it, as if to prevent him from snatching it away. He took a stab at reading the expression on her face—anger and suspicion, mixed up with something that might have been guilt—but there was too much going on behind her eyes for Bolan to trust his read. Without the benefit of psychic powers, he decided on the more direct approach.

"I'm leaving in about five minutes," Bolan told her. "If there's anything you want to talk about, before I go..."

"I think we covered everything," Palmer replied. "Of

course, I wouldn't mind a lift into the city if you're headed that way.''

"You'll be going into federal custody,'' he said, watching her blink as the announcement took her by surprise.

"For what, exactly?" she demanded.

"Material witness to racketeering and multiple murder should do it for now,'' he replied. "At least, it ought to keep you out from underfoot until we wrap this up.''

"Meaning Rory,'' she said. When Bolan made no reply, she said, "Suppose you get him. Then, what?''

"Not my call,'' he said. "I'd be surprised if you do any time. But, then again, you might be safer in a cell when word gets out.''

"Oh, yeah? What word is that?" she challenged him.

"You never know,'' the Executioner replied. "A deal like this, you've always got a few loose ends. Some little fish slip through the net, and pretty soon, they notice there's a shortage of big fish on top. That cheers them up, of course…until they start to think about the other loose ends, looking for a scapegoat to explain what happened.''

"Right,'' she said. "That's fucking typical. You set me up if I don't help you. Either way, I take the heat.''

"It won't be me,'' he said, "but I won't be around to baby-sit you, either. If you help us with the cleanup now, there could be fewer problems for you down the road.''

"Forget it, friend.'' The last word sounded like a curse from Palmer's lips. "I'll take my chances, okay? Whatever happens, then, at least I know I didn't rat my friends out, just to help myself.''

"Whatever,'' Bolan said. "You've got a few more hours here, before the switch, in case you change your mind.''

"I won't,'' she said to his retreating back.

He had the door half-closed behind him, leaving her alone, before he heard a ripping sound—like bullets shredding wood-work—from the living room. Bolan was reaching for his side arm, moving swiftly toward the sound, when he was halted by a crash of glass behind him, from the bedroom, followed by a scream. He doubled back and cleared the threshold in a crouch, the big Beretta 93-R in his fist, eyes narrowed as he saw a frag grenade wobbling across the floor between the doorway and the bed.

He had a choice to make: retreat and save himself or try to help Palmer. In less time than it took to formulate the thought, Bolan made his decision, letting instinct drive him forward. Two long strides, and he was past the small, green canister of death, diving headlong to sweep Palmer from where she sat, frozen, and drag her down beside him to the floor behind the bed.

The frag grenade went off a heartbeat later, thunder battering his ears, smoke churning through the room and out into the corridor beyond. He heard the ripping sound of shrapnel, slicing into furniture, the ceiling, all four walls, but they were shielded from the worst of it by Palmer's bed. The covers were on fire as Bolan rose to his hands and knees, but that would be the least of his concerns.

Someone had tracked them to the safehouse, and he didn't even care how that had happened, at the moment. All he cared about was getting out of there, taking Palmer and Petrov with him, while the three of them were still alive.

Petrov!

As Bolan dragged Palmer to her feet, deaf to her tearful protest, he heard more sharp, staccato sounds of automatic weapons' fire, reverberating from the general direction of the living room. It would become a dying room in seconds flat, and Bolan understood that they were swiftly running out of time.

In fact, he realized, it might already by too late.

MINDFUL OF BAKLANOV'S admonition, Hedeon Chapaev had selected fifteen soldiers for his trip across the river to New Jersey. Strictly speaking, they weren't his best—the best had been killed within the past few days—but even second-stringers in the small, select battalion were among the best—or worst, depending on your point of view—that Mother Russia had to

offer. Each and every one of them had learned to kill a hundred
different ways, at government expense, before the Communist
regime that nurtured them had finally collapsed and left them
to their own devices.

Now, the time had come for them to earn their pay.

His orders were to bring the woman back alive, if possible—
or, failing that, to silence her for good, along with anyone
found in her company. Given the time and opportunity, Chapaev was instructed to identify her so-called captors and report
whatever information he obtained to Rurik Baklanov without
delay.

Chapaev thought it was an optimistic order at the very least.
Palmer's abductors—or protectors—had already faced his soldiers twice in combat, killing ten and scattering the rest. He
had no reason to believe they would be lax this time, or yield
up any secrets after death. They were professionals; that much
was clear. And as such, they would take precautions, carry no
ID that would betray them to their enemies if killed or captured.

Still, Chapaev had his orders and was bound to try.

Their drive from Queens consumed the better part of ninety
minutes, and he worried that the woman might be gone before
they even reached the address in North Bergen. If there *was*
an address, and she hadn't simply laid another trap, for reasons
Hedeon Chapaev couldn't guess. She was a common whore,
of course, and that meant she would always choose the highest
bidder, but he found it difficult to picture anyone outbidding
Rurik Baklanov.

His first good news of that grim day came when they saw
the house, its address painted on the curb, black numbers sten-
ciled on a swatch of white. They drove on past, four cars in
line, with four men each, and parked downrange beyond the
line of sight from curtained windows in the target dwelling.
They unloaded in the shadow zone, between two widely spaced
streetlights, Chapaev briefing his commandos, even as he pon-
dered questions that had dogged him all the way from Queens.

If Palmer was a prisoner, how had she managed to com-
municate with Baklanov's service, in Manhattan? Were her

captors lax, or was this yet another trap counting on surprise to rout his soldiers once again?

If so, Chapaev was pledged to see them fail. He had already suffered more humiliation in the past few days than in the whole of his career with Spetsnaz, spanning nearly thirteen years. It stung him, and he craved revenge.

To that end, he had told his men exactly what would be expected of them. They should bring the woman out alive, if possible, but if they met resistance, no survivors. Under no circumstances would anyone be permitted to leave the house alive, except securely in his custody.

His troops were armed with submachine guns and side arms, and hand grenades obtained from one of Baklanov's contacts in the local Mafia. Trailing a few yards behind his men, Chapaev took the time to double-check his Skorpion and pat his pockets for the reassuring bulk of extra magazines.

This time, he thought. This time they would do it right.

He felt the lift that always came to him immediately prior to combat. It was something that had startled him, his first time out in uniform, mistaking it for fear. Experience had taught him to enjoy the feeling, use it to his own advantage. It was this enjoyment of his work, together with aggressive training, that had made Chapaev one of the elite.

He would have liked to lead his men inside the house, but rank had its responsibilities, and one of them was to observe, remain aloof and delegate the killing chores. If that meant missing out on some of the excitement, still, it reassured him that no angle of attack was overlooked, no problem unanticipated. If his soldiers were successful tonight, the glory would be his. And if they failed...

He heard the parting words of Rurik Baklanov once more: If you can't return Justine to me, let no one come back here alive. Chapaev understood that there would be no waivers or exemptions should he fail this time.

The pressure didn't trouble him; in fact, Chapaev thrived on it. What point was there in going off to war if it was simply shooting goats staked out for slaughter, with no risk involved?

Any street thug could do such work. It didn't take a soldier to crush rodents underneath his boots.

One thing the past few days had taught him: he was dealing with a worthy adversary in the unknown enemy who had come close to decimating his command. Revenge would be that much more satisfying after all the enemy had cost him—both in terms of manpower and the respect of Rurik Baklanov, so seriously damaged by the recent killings in New York.

Chapaev meant to fix all that. He meant to prove himself, make Baklanov understand that he was still the best for any job requiring martial skills and cunning. No matter who was fielded to oppose him, Hedeon Chapaev would prevail.

He reached the sidewalk opposite where they had parked the cars, and saw his soldiers fanning out to ring the house with guns, cut off retreat for anyone inside. Despite the draperies that covered every window he could see, Chapaev saw the lights were on inside—and knew that didn't mean a thing. If Justine Palmer was, in fact, a captive, and her keepers were aware that she had somehow used the telephone, they could have whisked her off to yet another hiding place by now, before the hit team made its way from Queens.

And he would know, within a few more moments, one way or the other.

He was standing well back from the house, the Skorpion concealed beneath his jacket, when his point men rushed the door. They didn't knock or ring the bell, but rather used a submachine gun with a sound suppressor attached to blast the locks. A swift kick, spilling light across the stoop, and they were through the doorway, well inside.

More gunfire from the house, and this time with no suppressor to muffle the reports. Chapaev cursed, and he was moving forward to assist when a grenade went off somewhere in back.

The Spetsnaz warrior broke into a run, his weapon drawn. Finesse was out the window, now, and it was killing time. The time he cherished most.

And he allowed himself no doubt in terms of who would finally prevail.

PALMER HAD TROUBLE breathing as the tall man dragged her from the shattered ruin of the room where she had been confined mere seconds earlier. Her head was spinning, ears still ringing from the blast. Her lungs were filled with smoke, and she was gagging on it, vastly different from the sweet taste of the cigarettes she favored,

Jesus Christ! A freaking hand grenade?

And there was something else before that. She had seen the tall man starting to react to it—a sound from the direction of the living room, like someone was hacking through the front door with a Ginsu power cleaver. Those were gunshots, Palmer realized, an automatic weapon, probably outfitted with a sound suppressor.

Her heart was pounding like a trip-hammer against her ribs, and she almost stumbled, as the big man hauled her down the corridor behind him. They were heading for the sounds of battle, so much louder now, and Palmer had an urge to pull away from him, retreat to safety, but she understood there was no safety to be found within these walls. The bedroom windows were all barred, impassable, and there were men outside who were apparently prepared to kill the occupants without distinction or discrimination.

Palmer felt a sudden need to vomit, but she swallowed hard and kept it down, focused on keeping up with the man who had just saved her life.

Those were Baker's gunmen outside, and she had brought them here. They were supposed to rescue her, and yet they came in shooting, lobbing hand grenades through the windows. If this tall stranger clutching her wrist had been one second slower, Palmer knew she would have been dead, maybe shredded by the blast and shrapnel.

Oh, God! Baker's soldiers really didn't care if she got out alive or not—which meant that Baker didn't care. The nausea hit her again, like a rabbit punch to the solar plexus. She nearly doubled over, breaking stride, careening off course toward impact with the nearest wall.

"Come on!" her savior snapped without a backward glance, still dragging her along.

She cursed him silently, then felt a sudden unfamiliar rush of guilt, sparked by her own ingratitude. This total stranger, whom she had betrayed, had saved her life and now seemed bent on keeping her alive, while Rory Baker did his best to rub her out. The tall man and his Russian sidekick had been right from the beginning. Baker didn't trust her, and his only thought for her revolved around insuring that she never had a chance to reveal whatever he supposed she knew.

She'd talk, all right, Palmer thought, with a flash of grim defiance. If she got out of there alive, just try to shut her up!

And getting out alive would obviously be the problem. Baker's people had them more or less surrounded, from the look and sound of things—at least one man out back, to pitch grenades, while more were shooting up the front. With windows either barred or covered, there were two ways out: the front door, or another on the side that served the kitchen, granting access to a strip of grass along the west side of the smallish house. Palmer had scoped the layout when they brought her in, a habit with new places, and she saw no realistic hope of getting out through either door. Two gunners, one for each, could keep them bottled up until...

Until what?

More grenades, Palmer thought. Maybe something to set the place burning. Or gas! The cops used it to flush people out, and she watched enough television news to know there were all kinds available, some of them lethal. Her boyfriend wanted her dead—wanted all of them dead—and she suspected he wouldn't be too particular about the methods used to realize that goal.

Another blast ripped through the house somewhere behind her. They were clearing out the bedrooms, one by one. It didn't matter, finally, if the grenades killed anyone, or simply drove them all toward the front of the house, where the shooters were waiting. One way or another, the end result should be the same.

Passing the entrance to the living room, she glimpsed the Russian who had pulled her out of the hotel that afternoon. He was crouched behind the sofa, popping up to spray the door and windows with a submachine gun, ducking back again as the return fire from outside hit all around him, cushions jumping, stuffing in the air like snowflakes.

Palmer felt a bullet ripple past her face and heard its sound a fraction of a second later, trying to catch up. The big man gave a sharp jerk on her arm, and she cleared the doorway, lurching after him, into the combination dining room and kitchen. It was dark there—darker, anyway, with no lights on, some spillage from the hall and living room—and her companion seemed to like it that way. Palmer bumped into him when he stopped short just inside the doorway.

"What the—"

When he shoved her, straight-arm from the shoulder, it appeared to cost him little in the way of effort, but Palmer, on the receiving end, was driven sharply to her left and downward, stumbling, sprawling on the vinyl floor. She bruised her hip and shoulder, banged an elbow, pain and anger flaring in her simultaneously.

"Damn you, what—"

Before she had an opportunity to chew him out, the kitchen door slammed inward, blasted off its hinges with a sound like thunder. Palmer heard it hit the floor, smack-rattle-bang, and then all hell broke loose, with automatic weapons hammering.

She brought her knees up, curled herself into a fetal ball, and closed her eyes, wishing she could recall some kind of prayer from childhood, when she still believed in something other than the power of the dollar.

And the best she could come up with was a kind of silent mantra, endlessly repeated in her mind: just make it quick.

PETROV WAS ANGRY at himself for having let his guard down, but he had no time to deal with the emotion now that they were under fire. If he survived the next few moments, he could always brood about it later, fix a certain punishment to help himself remember next time.

At the moment, though, he had to think about this time and how to keep himself alive.

He should have covered the approaches to the safehouse, somehow, rigged some kind of early-warning system that would have alerted him before his enemies were close enough to open fire and lob grenades. Too late for that, now, with their bullets chewing up the front door, smashing through the windows, shredding curtains. Petrov gave them credit for achieving the surprise, but marked them down for striking hastily, before they had clear targets marked and verified.

It was an error that, with any luck, might just allow him to survive.

He nosed around the left end of the sofa, squeezing off another short burst from his AKM. Petrov had nothing in the way of targets, either, but he wanted them to know at least one shooter was alive and well inside the house, to slow them and buy some time.

With all this racket, it was guaranteed that someone on the street had called for the police by now. The trick—and a demanding trick it was—would be to stall their enemies until the sound of distant sirens forced them to retreat, then slip away in the confusion without being spotted or arrested.

It was simple. All he needed was a magic ring or cloak to render him invisible.

Petrov had no idea if Mike Belasko and Justine Palmer were still alive. The sound of hand grenades exploding told him Rurik Baklanov was pulling out the stops, intent on silencing his girlfriend and rooting out his unknown enemies by any means available. He didn't have a clue how many soldiers were outside, but from the concentrated fire exploding through the door and windows of the living room, he made it three to five in front, alone.

Bad odds, but he had never been a quitter. Not an optimist, perhaps, but Petrov was a fighter. Knowing that surrender meant his death, the Russian's grim determination was increased tenfold.

If it came down to dying, he was ready for a last-ditch stand, and he would take as many of the bastards with him as he could. Besides the AKM and three spare magazines, he had the Skorpion beside him on the floor, and wore the P-9 semiauto pistol in its quick-draw shoulder rig. Of course, he needed targets first, in order to score hits, and Petrov made a mental note to save his ammunition for the rush he knew was coming any moment now.

Just one more burst to keep them on their toes…

As if in answer to his silent thoughts, the tempo of incoming fire increased, a veritable storm of bullets whipping through the tattered curtains, gnawing chunks the size of dinner plates out of the door. Petrov knew what was coming, more or less, but for the moment he could only keep his head down, grimacing as more rounds tore into the sofa, whittling his cover away.

If they didn't come soon…

While he was waiting, Petrov switched magazines on his AKM, feeding a fresh clip into the assault rifle. He would need every one of its thirty rounds when the shooters came for him, and there might be no time to reload before he fell back on the Skorpion machine pistol. So little time, perhaps, remained in his life.

It always ended like this for warriors, he reflected, suddenly and unexpectedly. Given a choice, Petrov wouldn't think twice about the way he chose to die.

But if he had a choice, when all was said and done, he wouldn't die tonight.

They came together, firing as they rushed the door and broad front window of the house. One of them cleared the window first, all tangled up in shredded curtains, thrashing with the muzzle of his weapon as he tried to clear a field of fire, another close behind him, in the clear.

Petrov was waiting for them, squeezing off a short burst at the second shooter first, because his view was unencumbered, and that made him dangerous. The armor-piercing NATO rounds tore through the shooter's chest—it made no difference whether he was swathed in Kevlar underneath his shirt—and blew him backward out the window he had chosen as his means of entry to the house.

One down, and Petrov fired a second burst, almost before the death of his first adversary registered. The point man had reached up with one hand, clawing at the strips of fabric stretched across his face, and cleared them just in time to read his death in Petrov's eyes. Still, he was quick enough to get off another burst from his SMG, before the AKM rounds ripped a bloody fissure in his chest and dropped him in his tracks. Nine-millimeter Parabellum rounds flew over Petrov's head and smacked into the wall behind him, raining plaster from a dozen tidy holes.

Two down. He swiveled toward the door and found it gaping open, one of his opponents well inside and dodging toward the cover of an easy chair, while two more double-timed across the threshold. Petrov scarcely had to aim at that range, simply point his AKM and hold it steady as he squeezed the trigger, tracking left to right across the open door, then back again.

His adversaries seemed to stop in freeze-frame, for a moment, as the bullets found them, hammering through flesh and fabric, both of them going down together in a snarl of twisted limbs, blood splashed across the doorframe and the nearby walls. Petrov couldn't be certain they were dead, but both of them were badly wounded, out of action for the next few moments, at the very least.

And that left one.

Petrov was lowering the muzzle of his automatic rifle toward the easy chair, prepared to finish it, when he was startled by the image of a green egg tumbling through the air, wobbling in flight, arcing directly toward his face. He recognized the frag grenade for what it was, recoiling in an instant, ducking behind the couch. It wasn't much, but it was all he had.

And it wasn't enough.

The blast slammed Petrov and the sofa back against the wall, ten feet behind him. For an agonizing instant, Petrov was the filling in a sofa sandwich. He felt a number of his ribs snap, followed by the deep pain of bone splinters puncturing a lung. He dragged himself through swirling plaster dust and smoke, unable to remember where the AKM and Skorpion had gone while he was airborne, using precious breath to curse in Russian, while he twisted in his pain and tried to reach the pistol slung beneath his arm.

He almost made it.

When the shadow fell across his face, Petrov had wrapped his hands around the warm grips of the P-9 automatic, flicked the thumb-break snap aside to free it, but he didn't have the time to draw and fire. Instead, he glimpsed a pair of hard eyes glaring at him over gunsights, heard what sounded like a Russian curse in answer to his own... and then, the world exploded in his face.

THE FIRST MAN through the kitchen door was dead before he knew it, Bolan squeezing off a 3-round burst from roughly fifteen feet away, the Parabellum slugs ripping through his target's jaw and cheek. The Russian went down firing. Bolan gave him points for sheer tenacity, but it was wasted effort, bullets chewing up the kitchen's vinyl floor to no result.

And he was ready when the second shooter came into view, already firing as he crossed the threshold, without any target clearly fixed in mind. Another 3-round burst from the Beretta 93-R took him down as cleanly as the first, and left the dead men sprawled within arm's reach of each other on the floor.

"Come on!" he snapped when there was no sign of a third commando in the doorway, reaching out for Palmer where she huddled in a corner to his left.

"Come on?" she answered, gaping at him. "You just knocked me down, for Christ's sake!"

"Do you want to live or not?" he asked, keeping both eyes on the dark rectangle of the kitchen door.

"I'm coming, dammit!"

Bolan caught her by the arm as she stood and pulled her

after him. He kept his gun trained on the doorway, glancing briefly backward as the sounds of gunfire from the living room spiked toward a fever pitch. There was no way to help Petrov and save the woman, too. There might be no way he could save her, period, but Bolan knew that he was bound to try...or die in the attempt.

"There might be more outside," he told her, speaking loud enough to make his message understood by ringing ears. "Stay low and follow me, no matter what."

"And if they take you out?" she asked him pointedly.

"Then," Bolan said, "you're on your own."

"The freaking story of my life," Palmer replied. "All right, let's get it done."

A glance outside the door might show him gunmen lurking in the night, or it might not, but it would certainly alert his enemies to Bolan's plan if they were standing by, on watch. He didn't like the thought of charging blind into the darkness, but it beat the flip side of the coin, which could be getting pinned down in the kitchen, trapped while his opponents closed their deadly pincers on him, finishing the play.

So Bolan moved, a shadow gliding through the doorway, pausing only long enough to lift an Uzi submachine gun from the dead hands of the second shooter he had killed. There was no time to check the weapon's load, but even if it only gave him one or two short bursts, it was a bit of extra firepower, and Bolan needed all that he could get.

Behind them, as he cleared the steps outside, he heard another hand grenade go off, this one a good deal closer than the others. In the living room? It angered him to think of leaving Petrov, but they had a common goal—destroying Rurik Baklanov—and he couldn't accomplish that if he and Justine Palmer died here. Worse, if he went back, then Petrov's sacrifice to stall the enemy and buy them time would be in vain, a total waste.

Bolan was halfway to the northeast corner of the house, facing the street, before a gunner stepped in front of him, out of the shadows, barking at him in Russian. Bolan let the Uzi rip without a second thought, stitching the silhouette from groin to breastbone with a burst that dropped him, limp and lifeless, on his back.

"Stay with me, now," he told Palmer.

"Like I've got somewhere else to go," she said, a measure of her spirit coming back despite the death surrounding her on every side.

"We need some wheels," he said, still moving forward, while the sounds of combat echoed from inside the house. "They might have our cars covered. Either way, no matter what, you stick with me."

"Like glue," she said. "And by the way, if you get us killed, I'll never speak to you again."

He hesitated at the corner of the house for just a moment, knowing once the move was made, once they exposed themselves to any shooters covering the yard, it would be all or nothing, do or die. His knuckles blanched as Bolan clutched the Uzi in a death grip, willing it to have enough rounds left to see them through, whatever happened next.

"Look, if we're doing this—"

He moved before she had a chance to finish, hearing Palmer's muffled curse behind him, footsteps running to keep up. The door and picture window on the front side of the house were gone, the siding pocked with bullet holes. The Ford Econoline van and Petrov's second rental car were waiting for them in the driveway. Bolan's pocket was heavy with the keys that fit the van. He made directly for the Ford, letting Palmer make her own way. His eyes and weapon swept the yard, alert to any opposition on the way.

A muzzle-flash erupted at the northwest corner of the house, immediately followed by a gruff voice calling out in Russian. Bolan didn't get the message, and he didn't give a damn. He let his captured Uzi do his talking for him, laying down a screen of cover fire—perhaps a dozen rounds in all, before it suddenly ran dry.

He ditched it, drew the 93-R from its armpit sling and fanned another 3-round burst in the direction of his enemy. Then he was at the van, his free hand opening the driver's door, and Bolan stood aside to let Palmer dive in, across the driver's seat and into the back.

Smart girl, he thought. She could lie down back there and have a better chance of dodging any slugs that pierced the van. Of course, it only took one lucky round, but, then again…

He got behind the wheel, jammed his key into the slot, then turned the engine over, slammed the van into reverse, released the brake and powered out of there. The rear end of the van struck something, and he heard a muffled cry, but that was someone else's problem. There were no civilian strollers out this time of night, not with a firefight in full swing, and any adversary dumb enough to stand in front of Bolan's van could take his chances with the rest.

A pair of guns were snapping at his heels, as Bolan put the van in Drive and left a trail of rubber on the pavement, heading out. No headlights in his wake, though, as he cleared the neighborhood and started looking for another place to hide.

Petrov was on his own, assuming he was still alive.

God keep, Bolan thought, as he drove on through the night.

14

As failures went, it wasn't Hedeon Chapaev's worst in recent days. He still had eight of his original fifteen commandos left, though one of them was barely conscious when they found him, knocked down by a fleeing vehicle as Justine Palmer and at least one of her guardians escaped. Chapaev didn't care, particularly, if the wounded soldier lived or died.

More to the point, his men had finally succeeded in eliminating one of their elusive enemies. Chapaev had them drag the body out and toss it in his trunk, for leisurely examination at a safer time and place. Sirens were drawing nearer by the moment, as the nine survivors of the raid piled into their four cars and got out of there before the frightened neighbors had a chance to make a note of license numbers.

Not that it would matter, since the plates on all four cars were stolen, anyway. Chapaev was a firm believer in preventive medicine, and while a string of rapid-fire humiliations had embarrassed him in recent days, his caution served him well most times. Just now, though, he was thinking past the moment, wondering what he should say to Rurik Baklanov when he made the inevitable, inescapable telephone call.

Baklanov's instructions had been crystal-clear and quite specific. If they failed to bag the woman, dead or alive, no member of the raiding party was permitted to return. That order brooked no compromise, but it was clearly open to interpretation. If Chapaev had been Japanese, for instance, he might have felt duty bound to kill himself in expiation of his shame. A Russian soldier viewed things in a different light, of course. To Chapaev, Baklanov's order clearly meant the hunters should remain at large until they were successful in their quest. The corollary to that proposition, clearly visible between the lines, was that the mob boss intended to annihilate any survivors if they failed.

There were degrees of failure, though, and thereby hung Chapaev's one hope of survival—even reinstatement to his master's favor. True, the whore had managed to elude them with at least one of her bodyguards, but they had finished off one member of the opposition team, their first score of the game. Dead men didn't talk, but they still carried tales from time to time, and Chapaev thought they might be able to identify the corpse, with any luck at all. Once it possessed a name, they would be one step closer to determining who pulled the strings, identifying those responsible for all the grief that had been heaped upon his head.

But first, Chapaev had to get in touch with Rurik Baklanov. Reporting failure was a dreary task at best; in the worst-case scenario, when lives were riding on the line, it might prove fatal. All the more important, then, for Chapaev to report before Baklanov began to pick up bits and pieces from the radio or television news. He had to tell—and sell—his version of the story first, with emphasis on what he hoped to gain from an examination of the corpse now riding in his trunk. If he was quick enough and cool enough, Chapaev thought there was a chance he could finesse the conversation, buy himself some time in which to track down the woman and her other playmate.

It had become a personal affair to Chapaev, the way Justine Palmer led them all around by their noses, baiting one trap after another. She had cost him seventeen men in less than twenty-four hours, an attrition rate that, if continued, would leave Chapaev on his own, single-handed, by week's end. The prospect troubled him, though he wasn't truly afraid.

Not yet.

But he was getting there.

"I need a telephone," Chapaev told his driver. When the young man took a cellular phone from his pocket, offering it to his chief, Chapaev shook his head. "A land line," he explained. "A public telephone. Something secure."

Secure for him, that was. Cellular phone communications were too easily monitored for Chapaev's peace of mind. Likewise, the telephones at Rurik Baklanov's retreat, in Queens, were all equipped with caller ID boxes, printing out the number of origin for all incoming calls. The device wouldn't work with a cellular phone, only the more secure land lines, and once Baklanov had the number in hand, it was a relatively simple matter for him to locate the telephone, using his Sicilian contacts, or even some corrupt policeman. By the time he traced a public phone booth, though, Chapaev and the remnants of his strike force would be miles away—and, hopefully, in hot pursuit of their elusive prey.

The former Spetsnaz trooper needed time, a longer lease on life, in which to find the woman and her bodyguards. If Baklanov tried to reel him in right now, or sent another team of hunters after him, Chapaev wouldn't have a chance to properly redeem himself, his honor. He would have his hands full, simply fighting for his life.

That simply wouldn't do.

"Gas station," his driver said, pointing. "There's a telephone."

"Pull in," Chapaev said, "and keep the engine running while you wait. I won't be long."

"SO, YOU WERE RIGHT."

It was the first time that Palmer had spoken since they fled North Bergen, following the Hudson River twenty miles or so, then veering inland, stopping at a cheap motel in Tenafly. She helped the man who called himself Belasko carry bags into the room—more hardware, by the weight and sound of it—and never once considered bolting when his back was turned.

Mostly, Palmer was worried that he just might let her go.

"I didn't know, okay?" She felt obliged to fill the silent void between them, start him talking. It would help distract him from the fact that she had killed his friend, the Russian who had saved her life at the hotel on 82nd Street, as certainly as if it were her finger on the trigger of the gun that did the job.

Instead of answering, the man took her purse away and dumped its contents on the bed. The cellular phone went into his pocket, and Palmer was worried for a moment that he might haul off and smack her, but instead, he walked back to a chair, positioned near the door, and sat.

"I'm out of time and out of patience," he informed her. "You'll be going to the Feds, as soon as they're available to take you off my hands. It's your choice whether you go as a witness or accessory to murder. Take your pick. You've got ten seconds."

"Jesus, how could I know they were—"

"Five."

She searched his face for mercy, found grim death instead, and had about one second left when she replied, "All right. I'll tell you what I know."

"I'm listening."

"It isn't much," she said. "But if that's not good enough, after I tell you what I know for sure, I can go back and make shit up, fill in the blanks."

"Just play it straight," he said. And Palmer thought she heard the rest of it, unspoken, like an echo in her head: *for once.*

"Okay," she said. "The truth is that I knew Rory was Russian—pretty hard to miss it, with that accent, right?—and I knew he was in the Mob. He didn't talk about his business. Wise guys never do, unless they're stupid or strung out on something. Anyway, I know he cut some kind of deal after he got arrested by the FBI. I didn't pay attention to the trial. I'm not that big on talking heads, you know? The fact is, I figured, even if he got a pass on that deal, we were done. You get a fresh start on a thing like that, you leave your baggage, right?"

"But then he got in touch," Bolan said.

"That's right. He said he missed me." Palmer felt a flush rise in her cheeks, uncertain whether it was some leftover from her fling with Baker, or a straight case of embarrassment. "I might not look like much to you right now," she said, "but lots of guys have missed me. You can take that to the bank."

"It's not about you," Bolan said, staring through her eyes, into her brain. "Get on with it."

"We were supposed to meet," Palmer continued, "but he kept on getting sidetracked, what with one thing and another. Anyway, we kept in touch by phone. I got a couple numbers— one in Queens, a service in New York—where I could get in touch with him."

"Give me the numbers."

She reeled them off from memory, noting that he didn't repeat them or attempt to write them down. Some kind of photographic memory, on top of everything. The guy was like a damned machine. Palmer had once, briefly considered flirting with him, maybe showing him a good time in return for letting her escape, but she had quickly given up on the idea. He didn't strike her as a sissy or a eunuch—quite the opposite, in fact— but there was something in his attitude that told her any play she made, involving sex, would be a waste of time.

And now, she realized that ditching him would very likely get her killed.

"Which number did you call tonight?" he asked. There was no condemnation in his tone; not much of anything, in fact. Belasko didn't strike her as a man who took his anger out on women as a rule, but she could see death in his eyes, deep down, where it was rooted in his soul.

"The service in Manhattan," she replied. "My cell phone wouldn't reach to Queens."

He thought about that for a moment. She could almost hear the wheels mesh in his mind, deciding whether he should have her make another call. But what would be the point of that, except to place them both in mortal danger? She relaxed as he apparently dismissed it, rising from his chair and moving toward the nightstand, where a plain black telephone was bolted down to keep the ritzy clientele from walking off with it. He fiddled with the jack for several seconds, hooking up some kind of plastic box, roughly the size of a cigarette pack. When he was done with that, he punched nine for an outside line, then stepped around to block her view and started tapping out digits in rapid fire.

She counted off eleven—a long-distance call—before he turned to face her once again and sat on the other bed. His flat gaze made her nervous, something Palmer rarely felt with any man, until she dropped her gaze and focused on the worn beige carpet.

Listening to one side of a conversation could be frustrating, at best, but Palmer followed this one well enough. She didn't care for the direction it was taking, but her choices were distinctly limited. Like, none.

"It's me," Bolan said into the mouthpiece when somebody picked up on the other end. "I've got her here... Not yet... I'll need a pickup... Right, ASAP... He's out of it... North Bergen..."

She could feel the flush returning to her cheeks. No question in her mind who "he" was, much less what Belasko meant by "out of it." The Russian's death was her fault. It wasn't the kind of thing you walked away from, if your conscience still had any life at all left in it.

Palmer was a bit surprised to find that part of hers was still alive and well. She wondered what that meant, and finally decided that she didn't want to think about it. Not right now.

"Okay," Bolan said, "if that's the soonest we can get it done... I'll baby-sit till then... No, I've still got a couple angles I can try... Two numbers I need traced... One in Manhattan, one in Queens..." He played them back from memory. "All right... Do that... Right... I'll be in touch."

He lowered the receiver, and Palmer locked eyes with him again. Whatever he had planned for her, she was determined not to run and hide from it.

"They can't send anyone to fetch you for about an hour," Bolan said. "You want to get some sleep, it wouldn't be a bad idea."

"Where will they take me?"

"Not my problem," he replied.

"So, what's the charge?"

"No charge," Belasko said. "Protective custody. You're being treated as a witness, like I said."

"That means I have to testify?"

It was the first time in their short acquaintance that the man had smiled, and when he did, it chilled Palmer to the bone.

"I wouldn't count on it," he said.

BOLAN RESTRICTED small talk to a minimum while they were waiting for the pickup team to show. It seemed to him that Palmer still had things to say, perhaps in a belated effort to explain herself, but he couldn't provide the absolution she desired. Her call to Rurik Baklanov, from the North Bergen safehouse, had resulted in another bloodbath, and as far as Bolan was concerned, Palmer could live with that until she found her own peace down the road.

It wasn't all her fault, of course. Petrov had failed to search her bag, while Bolan, in his turn, assumed the Russian would have done so, never pausing once to think that Palmer might still have some means of talking to the outside world. It was the kind of "small" mistake that got men killed. Petrov had paid his portion of the tab, in blood. Palmer, from all appearances, was paying hers in unfamiliar guilt.

As for the Executioner, he spent more time collecting tabs than paying them.

He had two numbers now, the one in Queens apparently a residence. The service in Manhattan was a fallback option, something he could try if Baklanov bailed out before he got to Queens, and Bolan had to wonder if his man would run again.

There were at least two different ways to look at it. In one scenario, the Russian mobster might decide his girlfriend was well and truly lost, a convert to the enemy, in which case he would have to figure that the hideaway in Queens was compromised. Departure with a minimal delay would be the only sure-fire remedy, and Baklanov had shown his willingness to pull up stakes when he was threatened, seeking out more friendly territory for his bivouac. If that turned out to be the case, another hour, waiting with Palmer, could give his adversary all the time required to get away. Before Brognola got back to him with a trace on the two numbers, they could both be useless.

On the other hand, his enemy had proved that he had confidence and nerve. Assuming Baklanov believed that Palmer was alive and had betrayed him, there was still a chance the Russian might stand firm, prepare himself to meet the unknown enemy in a decisive battle. Bolan didn't know how many soldiers Baklanov had left, or what kind of support he could expect from his connection to the Mafia.

If Bolan missed his man in Queens, that was an angle he intended to dispose of, stat. Once Baklanov was cut off absolutely from support and reinforcements, he became a drifter, forced to run and hide—perhaps to flee the country. Bolan didn't want him to escape, of course. But any soldier on the run immediately lost a measure of efficiency, compelled to focus on evasion and escape instead of nailing down the details on some broader, more insidious design.

He stretched out on the bed and closed his eyes, ignoring it when Palmer switched on the television for company. It crossed his mind that she might have her feelings hurt, but Bolan didn't care. She was alive, bound for protective custody, while Dima Petrov made his journey to a cold drawer in the Hudson County morgue. All things considered, Justine Palmer had the best part of the deal.

He didn't sleep. In fact, his mind remained alert to every noise around him, though a part of it was perfectly detached, at liberty to plan his movements for the next few hours. It would be dark when he got to Queens and started scouting out the target.

He had ample time to kill, assuming there was anyone or anything to find. If not, he would be forced to start from scratch, and Bolan had some ideas on that score, as well.

There was one angle of attack, one target, that he had neglected up to now. If he missed Baklanov in Queens, that over-

sight would be corrected with a vengeance. One way or another, Bolan was determined to shake something loose,
bulldoze a path that led directly to his enemy.

And once he met the Russian mobster, face-to-face, they
would find out whose lethal reputation passed the acid test.

The house in Queens was stylish, but it proved to be a washout. By the time the Executioner arrived, it had been cleaned out and abandoned. There was no one left to greet him as he roamed the grounds and let himself in through the tall glass sliding doors that faced onto a flagstone patio and swimming pool. No trace of paperwork was left behind to show him where his prey had run to, but he played a hunch and hit the redial button on a telephone he found in what appeared to be a well-appointed study. Bolan waited while the bright tones of eleven digits sounded—a long-distance call—and heard a gruff male voice respond after the second ring.

"Yeah, what?"

He played another hunch, trusting his gut, and asked, "Is Don Gaetano there?"

The other missed a beat before responding, "Nah, he went out for a while. I take a message?"

"Never mind," the Executioner replied, and cradled the receiver gently.

When he tried the service number in Manhattan, there was no response. Another wash, and Bolan saw the only course of action still remaining open to him. He was far from thrilled about it, but he had no choice.

He had to shuffle off to Buffalo.

THREE HOURS and nineteen minutes later, Bolan's flight from JFK touched down at Greater Buffalo International Airport, situated on the city's eastern outskirts, below Williamsville. He spent another quarter hour waiting for his suitcase to appear upon the luggage carousel. A rental car was waiting for him when he cleared the baggage area, and Bolan made his way outside with keys in hand, to find the gray Toyota Celica GT.

With the delays imposed on Bolan by his unexpected journey from Manhattan, it was well past nightfall by the time he left the airport, winding through the city on a north by northwesterly course. Gaetano Donatelli didn't live in Buffalo, per se. His home was on Grand Island, some twenty-five square miles in area, wedged between New York and Canada, flanked by the east and west forks of the Niagara River. In the old days, when the Mafia was young and thrived on traffic in illicit alcohol, Grand Island was a major port of call for rum runners—and an ideal escape route for indicted mobsters bent on hiding out in Canada until the heat blew over. These days, it was scenic and expensive, the ultimate bedroom community, isolated from the worst of Buffalo's urban problems by a natural moat.

It was half-past ten o'clock when Bolan paid his toll and crossed the South Grand Island bridge, rolling into Grandyle Village. He found a self-serve station and convenience store, topped off his gas tank and slipped into the men's room for a change of clothes. He looked no different, coming out, but now he wore the formfitting blacksuit underneath his civvies, ready for a final quick change when he reached his final target.

Seven minutes later, he was cruising through the stately neighborhood where Don Gaetano Donatelli made his home. A call to Hal Brognola had supplied the address, and he scouted the perimeter on wheels, as best he could, before finding a place to stash his car and going EVA.

The night was cool, just short of brisk, as Bolan stepped out into darkness. He'd finished with his war paint, slipped into his combat harness, then buckled on his web belt, double-checking side arms and grenades. The MP-5 SD-3 submachine gun with its built-in sound suppressor across his shoulder, he was ready for whatever happened next.

As ready as a man could be, at least, when it came down to facing unknown forces ranged on unfamiliar ground.

There was a chance he might have led himself astray, assuming Rurik Baklanov would run to his one unmolested ally in the Mafia, when things got too hot in New York. For all that Bolan knew, his quarry might have backup houses in New York—or other allies unidentified, so far—but the soldier had to play the cards he held, and Donatelli was the smart bet, at the moment. If he was mistaken…well, at least he had the chance to do some damage to the Family in Buffalo, maybe pick up a hostage he could question at his leisure and find out where else the Russian might have gone to ground.

But in the meantime, he was thinking positively, concentrating on the up side, as he made his way through darkness toward the tall stone wall surrounding Donatelli's property. Whatever happened in the next half hour, it would be life or death for some of those inside that wall.

And for Mack Bolan, right.

The Executioner hadn't come this far, just to fold his cards and walk away.

GAETANO DONATELLI was working on his third glass of wine since the Russians showed up on his doorstep, seeking sanctuary. He regretted giving Baklanov the go-ahead when he had phoned from New York, but Donatelli had been cornered, torn between the bargain they had struck some months ago, when everything was cool, and the misgivings that had inundated him within the past few days, as everything began to fall apart.

He had been tempted, for a moment, to refuse the Russian's plea for help. He would have been within his rights to slam and bar the door, tell Baklanov to take a flying leap and find his own way into Canada or wherever in hell he was going. Still, the boss of Buffalo had been brought up to honor promises—at least, the ones which stood to put cash in his pocket.

It would cost him little, in the long run, helping Baklanov to flee the country for a while, and when he thought about the benefits—a chance to cool the heat, if nothing else, before it wound up scorching him—he reckoned it would be a bargain. There was also still a chance, when all of this blew over, that he might profit handsomely from his arrangement with the Russian.

Fair enough.

The capo mafioso took another sip of wine and asked his Russian guest, "So, when are you crossing over?"

"Later tonight," Baklanov said. "I have a call in to my people in Toronto. They're supposed to meet me in Niagara Falls at 1:00 a.m."

Donatelli nodded, swallowing an urge to check his diamond-studded Rolex watch. Baklanov would leave when it was time, a few more hours. What was that, all things considered, in the course of life?

"You want another vodka?" Donatelli asked the Russian.

"Please."

The capo swiveled in his seat and nodded toward one of his soldiers, Louie, lounging at the bar, watching the man reach across to grab the bottle and pour another double over ice.

Louie was halfway to the couch where Baklanov was sitting, carrying the glass of vodka, when all hell broke loose outside. Somebody started shouting, one of Donatelli's soldiers by the sound of it, and then all kinds of automatic weapons opened up in unison, a blast of sound that made Donatelli flinch involuntarily. He bolted from his chair, saw Louie drop the Russian's glass and reach inside his jacket for his piece, already moving toward the French doors facing on the yard outside. The Russian was on his feet, as well, his own lieutenant leaving his bar stool, to stand at Baklanov's side.

"Check out this shit and see what's happening," the capo ordered Louie, who answered with a grunt before he stepped outside. The Don rounded on the Russians, felt the hot blood rising in his cheeks as he confronted them. "So what's this?" he demanded. "The way I understood it, you weren't followed."

"That's right," Baklanov's bodyguard said, almost sneering. "We were clean. If there has been a leak, it's not with us."

"Meaning I set you up? Is that what you're about to say?" Donatelli heard his own pulse thumping in his ears, like someone beating on a tom-tom. "Standing here in my house, asking my help with a mess you made yourself, you're gonna tell me I'm responsible for this shit, here?"

"I'm sure he didn't mean that," Rurik Baklanov replied, shooting an icy glare at his man, silencing him before he had a chance to squeeze the other foot inside his mouth. "Still, since there obviously is a problem—"

"Maybe we should bail," the capo said, a taste of bitter fury in his mouth.

"Indeed, it might be wise," the Russian said.

"I hear you," Donatelli told him, "but I can't just split before I know what's going on. You get your boys together, while I check this out. It shouldn't take too long."

"I hope not," Baklanov replied. "This unexpected problem—"

"Is in my backyard," the boss of Buffalo reminded him. "Those are my boys out there, and I can promise you, they didn't pick this time a night for fucking target practice."

Baklanov and his lieutenant left the den to round up members of their escort team, the dozen-odd men who had shown up with them at the gate. Gaetano Donatelli never would have let them in, that many guns together, if he hadn't been prepared for them, with twice as many of his own men waiting, dressed to kill. It was supposed to be a quiet night, the Russians hanging out until the time came for their run across the border, but now it was coming apart, blowing up in his face, and Don Gaetano still didn't know why.

How could this happen on his own turf, when he had the cops and everybody locked down tight? It was a slap in Donatelli's face, the kind of insult that required a swift, definitive response. Beginning now.

He stepped around behind the bar, reached underneath and came up with the SPAS-12 riot shotgun he kept hidden there. The piece was fully loaded, seven 12-gauge buckshot rounds inside the magazine, with one more in the chamber. All he had to do was thumb off the safety, and it was ready, not the lightest weapon in the world, but reassuring in its solid weight.

He left the metal stock folded, across the top of the receiver, as he headed for the French doors that had swallowed Louie moments earlier. It would have been a smarter move, perhaps, to wait inside and see what happened next, but Don Gaetano wasn't wired that way. When danger threatened him, he liked to face the problem head-on, eye to eye, and stare it down.

Of course, that didn't mean he was about to go play Rambo in the middle of the night. His soldiers had that action covered, and he didn't plan on getting in their way.

But he would join them for the kill, you bet your ass. And only then would he escort the Russians out of town, while his subordinates were cleaning up the mess.

Meanwhile, his not-so-helpful friend from Moscow could stand by and wait.

THE ONE THING Bolan hadn't counted on was Donatelli fitting his sentries with night-vision goggles. He had scouted the perimeter for closed-circuit cameras and motion detectors, had blown a silent dog whistle to scare up any canine defenders of the property—but all in vain. That done, he had assumed Donatelli's home defenses were conventional.

And that had been a critical mistake.

One of them spotted him when he was halfway to the house, gliding through darkness like a sentient shadow, taking full advantage of the night. This was the game that he had learned to play on foreign killing fields, and while he was a master at it, Bolan still wasn't invisible.

The sentry could have taken Bolan down without a warning, and that would have been the end, a short burst fired from thirty yards or so to drop him in his tracks. Instead, for reasons best known to himself, the button man picked up his walkie-talkie, thumbed down a button and sent a burst of static hissing through the night, as he attempted to transmit a call for help or seek instructions.

That was *his* mistake, and it would be the last he ever made.

Bolan squeezed off a sound suppressed, 3-round burst that hit his target in the chest, then moved toward him for a follow-up as the sentry slumped backward, rebounding from the smooth trunk of a tree. In his hand was a mini-Uzi with extended magazine, no sound suppressor attached, and as the shooter fell, his index finger clenched the trigger, rattling off a burst that would be audible all over Grandyle Village.

Bolan hit him with another close-range burst, uncertain whether he was down and out, or simply stunned. If they had infrared goggles, they might have Kevlar bulletproof vests, so he aimed the second burst of three slugs at his target's face and finished it, no further doubt as the Executioner turned away and kept moving toward the house.

It was the time to cut and run, he realized, before the home team had a chance to spread out and encircle him, but the soldier was determined not to let another chance slip through his fingers. Baklanov had managed to evade him for the best part of a week, and Bolan wouldn't rest until he found out where the Russian thug had gone to ground. If he wasn't in Buffalo, with Donatelli's people, someone there should have a fix on where he was.

Another sentry wearing big-eye goggles tried to intercept him when he was within a hundred yards of Donatelli's house. This gunner didn't give himself away by fiddling with a radio; instead, he came at Bolan through the darkness, charging like a bull, spraying the landscape with a semiautomatic Ruger Mini-14 rifle.

For a crude approach, it still worked fairly well. Bolan was forced to hit the deck, as 5.56 mm bullets swarmed through space around waist level, where he had been standing just a heartbeat earlier. Returning fire, he squeezed off two short bursts, aiming a hand's-width higher than his adversary's muzzle-flash. The mafioso fetched up short, as if a cable strung across the path had snagged him underneath his chin, and fairly somersaulted backward into death.

Bolan was up and running toward the house before the dust had settled on his second kill. Gaetano Donatelli might be paranoid enough to station men around his yard with automatic weapons every night, but something told the Executioner they didn't always come equipped with infrared goggles. That made this evening special, and the only reason he could think of for the palace guards to go all-out would be in the defense of special visitors.

Russians, perhaps.

Bolan could see the soldiers forming up into a skirmish line, between him and the house. Floodlights had been switched on around the house, high noon at midnight in the heart of Grandyle Village, and the glare would work against his adversaries who still wore night-vision goggles. None of those he saw ahead of him were so encumbered, though they all had shotguns, SMGs, or rifles, spreading out to form a ragged firing line before they started moving toward the trees.

And it was Bolan's turn to go on the offensive. He wasn't about to wait for them to find him, drive him through the night as if it were some kind of fox hunt. They were counting on their numbers to intimidate the enemy, but they had no idea who they were dealing with.

He switched mags on his submachine gun, opting for a fully loaded one, then palmed a frag grenade, left handed, and released the safety pin. His tight grip held the spoon in place as Bolan broke from cover, moving toward his adversaries. He had their blind spot, still beyond the outer limits of the floodlights' glare, while any soldier in the woods behind him, wearing infrared goggles, would be immediately blinded, facing the house.

He lobbed the frag grenade from thirty paces out and started firing with the MP-5, from right to left, across the skirmish line. At first, his targets didn't recognize the silent death that whispered through their ranks, one falling, then another and another. Then, just as they understood exactly what was happening, a smoky thunderclap enveloped three of them, while jagged shrapnel sprayed the troops still on their feet.

No more than half a dozen still remained to face the Exe-

cutioner, when he burst out of darkness, into light, and fell
upon them like the wrath of God.

SOME FANCY TALKING had been necessary after the fiasco in
New Jersey, and Hedeon Chapaev knew he wasn't fully back
in Baklanov's good graces yet. The long drive back to Queens
had been a torment, after Baklanov summoned him. Chapaev
half expected his own soldiers to be waiting for him when he
stepped out of the car, a bullet in the head to finish it, if he
was lucky. As it happened, though, his boss had finally had
enough, deciding they were cursed somehow, that it was time
to leave. He would reach out and punish Justine Palmer from
a distance, someday, when he had the luxury of time. Right
now, he wanted space between himself and his persistent,
nameless enemy. Chapaev might not be forgiven for his failures, but he was the best commander Baklanov had available.

So, they had come to Buffalo, en route to Canada, where
Baklanov thought they would be safe. Chapaev didn't share his
confidence, but he would do as he was told.

And now, the nightmare had begun once more.

Baklanov was ashen, bearing close resemblance to the victim
of a stroke, as they proceeded toward their waiting limousine.
Semyon Shurochka was already standing in the parlor with the
rest of their boss's bodyguards, a grim expression on his face.

"They've found us once again," he said. A simple statement, rather than a question.

"No time now for talk," Baklanov snapped. "We must get
out of here."

The white stretch limo had room for all of them. Two men
up front, eleven in the back, suitcases filled with money in the
trunk. Chapaev wished there had been any number of them but
thirteen, then cursed himself for thinking of a childish super-
stition when he should be focused absolutely on the task at
hand. Survival was the first priority—survival and escape. It
was a relatively short run to the border, but if they were forced
to make the journey under fire...

The shock wave of a small explosion rattled windows. Grenade, Chapaev thought, and tried to guess what other military hardware their opponents might be sporting this time. He no longer cared about allegiances, identities. Chapaev wanted out of there, and feeling that provoked a sudden flash of anger at himself.

He wondered if he had begun to lose his nerve.

His soldiers all had guns in hand, now. They were mostly pistols, since their host had balked at his self-invited guests bringing an arsenal into the house, but Chapaev reckoned pistols would do for the short run to the limousine. Inside the stretch, ready and waiting, there were AKMs and Uzis, shotguns, even a grenade launcher. If they could only make it to the limousine, Chapaev told himself, then they could fight their way past anyone.

He drew the Skorpion from underneath his jacket, small and light enough that it had passed inspection as a pistol when they first arrived. It was Chapaev's job to take the point and lead them out of there. Nobody had to tell him that, or urge him on. It went without saying, and he didn't hesitate as he brushed past his soldiers, issuing instructions to them as he passed.

They would surround Baklanov and Shurochka, protect the godfather at all costs, and his lieutenant with whatever means they had left over. In the circumstances, guarding two was no more difficult than guarding one. If they were hit by automatic fire and hand grenades before they reached the limousine, the chances were that none of them would make it through alive.

Chapaev had this opportunity to prove himself, make up for recent failures by insuring that his master was unharmed. If enemies were waiting for them outside, it was his job to cut them down—give up his life, if necessary, to protect the man who paid the bills.

Same old, same old, as the Americans would say.

He hesitated for an instant, with his left hand on the door-knob, glancing back to find a dozen faces ranged about him, staring, waiting for Chapaev to be brave. He felt like spitting on them, telling them to find their own way for a change, but kept the sudden anger to himself, rechanneled it in the direction of his unknown enemies.

Turning his back on the expectant faces, Hedeon Chapaev opened up the door and stepped out into artificial daylight, glancing left and right as he moved swiftly toward the waiting limousine.

BOLAN DITCHED the MP-5's empty magazine and fed a fresh one into the receiver, moving through a haze of dust and smoke kicked up by the grenade blasts. Donatelli's button men littered the turf around him, some dead or dying, others perhaps only stunned. He didn't care about them at the moment, knowing that his time was short and he was still some distance from the targets he had come to find.

Fifty paces from the house, and Bolan stopped short as he heard another man approaching. This one telegraphed his movements, shouting names in what the Executioner presumed was an attempt to rouse the palace guards. The shouter had no way of knowing most of them were down and out, the others either out of earshot or pretending not to hear, while they went looking for a place to hide.

Bolan was waiting when the loud guy came around the corner and confronted him. The Executioner recognized the mobster's face on sight. It was regurgitated from his mental file of mug shots that included ranking mobsters, terrorists and other human predators from all around the world.

Gaetano Donatelli.

The Executioner was looking at the Don of Buffalo.

The mobster had a SPAS-12 in his hands, and Bolan took for granted that he knew how to use it. There was hesitation, though, when Donatelli found himself confronted with a stranger dressed in military gear, face and hands painted black, a sound-suppressed SMG pointed directly at his chest.

"So, who the fuck are you?" he asked. And as he spoke, the capo swung his piece around, the shotgun's muzzle pivoting toward Bolan.

The Executioner let his submachine gun answer Donatelli's

question, stuttering a 3-round burst, immediately followed by another, for insurance. Coming late, the way he was, there was at least an outside chance the man had stopped along the way to don some kind of body armor. Bolan's first three bullets hammered Donatelli's chest and drove him back, off balance, while the second burst came in a heartbeat later, shearing off his lower jaw, clipping the spinal cord.

Enough strength still remained in Donatelli's dying hands for him to squeeze the shotgun's trigger once, as he was falling backward in a lifeless sprawl. The blast kicked up a storm of dust and mangled turf, Bolan recoiling as one of the pellets buried itself in his thigh.

He cursed and bent to examine the wound. No blood to speak of, and the bone was still intact. A simple flesh wound, then, most probably a ricochet. It pained him every time he took a step, but this wasn't the time for him to let a little inconvenience slow him.

The limp was barely visible as Bolan double-timed through pain and gun smoke toward the nearest corner of the house. Another moment, and he saw the broad loop of the driveway, counting three, four cars, besides a white stretch limousine. The stretch was loading as he got there, two more men still waiting for their chance to climb aboard, while several gunners stood around and covered them.

There was a difference between the two groups, to his eye, although he pegged them all as mobsters. Those who stood aside and watched the limo being loaded were predominately younger men, most of them sporting longish hair, well oiled and sculpted into styles that dated from the 1950s—Donatelli's men, still unaware that they had lost their capo moments earlier. The limo riders, by contrast, wore buzz cuts and suits off the rack. They were visibly older than most of Donatelli's crew, but still hard and fit. Soldier types.

Russian soldiers, perhaps.

It came together in a flash, the recognition that Donatelli's shooters wouldn't be guarding visitors—supervising their escape in the midst of such chaos, with their capo lying dead a few yards distant—unless those visitors were very VIP. An order from the boss would rate that kind of service, though, and Bolan suddenly realized, as surely as if he could see through the limo's smoked windows, that Rurik Baklanov was there, inside the stretch, prepared to slip away once more.

Not this time, Bolan thought, and came out firing. With the silenced SMG, he took down four of Donatelli's guards before the others recognized that they were under fire. It got a little hectic after that, three Sicilians and the last two limo riders all unloading on him, simultaneously. Bolan stuck it out, ducking and weaving, hearing bullets whistle past him, feeling one or two tug at his web gear, answering the fire with short precision bursts.

He finished off the mafiosi first, since one was carrying a shotgun and the other two had SMGs. One of the Russians was about to duck inside the limousine when Bolan shot him in the face and left him stretched out on the asphalt. Someone started barking orders from inside the stretch, and while Bolan was too far to hear the words, he was crystal clear about the tone. The speaker wanted out of there right now, and when he spoke, the limo driver listened, stamping down on the accelerator, roaring off before their final passenger had time to jump inside, or even close the door.

The Russian lost a fatal moment staring at the taillights of the limousine and mouthing curses, then remembered Bolan, turning back in time to catch a trio of 9 mm slugs in the chest. He went down like a rag doll, instantly forgotten as the Executioner ran over to the other cars, searching for one with keys in the ignition. Any wheels at all, as long as he didn't lose sight of the escaping limousine.

He scored on the first try, a midnight blue Chrysler LeBaron. Gunning the engine and wheeling out of there, he glimpsed a shooter—one of Donatelli's—rushing for him on the driver's side, some kind of handgun or machine pistol extended for a killing shot. Instinctively, the soldier swung the steering wheel and clipped his adversary, felt rather than saw the young man going airborne.

And then the driveway lay open before him, the limousine already clearing the gate, with a hundred-yard lead. Bolan stood on the gas pedal, hearing squeals from the tires as the Chrysler leapt forward and into pursuit.

16

A black rage had enveloped Rurik Baklanov. It took a conscious effort to refrain from lashing out at those around him, cursing them, or even bloodying their faces with his fists. He had been so close to evasion of his enemies, slipping beyond their grasp unseen, but now he was entangled in the net once more, and it was threatening to drag him under.

Someone was to blame for this—someone besides himself, of course—and Baklanov would punish those responsible, as soon as he could find out who they were. Assuming he survived, that was. And at the moment, even life itself was far from being guaranteed.

They had a lead, of course, and that was something. Let the bastards spend their time on Donatelli's people, mopping up, while Baklanov made his escape.

It was a fair plan, and it almost worked. The white stretch limousine was through the gate and running northward, toward the junction with Grand Island Boulevard, the bridge to Canada beyond it, when the driver said in Russian, "Someone follows us."

Baklanov swiveled in his seat so suddenly that he felt a white-hot stab of pain in one side of his neck, ignoring it as he focused on the pair of headlights trailing them, perhaps three-quarters of a mile behind. The distance seemed to make no difference, as the chase car swiftly closed the gap, running flat-out in defiance of the posted speed limit.

"Can we outrun them?" he demanded of the driver, shouting to compensate for the distance between them.

"I doubt it," the driver informed him. "This damn thing's too heavy."

"Well, try, anyway!" Unspoken in the order was the knowledge that each of them shared. This limousine, unlike his own custom model, had no armor plating, no gun ports, no bullet-proof glass or self-sealing tires. This one was designed for high-school graduation parties and the like, with no thought given to security beyond the driver's air bag and the seat belts, which from all appearances had never once been used.

They would be sitting ducks inside the limousine if someone opened fire on them. The tinted window glass would hide them, making it impossible to spot specific targets in the limousine, but once the glass was shattered, even that advantage would be lost.

Semyon Shurochka had a glass of whiskey in his hand, poured from the limo's mobile bar. He drained it in a single gulp and grimaced as the liquor seared his throat, bright moisture brimming in his eyes. Baklanov ignored his second in command and turned to Hedeon Chapaev, leaning forward to clasp the soldier's wrist in a grip of steel.

"You have to stop them," he demanded. "It's your chance to make amends." Not an endearing speech, perhaps, but he saw the words strike home, knew Chapaev understood their meaning and took it to heart. The soldier had failed him repeatedly in recent days, couldn't seem to perform the simplest task without getting caught up in a firefight, losing men and weapons wherever he went. Now, Baklanov was telling him that if he did only this one thing right, his debt would be wiped clean.

Chapaev nodded, understanding. "So be it," he said, and shifted seats to place himself in back, his Skorpion braced on the window ledge behind the broad rear seat.

There was a problem with the car's design when it came down to personal defense. From the outside, the limo appeared to be a normal car, vastly elongated, with darkened windows normally positioned on both sides. Most of them couldn't be opened—none at all along the left, except the driver's window, and only two on the right, those attached to doors flanking the wet bar.

What that meant, in concrete terms, was that aside from the driver's window, way up front, they could only return fire on the left—the side most likely to be strafed by any chase car overtaking them—if they smashed out the stationary window glass. Three windows altogether could be lowered on the right side of the car, facing the shoulder of the highway, where no vehicle could overtake and pass. It would be fine for drive-by shootings, picking off pedestrians, but in the present circumstances, they were screwed.

"Slow down!" Chapaev told the driver, raising his voice to be heard without taking his eyes from the highway behind them, the headlights approaching at speed. Another moment, and he dropped the Skorpion onto the seat beside him, reaching backward with an empty hand. "A rifle, quickly."

One of his subordinates passed him a stubby AKSU, and Chapaev unfolded the skeleton stock, scooting back to the edge of his seat to make room for the weapon's long, curved magazine. He braced his forward elbow on the seat cushion, sighting along the barrel at his target. Even with their headlights switched to high beams, the pursuers couldn't see him through the limo's blacked-out glass. Another moment, now, and it would be too late for them to save themselves.

When Chapaev cut loose with the Kalashnikov, it filled the passenger compartment of the limousine with thunder, battering eardrums, filling nostrils with the acrid stench of cordite. Smokeless powder it might be, but there was no escaping the smell that Rurik Baklanov always associated with sudden death.

This time, he thought, it was the death of nameless, faceless adversaries who had plagued him far too long.

The first short burst of automatic fire blew out a section of the window, and the headlights of the chase car instantly grew brighter, as the tinted glass was swept away. Besides the smell of cordite, now, there was an odor of exhaust fumes, heated rubber, asphalt—all the smells, in short, that went with highways in America.

The chase car swerved but didn't seem to lose momentum. It was staying with them, closing by the moment. In another instant, Baklanov picked out the winking blips of muzzle-flashes, as their pursuers began returning fire.

BOLAN WASN'T SURPRISED when someone in the limo started shooting at him. He had been expecting it, in fact, but he was startled when the first shots came directly through the broad rear window of the limousine. The spray of rifle fire made Bolan duck and weave, but it supplied two bits of vital information simultaneously.

First, the limo wasn't bulletproof. If passengers could fire through the windows, that meant Bolan could fire in.

Second, if it wasn't in fact a tank, designed for personal security, there would be no gun ports along the driver's side.

The second piece of information didn't help him much, since Baklanov and company had shown a willingness to shoot out the big car's windows, but Bolan had observed enough stretch limousines to have a fair idea of how this one was built. The seats, most likely, would be laid out on three sides of an extended rectangle, most of them facing toward the wet bar and the doors, to starboard. Firing to the left meant passengers would have to turn around, perhaps kneel on the seats, to face the tinted windows on the driver's side. It was an awkward posture in the best of circumstances, all the more so under fire, and Bolan thought it might be used to his advantage now.

Another burst of automatic fire came from the limousine, and the soldier swerved to avoid it, running up behind the stretch in the highway's south-bound lane. A sudden flash of déjà vu took him back to his first encounter with Rurik Baklanov, the wild chase in New Jersey a lifetime ago, and Bolan was determined to see a different outcome this time. If he let the Russian slip away once more, escape to Canada, there was no telling where or when he could pick up the scent again.

Bolan made up his mind. One way or another—win or lose, live or die—the game would be finished tonight.

He let the LeBaron unwind, closing in on the limo, thankful for the power windows that let him lower panes on both sides of the car without budging from his seat. Bolan felt the wind whip at his hair, roaring in his ears, but he could live with it. The alternative meant waiting for a lucky round to crack the glass and send it flying in his face like shrapnel. There was nothing he could do about the windshield, short of blowing it away himself, and Bolan passed on that for the moment, focused on his target as he drove with his left hand, raising the MP-5 SD-3 submachine gun with his right.

He could picture the confusion in the limo as he pulled alongside, the rear-window gunner forced to shift positions, looking for another angle of attack, the other passengers ducking and dodging in an effort to avoid potential cross fire. Bolan didn't know how many men were riding in the stretch, but any more than two or three would feel like a mob, when they started scrambling around under fire, seeking cover on the floor, below his line of sight.

He thumbed the SMG's selector switch from burst mode to automatic fire, leaning over just enough to brace its heavy muzzle on the starboard windowsill as he drew even with the rear of the limousine. Glancing up the road, northward, he saw no headlights bearing down on him. The way was open for the next few miles, leaving the Executioner to concentrate on taking out his enemies.

He stroked the trigger, rattling off ten or eleven rounds, a couple of his bullets striking low, the rest on target, taking out a three-foot stretch of tinted glass. He glimpsed a startled face in profile, there and gone, uncertain whether he had nailed one of the passengers, or simply spooked the man into a headlong dive for cover. Either way, it added up to more confusion for his enemies, and that could only work to his advantage in the end.

One of the shooters in the stretch was now returning fire. It sounded like the same Kalashnikov. Bolan squeezed a few more miles per hour out of the LeBaron's power plant, feeling the car surge forward. Half a dozen bullets struck his ride, but they were punching through the back door on the other side, spending their force against the body work, or in the cushions of the vacant seat.

Bolan, meanwhile, was firing off another burst, all of the shots on target now, as blacked-out windows suddenly imploded. Even with the noise of the Kalashnikov, he heard a male voice scream in pain or fear, the sound immediately whipped to shreds and blown away.

The best thing he could do was try to stop the limousine, and that meant taking out the tires or driver. Going for the tires wasn't a possibility, as long as they were running side by side. To make that shot—assuming he could make it in the dark, racing along a rural highway—he would have to fall back, let the limo pull ahead and take his best shot from behind.

No good.

Retreating gave his enemies a chance to pull away from him. It also gave the shooters in the limo a perfect chance to take him out, gun Bolan off the road, as they had done in New Jersey.

No.

He fired another burst to keep their heads down, emptying the SMG, and dropped it in the seat beside him. He drew the Desert Eagle semiauto pistol, thumbed the hammer back and held it ready as he bore down on the gas and made the Chrysler wail.

The limo's driver did his best to pull ahead, but he was dragging too much weight—the vehicle itself, plus human cargo—to make his wounded work horse perform like a Thoroughbred. Bolan couldn't see the wheelman as he pulled alongside, but he didn't need to. There was only one driver's seat in the limo, only one steering wheel, one accelerator, and his target would be right there waiting for him, shielded only by a door and tinted window.

Bolan sighted quickly down the Desert Eagle's slide and emptied the magazine in rapid fire. Eight rounds of .44 Magnum express loads, semijacketed hollowpoints, punched through the flimsy shield of glass and steel at something close to 1,200 feet per second, seeking flesh and bone inside. One hit would be enough to take out the driver, and Bolan counted on a better score than that, rewarded when the limo lost momentum, veering sharply to the left.

He saw it coming and swung the Chrysler's steering wheel to meet it. Despite the limo's greater size and weight, without a pair of living hands to guide it, Bolan sent the stretch careening toward a roadside ditch and barbed-wire fence beyond.

He pumped the Chrysler's brakes, swung it around on smoking tires and lined it up so that his headlights faced back toward the limousine, nosed down into the ditch. Before he left the car, Bolan returned the Desert Eagle to its holster, reaching out to grab his SMG and feed the stuttergun another magazine.

IT TOOK A MOMENT for Hedeon Chapaev to realize that most of the blood smeared across his face and suit wasn't his own. He had been tumbled from his seat when they veered off the roadway, dumped on his backside with others sprawling around him, and at least one of those others was bleeding profusely. Whether the blood sprang from superficial cuts or mortal bullet wounds, Chapaev neither knew nor cared. It was enough to feel his own limbs respond to his mental commands, assuring him that he could still defend himself, defend his master.

Rurik Baklanov was huddled on the floor, back toward the limousine's rear seat. He had a dazed look on his face, but suffered no apparent injury beyond whatever bruising was occasioned when he tumbled from his seat. In other circumstances, Chapaev might have smiled at Baklanov's discomfort, maybe even laughed aloud, but this wasn't the time or place.

Ironically, he didn't fear the mobster's wrath, just now. Chapaev was intent, however, on repaying their assailants for the grave indignities he had been made to suffer during recent days. The fact that they were stranded now, their only means of transportation hung up in a ditch, riddled with bullet holes, meant no more to Chapaev than the buzzing of mosquitoes in the good old days, when he was out on night patrol with Spetsnaz.

It was kill or be killed, and he could think about obtaining other transportation later, when their enemies had been eliminated.

First things, first.

He scrambled for the nearest door, but couldn't get it open far enough to let him out. It jammed against the ditch embankment, and Chapaev didn't fancy getting stuck there, like some comic movie actor, while his adversaries stood back in the dark and picked him off.

He made it to the other door and kicked it open. This one struck the grassy bank, as well, but there was room for him to wriggle out, once he turned sideways, shoving the Kalashnikov ahead of him. Outside, he thought about the Skorpion, wished he had thought to bring it, too, but there was no time to duck back inside the stretch and find out what had happened to his SMG. Chapaev had his Walther automatic in a shoulder holster, if he needed backup, and before it came to that, he hoped a number of his men might join him in pursuit of their assailants.

In his haste, Chapaev hadn't ordered anyone to follow him, and now he wondered—only for an instant—if he might have made a critical mistake. Downrange, the chase car had reversed directions, headlights glaring in his face, half blinding him, and he couldn't make out how many men and guns were ranged against him. From his quick glimpse of the car, in passing, he decided there couldn't be more than four or five...and something told him that there might be only one.

A warrior like himself, perhaps, who carried battle to the enemy, regardless of the risks involved. It would be fitting, in more ways than one, if this turned out to be the adversary who had dogged his men from New Jersey to Cleveland, and back again to New York. They could finish it here, settle the matter once and for all. Just the two of them.

Chapaev edged around the left rear fender of the limousine and fired a burst downrange, taking out one of the chase car's headlights. The answering fire was silent, but he saw a muzzle-flash, there and gone before bullets started knocking divots in the fender, inches from his face.

They could go on like that all night, Chapaev knew—or until police arrived with flashing lights and sirens. In that case, there would be no realistic hope of anyone escaping from the scene. They would be charged with sundry weapons violations, at the very least—possession of machine guns, the grenade launcher—and Baklanov…

The grenade launcher.

Chapaev scuttled back down to the open door and thrust his head inside. One of his soldiers blinked at him, a dazed expression on his blood-streaked face.

"The grenade launcher!" Chapaev snapped at him. "Quickly! Where is it?"

The soldier muttered something, turned away, groped under moving bodies for a moment, coming back with the weapon Chapaev sought. He passed it over, then realized his mistake and went back for the bandoleer of 40 mm high-explosive rounds.

The weapon was a modified version of the American M-203, resembling nothing so much as an oversized flare gun or an inflated pump-action shotgun. It was breech loaded, single shot, and had a folding metal stock. Instead of being mounted underneath the barrel of an M-16 assault rifle, this model was designed to stand alone, a piece of compact field artillery for the modern infantryman. It was exactly what Chapaev needed to break the standoff.

Crawling back to his former vantage point at the rear of the limo, he broke the M-203 open and slipped a stubby HE round into its breech before closing the action. He unfolded the stock, raised the launcher's folding sights and edged his way to the corner of the leaning vehicle.

It would have inconvenienced some men, being forced to aim and fire left-handed, but Chapaev had trained both ways with Spetsnaz, becoming effectively ambidextrous with firearms. The talent didn't extend to penmanship, but the message he meant to send his enemies would be written in blood.

He risked a glance around the bumper, checking up and down the road for flankers, worried that someone might have advanced while he was retrieving the launcher from the limo. There was no one in sight, just the chase car, some thirty yards north, its single headlight glaring at him like the great eye of a cyclops.

Time to sleep, he thought, and brought the M-203 to his shoulder, squinting through the elevated sights. He aimed a bit above and to the right of the remaining headlight, where the juncture of the hood and windshield ought to be. He inhaled and held it, taking up the trigger slack.

Good night, sweet prince, Chapaev thought.

And squeezed the trigger.

BOLAN WAS ADVANCING through the tall grass of the roadside ditch when he heard the familiar sound of a grenade launcher firing in the breezy darkness of the open highway. Instinctively, he hunkered down and waited for the blast, now long in coming. Bolan didn't have to lift his head to know the Chrysler had become a casualty, the shock wave rolling over him, heat close behind as the gas tank blew in a secondary explosion.

Dammit!

That meant hiking out, but first he had to finish the task at hand, and he was nowhere close to finished yet. Not while the enemy was still alive and armed with heavy weapons.

Still…

If they wanted grenades, Bolan thought, he could give them grenades. Unclipping one of the lethal green eggs from his web belt, he shifted the SMG to his left hand, taking the grenade in his right. He pulled the pin and ditched it, the curve of the spoon warm and smooth against his palm. Once he released it, detonation would follow within six seconds.

Not much time at all, but a lifetime, for some.

He edged in closer to the limo, twenty yards and change, thinking that anyone who peered out through the windshield now might see him coming. Still, the darkness served him well, and no one opened fire on Bolan as he knelt in the weeds and wound up for his pitch.

The move he had in mind required some planning and finesse. It might be possible to lob his frag grenade through the unbroken windshield of the limousine, but Bolan also recognized a fifty-fifty chance that it would bounce back at him, maybe wind up in his lap. Likewise, he had the strength to make a toss beyond the stretch, where one or more survivors of the crash were huddled in the dark, but if he overshot too far or dropped it in the middle of the road, it would be wasted effort. What he needed, at the moment, was a high lob, up and over, dropping inside, through one of the shattered windows on the driver's side. No matter where the frag grenade went in, its blast should finish anyone inside the car—or leave them dazed and helpless for the mopping up.

The trouble was that Bolan had to rise and fully expose himself, to make that pitch. If he attempted it from where he was, hunched in the ditch, the odds were fair to excellent that he would miss the windows, bounce it off the limo's side like a pathetic spitball fired at Moby Dick. And even though he still had more grenades, a miss would show them where he was, bring every gun inside the limousine to bear on his position, while he scrambled for a second chance.

Fair enough. First time or nothing, then.

He rose up from his crouch, until the dark squares of the shattered windows were revealed. He chose the windows to the rear, mindful that most stretch limos had partitions separating passenger compartments from the driver's seat, drew back his arm and let it fly.

And almost missed.

The egg fell short, an inch or so, and struck a metal window post. It could have wobbled off across the door, or gone the other way and caromed off the limo's roof. Instead, it spun like a demented top, tipped over on its side and disappeared inside the car.

Bolan retreated, dropped prone in the weeds and waited for the blast. It came on schedule, running down the numbers, sudden thunder ripping through the inside of the limousine. A body spewed out through the windshield, smoke and flame erupting from the windows all around.

And still, it wasn't finished.

Even as he scrambled to his feet, advancing on the limousine, Bolan made out a figure rising from behind the car, back toward the rear. He counted only one, then had to dodge a stream of automatic fire as that one cut loose on him through the drifting smoke and dust, with a Kalashnikov.

He had a choice of dodging left, into a barbed-wire fence, or right, onto the open road. It was no choice at all, and Bolan hit the highway, running in a crouch, placing the shattered limousine between himself and his opponent for a crucial breather, gaining ground. His MP-5 was ready when the shadow figure showed itself again, emerging from behind the limo, and he didn't hesitate. A stream of Parabellum slugs met the Russian as he tried to leave the ditch, drilling his chest and torso, tumbling him backward into the weeds.

The man was dead when Bolan reached him, lying crumpled like a broken mannequin. Someone was screaming from inside the stretch, trying in vain to quit the flaming hulk. Bolan unclipped another frag grenade, armed it and dropped it through the nearest open window, edging backward swiftly, out of range, before it blew.

All was quiet now inside the stretch, except for the incessant crackle of the hungry flames. And sirens, right. Still far away, but drawing closer by the moment.

Bolan scaled the nearby fence and hiked a hundred yards into the middle of the field before he started back toward town.

The more things changed, the more they stayed the same.

EPILOGUE

"We won't get any new indictments out of it," Brognola said, "but what the hell. I never thought we would."

It came as no surprise to Bolan. The survivors of the game, two days and counting down the road, were mostly small-fry. It would do as well to keep surveillance on them, as before, and see who started moving up the ladder now that spaces had been cleared in several of the Mafia's surviving Families. Inevitably, those who made it to the several shaky thrones would ultimately make their own mistakes.

"So, what about the woman?" Bolan asked.

"We cut her loose," Brognola replied. "No one for her to testify against, the way it is. She might have problems coming up with the IRS, but that's another story."

Bolan thought about Justine Palmer and tried to find a soft spot in his heart, but came up short. She had been ready to betray him in a heartbeat—had, in fact, sent Dima Petrov to his death—and only switched allegiance when she could no longer doubt that Rurik Baklanov was working overtime to have her killed.

"Her problem," Bolan said at last. And then added, "You're sure about the Russian?"

"Dental charts," Brognola said. "Marx had a dentist take a set of X-rays, before he overhauled the face. He's done, all right."

"That's it, then."

"For the moment," the big Fed replied. "One faction, anyway."

He didn't have to say the rest. Bolan already knew the punch line, how the Russian mob had grown so strong and spread so widely since the fall of communism that it posed a greater threat today than all the mafiosi of past generations ever had. Eliminating Rurik Baklanov had stopped a merger of two evils, but without eradicating either one.

The war went on, and Bolan would be waiting when the enemy revealed himself again, next time.

But for today, his work was done.

Tomorrow, and the evil that it brought, would take care of itself.

James Axler

OUTLANDERS™

ARMAGEDDON AXIS

What was supposed to be the seat of power after the nuclear holocaust, a vast installation inside Mount Rushmore—is a new powerbase of destruction. Kane and his fellow exiles venture to the hot spot, where they face an old enemy conspiring to start the second wave of Armageddon.

James Axler

OUTLANDERS™

OUTER DARKNESS

Kane and his companions are transported to an alternate reality where the global conflagration didn't happen—and humanity had expelled the Archons from the planet. Things are not as rosy as they may seem, as the Archons return for a final confrontation....

Book #3 in the new Lost Earth Saga, a trilogy that chronicles our heroes' paths through three very different alternative realities...where the struggle against the evil Archons goes on....

An old enemy poses a new threat....

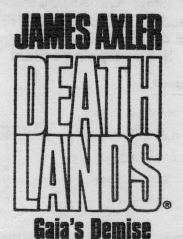

JAMES AXLER

DEATH LANDS®

Gaia's Demise

Ryan Cawdor's old nemesis, Dr. Silas Jamaisvous, is behind a deadly new weapon that uses electromagnetic pulses to control the weather and the gateways, and even disrupts human thinking processes.

As these waves doom psi-sensitive Krysty, Ryan challenges Jamaisvous to a daring showdown for America's survival....

Book 2 in the Baronies Trilogy, three books that chronicle the strange attempts to unify the East Coast baronies—a bid for power in the midst of anarchy....

Shadow THE EXECUTIONER®
as he battles evil for 352 pages of heart-stopping action!

SuperBolan®

#61452	DAY OF THE VULTURE	$5.50 U.S.	☐
		$6.50 CAN.	☐
#61453	FLAMES OF WRATH	$5.50 U.S.	☐
		$6.50 CAN.	☐
#61454	HIGH AGGRESSION	$5.50 U.S.	☐
		$6.50 CAN.	☐
#61455	CODE OF BUSHIDO	$5.50 U.S.	☐
		$6.50 CAN.	☐
#61456	TERROR SPIN	$5.50 U.S.	☐
		$6.50 CAN.	☐

(limited quantities available on certain titles)

TOTAL AMOUNT	$
POSTAGE & HANDLING	$
($1.00 for one book, 50¢ for each additional)	
APPLICABLE TAXES*	$
TOTAL PAYABLE	$
(check or money order—please do not send cash)	

To order, complete this form and send it, along with a check or money order for the total above, payable to Gold Eagle Books, to: **In the U.S.:** 3010 Walden Avenue, P.O. Box 9077, Buffalo, NY 14269-9077; **In Canada:** P.O. Box 636, Fort Erie, Ontario, L2A 5X3.

Name: _____

Address: _____ City: _____

State/Prov.: _____ Zip/Postal Code: _____

*New York residents remit applicable sales taxes.
Canadian residents remit applicable GST and provincial taxes.

GSBBACK1